IN THE HEAT OF BATTLE . . .

The firing had suddenly ceased. A strange silence had seized the ship, a funereal silence for all the dead. The rest of the men were in a state of depression and shock.

A blaze of daylight greeted the men and caused them to forget their ordeal, to forget any fears of the immediate future, and to fill them with an awesome sense of being. The men knew that they had witnessed a new chapter in history . . .

⚓

BULLER'S DREADNOUGHT

RICHARD HOUGH

ACE CHARTER BOOKS, NEW YORK

An Ace Charter Book

Published by arrangement with William Morrow and Co., Inc.

ISBN: 0-441-08930-5

First Ace Charter Printing: February 1983
Published simultaneously in Canada

Manufactured in the United States of America
Ace Books, 200 Madison Avenue, New York, New York 10016

Acknowledgments

For special advice and guidance I would like to thank Warren Tute, Michael Rubinstein, Lieutenant Colonel C. C. Mitchell, Walter Lord, Philip Pollock, my daughter, Sarah Garland, and F.W. Manders, the Local Studies Librarian at the Newcastle-upon-Tyne Central Library; and for advice on cameras and photography, Alan Maxwell of Wallace Heaton Ltd., and David Higginbottom.

Contents

Chapter I

⚓

A Yank at the Court
of King Edward

COMMANDER WHITNEY KYLE CAMPBELL U.S.N., age thirty-six, from Rutland, Vermont, had never lost his bearings at sea. But here in London, after losing his friends, he had no idea where he was, nor the direction of Buckingham Palace. The crowds pressed tightly about him, women wearing veils and smart hats with peacock feathers, women in shawls, men in silk top hats, bowlers or workingmen's cloth caps, bareheaded children, people of all walks of life, all friendly, all anxious.

In this summer of 1902, Whitney Campbell had been sent from Washington by order of President Teddy Roosevelt to be special United States Navy representative at the coronation of King Edward VII. Whitney had never been to England before, and as a Scots-American whose family had emigrated from the Highlands after the second Jacobite rising in 1745, he had inherited a deep suspicion of everything English. "Damn Limeys!" was the accepted expression when the subject came up, whether at home or school as a boy, at Groton and Annapolis as he became a man, and during his seagoing service in the navy.

1

Unlike some of his Irish friends, he felt no violent antagonism toward England. If he had been asked what he thought of the English before this surprise appointment came up, he might have said, "Snobbish, greedy bullies who think they're all-powerful and ought to rule the world." A few thousand Boer farmers, holding out against the British Army for three years, had shown that they were not invincible.

But Whitney had noticed since his arrival in London that English pride remained apparently undented by the military fiascos in Africa, and the plans for the coronation of their king were as elaborate and extravagant as for any Roman emperor. And now with the coronation just two days away, with the streets of London and every town and village in the kingdom decorated, scores of festivities already beginning, thousands of subjects from all over the world assembled in the capital—now, today, this June 24, 1902, the king had been struck down and an emergency operation performed only hours ago.

Whitney had been at a party at the United States Embassy when the rumor had flashed through the ballroom like an icy draft on that warm summer night: "The king is seriously ill . . . they say it's peritonitis . . . it's sure not lumbago as the newspapers were told . . . somebody at the palace said it is very, very grave. . . . Gee, do you think he's going to die?"

Within the hour many of the Americans present believed that King Edward was already dying. "He'll never make the coronation." The official news that there would not be a coronation, at least for the present, was made known in the very place where the ceremony would have occurred forty-eight hours later. Whitney Campbell, in the dress uniform of a commander U.S.N., was among those in Westminster Abbey for a full-scale rehearsal of the ceremony, when the Bishop of London had announced to the emperors and empresses, kings and queens, princes and princesses, grand dukes and grand duchesses, and lesser mortals of every color and creed and from every nation on earth, that the king was about to undergo a most serious surgical operation . . . "Let us pray."

And this august assembly, colored by robes of ermine,

glittering with crowns and tiaras, orders and epaulettes, had sunk to their knees and prayed for the life of King Edward VII.

The operation for peritonitis, it was said, had lasted forty-five minutes under the surgical control of Sir Frederick Treves, and the king continued in grave danger for the remainder of the day. At the embassy Whitney, as one of a party of half a dozen younger Americans—the ambassador's pretty niece and the naval attaché's son among them—drinking highballs, watching the sun set late in the evening, commented on the number of people in the streets.

The ambassador himself joined them briefly, and Whitney asked him about the crowds. "The whole city seems so restless, sir."

"The king is a great father figure to the English," the ambassador said. "He's like some tribal chief, and they really do love him—the fat, self-indulgent old reprobate. And I guess that's one reason. You see, all these people are going the same way, all to the palace to stand outside as a mark of concern. They'll be there all night."

"Why don't we join them?" a girl said with a giggle. She was well into her second drink. "Let's have a party outside Buckingham Palace—that would be swell."

So they had left, arms linked, and for a while across Green Park had remained together. But soon the press of numbers had broken them up, until as darkness fell at last after 10:00 P.M., Whitney found himself among strangers, half seen in the intermittent gaslight from the tall park lamps.

Whitney felt tired yet still amazed that these people were so reverently concerned for their sovereign. No one was drunk. No one was shouting. The sound from this vast concourse of people was no louder, no more threatening, than the lapping of a slow-moving river. And Whitney was being swept along like a stick on this current until he could see, not three hundred yards away, the outline against the last of the dying day in the west, the slab silhouette of Buckingham Palace, the faint glow of light behind curtains at its many windows.

Everyone wanted to be as close as possible to the iron

railings flanking the palace's forecourt, the nearest they could approach in order to offer the support of their presence to their king. Then they would drift away on the tide, and others would take their place, some climbing on the shoulders of others to peer into the empty forecourt.

The greatest press was about the board secured to the inside of the railings carrying the latest bulletin on the king's condition. With the aid of a stout woman carrying a wicker basket before her like a ram, Whitney found himself within a dozen yards of the railings, and at eleven o'clock he was among those who saw a figure in a bowler hat walking across the gravel from the Privy Purse entrance to the palace, a new board in his hand.

Around Whitney the hum of the crowd rose in volume, and he heard voices behind him calling out, "Let's know what it says," "Tell us 'ow 'e is," and simply "'ow's the king?"

With steady, unhurried hands, the official removed the old board and prepared to secure the new one. If it pronounced the death of the king, its thick black border would be instantly recognizable.

Commander Archibald Buller D.S.O., R.N., age thirty-six, from Wyston Court, Gloucestershire, and Clarges Street, Mayfair, London W., had also never lost his bearings at sea. After the two bottles of Mumm's Extra Dry he had consumed at the Marlborough Club that evening, it would have been understandable if he had wandered off course in the streets of St. James's. But like most naval officers, he had acquired a good head for drink and was well below his capacity level.

The baccarat table at which Buller had been playing since noon, and losing rather more than 200 sovereigns, had been a subdued one. The Marlborough Club in Pall Mall had been created by the king when he was Prince of Wales, and he had been its virtual dictator ever since. Its reputation for scandal and gambling was a reflection of the king's own reputation—deplored by his late mother, Queen Victoria, the Church establishment, and all those of a puritanical disposition.

The news of their patron's grave illness and operation,

with the canceling of his coronation, caused a shock throughout the club. The servants froze in their tracks, the croupiers
held their counters, gentlemen put down their cards and their
glasses, and for almost a minute silence prevailed throughout
the paneled rooms. The Marlborough Club was not normally
associated with prayers to the Almighty, but there was no
doubt of the sincerity and depth of the members' and servants' feelings.

Buller's first words were as banal as most people's. "It's
not possible! He's only been king for a year." Then an
elderly duke arose from the leather armchair in which
everyone thought he was asleep and, in ringing tones that
silenced the room, proclaimed, "God save the king!"

Like everyone else, Buller said, "Hear, hear!" then sat
back at his table, unable to concentrate on the game in
progress, remembering the king when he was Prince of
Wales and "Bertie" to his intimates, with his lovely but half-
crippled queen at Dartmouth. He remembered the charm that
emanated from him when he spoke, as if he, Archy Buller, a
twelve-year-old cadet, were the most important person in the
world. "My sons would like you to stay with us at Osborne
. . . ."

Another picture of him, the most memorable of all: the
journey in the royal train from Sandringham to London,
alone with this renowned and powerful prince, though almost
asphixiated by the smoke of his cigars, as the portly figure ran
his eyes down the columns of the newspapers and impatiently
turned the pages of *The Illustrated London News*.

The Prince of Wales at receptions and garden parties and
banquets, and so often in the company of his magnificently
beautiful and gifted mistress, Mrs. Keppel. The Prince of
Wales, only weeks before he succeeded to the throne, ribbing
Buller about the scar on his cheek and then saying, "Your
father would have been proud of you today—a grave pity he
is not with us," the "prrroud" and "grrrave" heavily guttural. And then he had pinned on the Distinguished Service
Order "for exceptional bravery and qualities of leadership at
the Battle of Colenso."

Buller had been comfortably winning at baccarat before

the news of the king's operation spread through the Marlborough Club. Then three times he had gone banco without considering his cards sufficiently, and each time had lost.

But Buller hardly considered his losses as he left the table early in the afternoon and returned on foot to his house. Later, with the coming of darkness and after dining alone, he had told Randolph, the butler, that he was going out and that he should reassure his wife when she arrived from the country with the children and nursemaids that he would not be late.

Like so many Londoners, he longed for news of his sovereign, and the latest would be on the Buckingham Palace bulletin board, though with his privileged connections he could obtain all the information he needed on a more private level.

Buller's wife, Clemmie, considered that her husband lacked imagination. It was true that even as a boy he had not been introspective. He took life as it came, had certain clear-cut likes and dislikes, especially a dislike of cruelty and unkindness, bullying and snobbism. But from time to time, usually when suffering from the remorse of a particularly bad hangover, he did consider his faults with a fleeting sense of shame—his selfishness, his neglect of his children, his re-laxed moral attitude, even by the standards of the time. He gambled too much, drank too much, ate too much, and slept with too many women.

Clemmie was right about Buller's lack of imagination. But at times his feelings ran deeper than she gave him credit for, and as he left his house again and walked down Clarges Street, he was aware of the somber and anxious mood of the great city, and of his own feelings of sadness at the threatened loss of this patriarchal figure with all his human qualities and failings. Buller had often seen evidence of his own character in King Edward VII, and that was the reason (he had once considered during another moment of reflection) why he felt so fond of him.

The crowds were already thick around the "In and Out" Club and the Ritz Hotel, and, like Whitney Campbell before him, he had difficulty in keeping his sense of direction and finding a way through toward the palace. Some families had brought rugs and were clearly making a night of it. On any other royal occasion there would have been a lot of drinking and shouting and singing. This crowd, which was of all classes, was as sober and well-behaved as the crowds celebrating Mafeking Night had been riotous and libidinous a year earlier.

Ten minutes later Buller bumped into Whitney Campbell. In the half-light of the lanterns set above the railings, they met head on, under the pressure of the throng trying to get near the bulletin board, and both apologized simultaneously. Buller caught the accent at once and said laughingly, "You must be the only Yank in this crowd!"

"Not quite true, sir. There were others in my party, but we've been separated for some time."

They were jammed like logs in a Canadian river, and Buller's social sense led him to continue the conversation. "Did you read the bulletin?"

"It says his condition remains grave and unchanged."

Buller could make out a pleasant-looking face. There were freckles on his nose, which added to the seeming youthfulness, and unlike almost everyone else, he was bareheaded, a full head of red hair tousled perhaps by the crowd which had also been responsible for the loss of his hat. The accent when he spoke again, Buller judged, was not a strong one, just a mild twang with sharp *a*'s.

"Perhaps I may introduce myself," said the American, "before we get swept away and separated. I'm Commander Whitney Campbell, United States Navy, over here officially for the coronation."

They were being forced apart again. Buller raised his voice. "My name's Buller, same business as you, same rank, too. Very decent meeting you—but very short meeting."

With a great effort Whitney Campbell forced his way between two big men and regained station on what he immediately referred to as Buller's port beam.

"Stout fellow!" said Buller. "I'm going to find out what's

really happening. Do you want to come with me?''

On the southwest corner of the Buckingham Palace grounds, there is a door let into the high wall and a small lodge which in the press of street traffic not one passerby in a hundred even notices. It is otherwise a blank length of wall on a busy length of road unassociated with royal comings and goings. If anyone had happened to have an interest in this door and possessed a room with a view overlooking it, from time to time—mostly at midday or late in the evening—he would have seen carriages or hansom cabs stop here. But only for a moment. Just long enough for a figure to hurry from the vehicle to the door, not furtively but swiftly.

There were still crowds making their way along Buckingham Palace Road toward the palace, spilling from the curbs into the dusty streets, where they risked being run over by hansoms, carriages, carts, and the occasional horse bus. Buller and Whitney forced their way against the tide, using the road when necessary.

"Here we are—follow me." Buller drew a long key from his waistcoat pocket, slipped it into the lock, and they were inside.

"It's like going backstage at the theater." Whitney laughed and leaned against an iron lamppost. Above him, a single gas mantle radiated a soft light over a gravel path, a seat, the corner of a bed of bush roses and trim-edged lawn. They could even hear the hiss of the gas, so insulated were they from the sounds of the street and of common humanity.

"If this is like backstage, it is a sort of play they're acting in there." Whitney nodded toward the great bulk of the palace rear, where curtained windows revealed rectangles of subdued light and the curve and columns of the projecting main drawing room could just be made out.

"It may be a play," said Buller briskly, "but the death scene is real tonight. Or it may be. We'll soon find out."

A policeman apprehended them before they had walked a hundred yards. He was very obsequious, explained why they had to be on special alert tonight—"All them riffraff, sir"—and directed them to the side door, which led directly into the Prince of Wales's offices.

"Yes, I know the way," Buller said.

"You're telling me you know the way," said Whitney, unable to conceal how impressed he was by this performance. "Now I suppose you're going to call the Prince of Wales by his given name."

"Not when there're people around." Buller laughed as they crunched fast along the gravel path. "I'm not connected with the royal family. It's just that I was a cadet with the prince and his elder brother—the one who died. They weren't treated very well. In fact, some of the cadets bullied them without mercy. And I didn't like that."

"So you became royal protector."

"Not at all," said Buller indignantly. "We became friends, and I saw quite a lot of his father, who was Prince of Wales then."

"Gee, I'm sorry. We Americans always say the wrong thing when it comes to your royal family. I guess it's because we're not used to it. You really like the guy—I mean both of them, father and son?"

"Yes, I do." Buller put an arm on Whitney's shoulder as if to guide him into the porch. "I don't suppose we'll see him. But at least his secretary can give us any news."

He opened the door to let Whitney inside first. Just as they had been struck by the silence inside the palace's walls, within the palace itself Whitney was aware of a heavy sense of formal reverence as if they had entered an ultraluxurious monastery in which the sacrament of extreme unction was being administered.

A gentleman usher in morning dress stood up from behind a low mahogany desk, recognizing Buller at once. "I'm afraid His Royal Highness is still with His Majesty, sir. But his secretary is in his rooms if you would care to see him?"

They were being escorted to the secretary's quarters along corridors heavy with purple hangings and carpets so thick that their footsteps were inaudible, past dim, giant paintings of royal palaces and royal landscapes and royal portraits, and gray busts of distant Hanoverian ancestors.

Whitney saw their escort flatten himself against the wall as they turned a corner, and there in front of them was a figure of medium height wearing a black suit and a dark gray cravat. The man halted as Whitney and Buller stepped aside to let him pass. Whitney recognized the prince at once, deep blue eyes, full sailor's beard already slightly flecked gray, a kindly but grave expression turning to a smile of recognition as his eyes met Buller's.

"Archy—how good of you to come! Always rely upon you in an hour of need." His arms opened wide, and Buller stepped forward, five inches taller and burlier, his embrace at once protective and affectionate.

"How is he, Georgie? The bulletins tell us nothing." Buller broke away. "I'm so sorry, this is Commander Whitney Campbell of the United States Navy—over here for the coronation, of course."

The Prince of Wales extended a hand, and after only a second's hesitancy and with a nod of respect, Whitney seized it. "So you're one of the multitude of the disappointed. I'm sorry, commander." He turned back to Buller. "Father has been wonderful—like a lamb as soon as he knew that it was his duty to give way. He walked in in his tattered old dressing gown to the special room prepared for Sir Frederick Treves to perform the operation. He wanted his dog to stay with him, then lay down, and said impatiently, 'Well, get on with it.'

"You know, it was terribly dangerous, Archy. Lord Lister was very doubtful about it but was overruled by the others. And afterward, when he came around about an hour later, do you know what his first words were, 'Where's Georgie?'"

"Well, I was there, of course, and he was like a baby. He thought he was going to die. So did I."

"And now he's safe?" Buller could not resist interjecting.

"No, but he's holding up well. Papa's very strong and has the will, too. Unless anything terrible happens, like a new infection, I think he'll pull through. I know he'd like to see you—but perhaps tomorrow."

"Thank God," Buller exclaimed. He seized the prince's hand and shook it. "I'm so glad. And now for your own sake, take some rest. You look all washed out."

"It has been a long day." The Prince of Wales smiled at them in turn, and they stood aside to let him pass.

Whitney waited for him to disappear through a door and then breathed out slowly. "Well, I guess that's straight from the horse's mouth. They won't believe me when I get back to the embassy."

They were led by their escort along a wide corridor through a great hall to the Privy Purse entrance.

"Come home with me before you go back," said Buller. "London won't be sleeping tonight, and my wife should have arrived home from the country. Let's take a cab, we've had enough walking to last the week."

And Archy Buller sank back on the hard leather seat of the growler. He was never a man for taking unnecessary exercise, as his waistline plainly showed to the world.

Only on invitation cards, in Debrett, and on the account lists of the better couturiers of Paris and London, was Clemmie Buller recorded as Lady Clementine Buller, wife of Commander Archibald Buller R.N. To her friends, relations, and acquaintances, she was always Clemmie, the sensible, down-to-earth, tall, handsome only daughter of the last and now deceased Earl of Huntley.

People in society used to ask, "How can anyone as mad as Lord Huntley have such a sane daughter?" And then answer it themselves: "The good Lord took one look at the father and said, 'Let there be none of this man in any fruit of his loins.'"

Clemmie had never known her mother, who had died (some said it was an act of mercy) when Clemmie was a week old, and she had been brought up by a succession of nurse-maids and nursery governesses. She remained the only person to understand and certainly the only one to love her fiercely eccentric admiral father.

With her fine head of fair hair with early flecks of gray, her stately figure, and air of innocence, which was not as deep as at first it seemed, Clemmie Buller was popular with men and women. She was loved by the multitude of servants—from gardeners and laundrymaids to housekeepers and butlers—and by the nursery staff who looked after the children at the town house in Clarges Street and the country house near Cirencester.

To them all she was an admired mistress, mother, and wife to the burly, notable, and heroic naval commander. While most of her social set assumed that Clemmie's moral life was as full of infidelities as their own, only her intimate friends knew the ever-changing pattern and the rises and falls in the passions of Clemmie's life. Long ago, in the early days of her marriage, she had been shocked to learn for the first time of her husband's affairs. Her cousin Marie told her she must expect them if you marry a sailor. But Clemmie was soon to learn it would have been no different if Buller had been a businessman or merely a country gentleman. Her husband was a born philanderer, and she was prepared to put up with that so long as there was nothing serious or lasting in his affairs.

For the fact was that while adultery was condemned in palace and pulpit and judged disgraceful among the laboring classes, the higher the social scale, the freer was the interpretation of the rules. As opportunity occurred in the social round, in her own house when Buller was absent, at country seats and town houses during the season, if a gentleman pleased her and she pleased a gentleman (and she almost always did) a pleasant flirtation might well lead to bed.

It was a very common arrangement about which men spoke little and women (at discreet times) a great deal. If infidelity were too brazen, too sustained, or too serious, marriages could be broken. Usually they were not, divorce being a very serious and damaging experience. In 1902 the Buller marriage, which was a very happy one, was not in the least threatened by the transient affairs of husband or wife. In fact, they both preferred sleeping with one another than with anyone else, and from time to time said so.

On the evening of the day of the king's operation, Clemmie arrived at Paddington Station with her children, governess, two nursemaids and her personal maid, Nona, at 10:15 P.M. The coachman was quick to spot them through the smoke haze of the station, two porters helping with the luggage.

Clemmie greeted him anxiously. "Good evening, Grant. We heard the terrible news before we left. How is the king?"

"It's said he's fighting bravely, ma'm. The master went off to Buckingham Palace to see what he could learn. It's an awful business, ma'm."

The sleepy children were helped into the carriage, smart in their town clothes and in strong contrast with the barefoot Paddington urchins who, pushing and shoving one another, cried, "'elp carry the bags, ma'm? 'elp with the luggage, sir?"

Although it had been a warm day, Randolph had ordered a fire to be lit in the drawing room, and when Clemmie entered it in her traveling clothes, the two men were standing with backs to it, sipping a brandy nightcap. She hesitated a moment at the sight of the American and at once smiled socially and inquiringly at him.

Buller stepped forward and briefly embraced his wife. "Darling, here is an American I have rescued from the crowds—quite lost he was, as I was, too. Commander Whitney Campbell of the United States Navy."

"Very pleased to meet you, ma'm." Whitney bowed and shook Clemmie's hand.

"And how is the king, Archy?"

As Buller recounted the meeting in Buckingham Palace and described the crowds and their subdued concern, Clemmie glanced from one to the other of the two men, first at her burly, good-looking husband, clean-shaven now, brown hair noticeably receding; and then for rather longer at the tousle-haired American with the boyish freckles and the high color in his cheeks, accentuated perhaps by the fire on this warm evening. Clemmie liked what she saw, liked the look of his hands holding the brandy snifter, the slimness of his figure in the American-cut dark suit, the way he laughed when Buller told of their near separation after no more than an introduction outside the palace. Yes, she could well imagine his being lost: it went with the vulnerable air of innocence.

"You and your wife must come to dine before you go home," Clemmie said.

"That's extremely kind of you, ma'm. Unfortunately I'm alone."

"How naughty of you to leave her behind," Clemmie teased. "How she would have loved all this drama!"

Whitney flushed with embarrassment. "No, I'm sorry—I mean I am not married."

Clemmie was quite able to deal with that. "What a lot of foolish women there must be!" she said with a laugh. Then she excused herself in order to change from her traveling clothes. She had already taken off her hat and veil, shaking out her long fair hair, and now left the room to join Nona in the hall. That's rather odd, she was thinking. He must be older than he looks to be a commander. Mid-thirties, like Archy? But not married, and yet her well-developed judgment on these matters had decided within seconds that this man was pure heterosexual.

Clemmie's social mind raced ahead over the next two weeks of their calendar. They were giving a dinner party on the following Thursday, a recovery from the coronation festivities dinner party, she had called it. Eighteen people, just close friends. She would make it twenty, and call on her cousin Maude to make up the numbers so that she could have this American. He came from a good East Coast family, she guessed, and with that name, clearly with Scottish connections. And very attractive, too.

Chapter II

⚓

Russian Crisis

IT WAS SAID by neighbors that so strong was the naval strain in the Buller family, the servants at the family seat, Weir Park, "showed a leg," holystoned the floors on their knees, and worked in watches; that the master was "piped on board" when he arrived home. It was true and not hearsay that Weir Park had been run more like a ship than a country house since it had been built by Captain Alastair Buller R.N. with prize money he won in an engagement with a Spanish treasure ship in 1743.

Since then, generation by generation, the walls were decorated with portraits of Buller sailors, some missing an eye or an arm, who had fought with Howe at the Glorious First of June, with Rodney at the Battle of the Saints, with Nelson at Trafalgar; and all the portraits showed the Buller characteristics of powerful shoulders, heavy nose like the prow of a three-decker, and all-round configuration of a John Bull. Captured ensigns, ugly chipped sabers, a French musket or two added to the warlike nature of the house, whose main entrance was flanked by a pair of cannon—4.5-pounders from the French three-decker *La Belle Poule*. On a softer note there were also portraits of Buller wives, and of children unfortunate enough to be born daughters, by distinguished

15

nineteenth-and eighteenth-century artists, notably Thomas
Gainsborough. These were more usually found in the
feminine environs of upstairs drawing rooms.

Of the long line of naval Bullers, only Archy Buller's
father, George, had died without seeing action, to his lifelong
regret. Archy himself had sustained the family's martial
reputation at the bombardment of Alexandria in 1882, in the
Egyptian War that had followed, and more recently in the
South African War, where he had earned his decoration.

Weir Park, built just below the summit of a south-facing
hill in the heart of the Cotswolds, had been inherited from
George Buller by his twin sons, Guy and Henry Buller, both
naval officers of forty-four years and both post captains. Old
George Buller's widow, Lady Cecily, never could remember
which twin had been born first, so the brothers had cheerfully
tossed a golden sovereign, the winner taking the baronetcy,
the loser the sovereign. Guy had won, but as there was plenty
of room and the brothers and their wives were devoted to one
another, when they were not in town and the officers not at
sea, they lived together at Weir Park, with their mother in one
wing of the house with her own personal servants.

On his father's death, Archy Buller had therefore bought
Wyston Court, a half hour's ride from Weir Park. It was a
modest Queen Anne manor house with a dozen bedrooms, a
nursery suite, and a home farm of some 500 acres. The three
brothers—when they were not at sea—and their wives hunted
with the Mid-Gloucestershire Hunt, their children mixed at
parties, their parents at balls and dinners. In their country life
the Bullers conformed to the semifeudal, benevolently aristocratic pattern which had existed for centuries, and ignored
the Industrial Revolution, the advent of the twentieth century, and the rise in strength and wealth of the new industrial
powers, the United States, Germany, and Japan.

The Bullers, like the landowning gentry and aristocracy
throughout the land, like their tenant farmers, their laborers
and servants, had grown up and lived in the assumption of
national and imperial power, and in the knowledge that no
empire had ever been as great nor as strong as the British

Empire. The villagers and laborers and craftsmen of the Cotswolds, and elsewhere throughout the countryside, had lived all their lives with the comforting belief that out there and far beyond the boundaries of their parishes and England's shores, their country owned vast areas of the world, and that they were protected by the Royal Navy and safe under the steady regal splendor of their monarch.

No one should have been more conscious of this comforting state of affairs than Archy Buller, whose service in the Royal Navy had taken him to every corner of the world. Wherever he went, from remote coaling stations in the Pacific or the sub-Antarctic to the great British naval bases at Simonstown and Hong Kong, Gibraltar and Singapore, the Union Flag flew above official establishments, the White Ensign from the masthead of British men-o'-war.

But Buller's naval service had also taken him to the South African colonies in 1899. And there in Natal, close to the village of Colenso, he had witnessed the shattering defeat of the British Army by nonprofessional Boer farmers armed with rifles and a few pieces of artillery. Buller himself had commanded a battery of naval guns, hauled up-country by train and ox team. He had lost half his men and all his guns.

Defeat on this scale was an unnerving experience for Buller, less so for his chief gunner, and friend, whose life he had saved after the engagement. Warrant Officer Rod Maclewin, from Newcastle-upon-Tyne, represented in the Royal Navy the harsher face of life in Britain at the turn of the century. By contrast with the timeless security, the spaciousness and seasonal beauty, of a Weir Park or a Wyston Court, Rod Maclewin had grown up in the world of a smoky industrial city, where the men drank to dull the harsh edge of their working life, or their lack of work, and the women bred too fast and suffered too much.

Rod Maclewin had joined the navy as an escape and a necessity, had suffered the rigors of the lower deck in the 1870s and '80s, had risen by merit and determination, and by chance and design had found himself sharing the crises of shipwreck and action with Archy Buller.

For Buller, as for his twin elder brothers, to enter the Royal Navy was as inevitable as growing up. To join the training ship *Britannia* at twelve years was as unquestioned as being weaned as an infant. First cadet, then midshipman, and then a commission as a lieutenant, followed by a career of privilege and authority as a Royal Navy officer. But always sharing the dangers and discomforts of the lower deck, and putting their interests before his own. Old Clarke, the head groom at Weir Park, had taught Buller as a boy always to consider his horse first, whether out hacking or hunting, and himself a very poor second. It came easily to Buller in the Navy to accept that his men came first, in calm or storm, at sea or on land, in battle practice or in battle.

Buller could remember from early childhood his father saying, ''You know why we always beat the Dons and the Frogs? I'll tell you why. It's because their officers thought they were better than their men, who were scum. But a British naval officer knows his men are more important than he is and have to be looked after. You remember that, Archy.''

It seemed the most natural thing in the world that such a close friendship should develop between Buller and the man with whom he had shared so many voyages and dangers. Rod called Buller ''sir,'' messed in the warrant officers' mess and not in the wardroom, went home on leave to his wife in a four-roomed Tyneside flat in the poorest part of Newcastle, while a carriage met Buller at Cirencester to take him to Wyston Court. But the two men were closer to one another in spirit and experience than any of their fellow officers and warrant officers.

In the strictly class-divided society that was Britain at the turn of the century, the structure of rank was as secure in the Royal Navy as the bulkheads of the ships in which officers and men served. But nowhere were the links of loyalty and common purpose stronger than in the senior service.

In a modern war Buller was confident that the spirit and fighting strength of the men would be as powerful as in Nelson's time. But in the ninety-seven years since Trafalgar had been fought, when Britannia really had ruled the waves, she had also grown arrogant and complacent. The colonial wars had shown the weaknesses of leadership in the army. Buller's own experience at the Battle of Colenso made him wonder if Royal Navy leadership would be any better in a major war.

Last month the Boers had capitulated and signed a peace treaty with Britain. Yes, victory for Britain. But it had taken nearly three years to defeat the Boer farmers, while the world mocked at the imperial humiliation. Five months before that, Britain had signed another treaty—a treaty of friendship with Japan. The great empire upon which the sun never set was climbing down from its isolated throne and seeking allies. The French Navy was a constant threat across the channel. Germany was already building a fleet to threaten the omnipotence of the Royal Navy. On the other side of the Atlantic, the American fleet grew year by year.

The Pax Britannica which had granted the world its most peaceful hundred years was showing signs of age, signs of cracks and imminent breakup. The near-death of the king-emperor so soon after Queen Victoria's funeral symbolized the fragility of the imperial structure which had held together the peace for so long, confirming the old saying, "Empires are only sandhills in the hourglass of time."

The cancellation of King Edward VII's coronation was also like a giant wedding at which the bride fails to appear. After the shock among the assembled guests, there were embarrassment and confusion. Will the bride make a delayed appearance—or, will the king recover to be crowned soon? No one was quite sure whether to stay, or go home. The higher the rank of these foreign guests invited to the coronation, the more pressing was the need to return home, to interrupted duties and engagements; and for a number of rulers of less settled states, the urgent need to go back in case of revolution and the discovery that they were returning to their execution rather than to their thrones.

Affairs of state were especially demanding on Kaiser

Wilhelm II, Emperor of Germany, King Edward's nephew, who, as one of the family, was a personal guest of the sovereign at Buckingham Palace. But it was the kaiser and the officials at the German Embassy who acted first and with typical German decisiveness after the shock of the cancellation. In the kaiser's party there was that toadying distant relation and naval A.D.C., Count "Sonny" Reitzberg-Sönderlong, Korvettenkapitän in the Imperial German Navy, also known as "the leech" for his capacity to retain at all times his hold upon his all-powerful master.

As soon as the bulletins indicated that the king would recover from his operation, the kaiser turned to his naval A.D.C. and stated emphatically, "Now we shall go home—but first we shall have a great reception at the embassy."

"A thanksgiving reception, sire?"

"No, Sonny, that sounds too ecclesiastical, as if the Archbishop of Canterbury were officiating. I shall officiate. We shall call it 'a soirée,' and everyone will come because all other arrangements have been cancelled. I shall enjoy it, Sonny."

And the emperor gave his upturned waxed mustache a quick twist with his good right hand and smiled with satisfaction. From his uncle's misfortune he would derive great kudos—as the man who saved the coronation from disaster.

It was as grand an occasion as the kaiser had predicted. All the crowned heads who had not already returned to their palaces were present, as were the more esteemed princes and princesses, grand dukes and grand duchesses, peers and peeresses, presidents and military dictators of the better-class republics. From the American Embassy came the ambassador and his wife, the naval attaché, and the special Navy representative of the president, Commander Whitney Campbell U.S.N. And Buller and Clemmie were invited as friends of the Prince of Wales.

The reception began at 9:00 P.M., and the Emperor of Germany was blessed (as always, it seemed) with perfect weather. Count Sonny had surpassed himself as organizer; Pol Roger '92 and Eitelsbacher Karthauserhosberg '86 flowed like the Rhine. *Cuisses des nymphes á l'aurore, crépinettes foie gras au truffle, volailles en gelée, pigeons en crôute,* and *fraises des bois* were served on silver platters by liveried footmen on the terraces and lawns overlooking the mall and in the drawing and reception rooms of the embassy until 2:00 A.M. Guests listened to or danced to the music of two orchestras.

Buller always remembered two incidents during that long summer evening in Carlton Terrace, with the sound of a Strauss waltz emerging from the open windows of the ballroom, and the mixed male and female scents of Havana Havanas and lavender blending with the smell of the roses in the gardens. He and Clemmie spotted Whitney, alone and looking somewhat forlorn by the lake. Whitney was transparently pleased to see them again, and they were talking of the Buller dinner party the following week, when Count Sonny joined them, uninvited but using the excuse of his acquaintance with Buller.

The first indication of his presence was the click of heels. Buller turned and recognized the tall, fair, and immensely handsome figure with the three saber scars on his cheek. His German accent was barely discernible as he spoke to Buller:

"Forgive me, commander. May I take advantage of our earlier meeting to persuade you to introduce me to this lovely lady—your wife, perhaps?"

Buller effected the introduction coolly. "And perhaps you already know Commander Whitney Campbell of the United States Navy? He is a considerable linguist, so you may talk to him in your own tongue—or in Italian or Japanese for that matter."

There was more clicking of heels, while Whitney in his relaxed and informal American manner smiled agreeably, offered a firm handshake, and said, *"Guten Abend."*

"Ah now, commander," said Count Sonny, "His Imperial Majesty is most anxious to meet you. He told me just so when he glanced through the guest list." He nodded at a nearby *Diensboten* and spoke briefly into his ear.

The count's handsome and stately wife, Miranda, joined them, giving Buller a brief, appraising glance before turning to talk to Clemmie. A moment later Buller became aware of the imminent arrival of a personage of great importance. Voices about them fell, there were hasty movements among the nearby guests, and a passage appeared as if Moses had parted the water of the Red Sea.

The bowing and curtsying over, the kaiser bent to Clemmie's hand and kissed it. "I know that your husband is a great friend of my cousin Georgie." He turned toward Buller but continued to address Clemmie. "And that he performed feats of great heroism in your most unfortunate war in South Africa. It is a pleasure to meet you both."

Buller murmured, "Your Majesty," and bowed again briefly. He had seen the kaiser several times before, had observed the pallor of his complexion, the eyes as shrewd and as brown as those of his uncle, King Edward VII, the Hohenzollern stance of inherited authority, and the charm in the voice and the glance.

"And this American is your friend, too, Commander Buller? I would like to talk to him." Then, as everyone except the military A.D.C. who was accompanying him and Count Sonny withdrew, the emperor indicated that Buller should remain.

"Commander Campbell, please convey my warmest felicitations to your president." He chuckled as he remarked in doubtful taste, "And advise him to be more careful than his predecessor. We want no more assassinations, do we, commander? And if he requires advice on personal security, tell him I have the best man in the world. Not that I have enemies, you understand. But there are always the insane among us—yes?"

"Yes, sir—that is true."

"And please tell him with my compliments that I fear he is not wise to superimpose the eight-inch guns in his new battleships on the top of the twelve-inch gun turrets. The blast of one will adversely affect the working of the other guns. It stands to reason. Admiral von Tirpitz agrees with me—and I make a study of these matters, Commander Campbell.''

Buller watched Whitney's expression with amused interest. The five new battleships at present being laid down in American East Coast yards were still highly secret in their design, and nothing had been publicly divulged about them. The kaiser was clearly enjoying showing off his knowledge. ''Now with our new eighteen-knot battleships, we believe we have the best arrangement of heavy guns, with primary and secondary armament not interfering with one another—no blast effects, you understand, commander.''

Buller admired the way Whitney replied so spiritedly and as if he were talking to a superior officer rather than to one of the most powerful men on earth. Half laughing, the American replied, ''I guess I won't tell President Roosevelt that our battleships are no damn good, sir. I might not get very quick promotion. But I'll remember to convey your anxieties to him and I know he will be grateful.''

Emperor Wilhelm II turned away with a grunt that suggested he had dismissed the subject for all time, there being more pressing demands on his attention, nodding at the two women before drifting away into the darkness of the evening.

''Well, I'll be jiggered,'' exclaimed the American. He turned to Buller. ''Why did he say all that to *me?* I always thought kings and emperors were polite to common citizens, especially their guests. Anyhow, what does he know about battleship design?''

''A very great deal, I believe,'' said Buller. ''The Prince of Wales tells me he's always talking naval architecture and drawing designs. He's got a jealous obsession about the British Navy being the biggest in the world.'' Buller mimicked (not very well) the Kaiser's accent. '' 'I vill not rest till I haf brought my Navy to ze same height at vich my army stands.' It's true—that's what he's saying. And his Army is known to be the most powerful in the world. We English have got only a token army, as you know. Our navy's our shield—we live by the sea and our empire all over the world. For Germany a fleet's just a luxury—a toy to spite us and his uncle. And a damn dangerous toy.''

Out of the half-light of the garden, two figures had appeared, and Buller recognized his wife in a long, white silk dress, and the even taller figure of the Countess Miranda Reitzberg-Sönderlong. Clemmie said rebukingly, "Come now, this is not a naval conference. It's a party and you're to entertain us and give us some fun.''

Buller and Whitney stepped toward the women, Buller apologizing and Whitney asking Clemmie if she would honor him with a dance.

Buller found himself standing alone with the countess and feeling gauche and discomfited, which was unusual for him. At six feet two inches, he was accustomed to looking down on women, usually some distance down, even on Clemmie, who was tall for a woman at five foot ten. But this German woman was over six feet tall, an Amazonian figure, finely proportioned in a heavy Germanic way, with powerful shoulders, a long neck decorated with a necklace of pearls of immense size and value, and a face chiseled into features of considerable beauty. Her hair was the color of newly quarried Cotswold stone, straight and swept back tightly into a bun, and she emanated the tangy smell of some rare lemon scent.

Buller felt uneasy at her side and could make only small talk. At first, he could think only of the bigness of her—her big bones, big (but finely shaped) hands, her big facial features, the nose uncompromising, the exposed ears like a man's. It was Buller's first encounter with a woman as tall as this countess, and his sexually alert mind raced with images of intimate contact.

"Would you care to dance this waltz with me, countess?'' Politeness obliged Buller to ask the question. Tingling curiosity added spice to it. They went inside, and she slipped into his arms, and he discovered at once what a light and effortless dancer she was, as if trained for the ballet. The fact that they were so nearly the same height made their matching as a pair seem in even closer harmony, pivoting and crossing their feet in reverse turns on the ballroom floor.

In their first dance they talked continuously, asking trivial questions of one another, sometimes laughing lightly at the answer, Buller resisting the urge to comment on how pleasant it was to talk to someone on his own level. Then the orchestra broke into "The Blue Danube," and both partners were content to remain silent as they gave themselves up to the haunting rhythms of the Strauss music.

Buller became increasingly overcome by desire mingled with curiosity about how it would be to lie with this tall, full-fleshed woman with her long limbs and heavy breasts, and the sharp—even challenging—scent of lemons. A last brush againt her leg, a final electric flash of lust, and they broke apart, to fall into the formalities of the dance's conclusion—a slight bow, a shadow of a curtsy. There were many eyes upon them as they smiled and broke apart.

Count Sonny broke in between them, nodding coolly in Buller's direction. "Forgive me for recovering my wife. Darling, you must meet Lady Churchill, the mother of Winston Churchill."

The following day, as Buller was about to enter his club for lunch, he saw a big yellow Benz motorcar coming down Pall Mall, thrusting its way through the growlers and hansoms, the carts and carriages and big horse buses, and raising some cries of protest from cabbies. Count Sonny himself was driving, goggles raised to his forehead, the countess at his side in a great flowered hat and motoring veil, looking like some twentieth-century Boadicea tearing into battle.

Buller raised his top hat as they passed the Marlborough, but neither the count nor his countess recognized him.

A party, which took place on Buller's return from the Marlborough, could not have been in stronger contrast with the ostentatious affair at the German Embassy. Warrant Officer Rod Maclewin had been detailed to lead in the coronation procession one of the parties representing the Naval Divisions which had fought in the South African War. His wife, Rosie, had insisted that she and the children—Tom, age nineteen, and the girls, Sarah and Mary, seventeen and fifteen—should come to watch the procession and cheer their father and Newcastle's hero, who would be wearing his Conspicuous Gallantry Medal in public for the first time.

The family had been living for a week in two rooms in a boardinghouse near Rod's barracks before the cancellation of the coronation. They were preparing to go home, as disappointed as all the other thousands who had looked forward to the festivities, when they received an invitation to visit the Bullers in their Clarges Street house before the family traveled north again.

It was Clemmie's idea. Buller asked if she thought it was fair to the Maclewins. Wouldn't they dread it in anticipation and be embarrassed when it happened? "Of course we're old friends, darling. But it doesn't mean you and Mrs. Maclewin have anything in common—or the children."

Clemmie always got her way in domestic matters. "Rubbish," she exclaimed in her downright manner. "It'll be all right—you will see."

And she was right. The Maclewins turned up for tea in a hansom cab, which cost Rod a day's pay. Clemmie brushed aside her own servants, ran down the steps to meet them herself, put everyone at ease with her natural charm, had Rosie laughing in no time and telling about the boardinghouse.

The Maclewin girls and Lucy Buller had tea in the drawing room, while the two men and the boys were taken by Buller up to his study, where he showed Rod his collection of ship models, including the battleship *Victoria* in which both men had served nine years earlier.

Then he took a picture down from the wall and showed it to Tom Maclewin. "Have you ever seen that before?"

Tom shook his head. "What ship is it? It's difficult to tell."

It was indeed. The picture was a photograph of a sinking ship with only the end of the keel, the upside-down stern and the twin propellers showing above water. There was much steam and black smoke rising from the doomed vessel, and you could see a number of men clambering down the underside to reach the sea.

"That's the *Victoria* going down in the Mediterranean," said Buller, "and we were both on board, as your father has probably told you. The only difference between us," Buller added with a laugh, "was that one of us could swim and the other couldn't."

"Pa can swim all right—I've seen him," said Tom.

Buller laughed. "And I know it. Because on that day he swam for both of us, and saved my life."

Buller glanced at Rod, who was clearly embarrassed. It was twenty years since they had first served and fought together, and now they were both approaching middle age— "Lucky Midge," as Admiral Lord Charles Beresford used to call him, no more than five feet four inches tall, his face lined now, the brown eyes as keen and alert as ever, practiced in the skill of estimating the bearing of a distant ship and bringing a Barr & Stroud range finder onto it as fast as any gunner in the navy; firm and tactful in the management of tough ratings in his gun turret; a good family man; and a good man to have at your side at sea, in peace or war.

Downstairs, they joined the women and girls for tea. Clemmie said, "Isn't it a pity we're all too old for hide-and-seek. It used to be lovely in this house when the children were young."

"Never mind how old we are, Lady Buller," said Rosie in her soft Scottish voice. "Let's play anyway. Do you mind?"

"Mind? I'd love it."

So for the first time in years, the rooms and corridors of 13 Clarges Street, Mayfair, echoed to the shouts and screams of grownups and children usually considered too old for parlor games as for more than an hour the two families searched for their victims. It was the talk of the kitchen and of the neighbors for days.

Then Buller, still feeling hot and breathless after such unaccustomed exercise, hustled both families out into the small paved garden at the rear of the house, lined them up, and took his new Kodak folding camera out of its case.

"I'm not going to lose a moment as historical as this," he said. "All Maclewins and Bullers together at last." He checked his camera, set the focus, and called for the butler. "Now Randolph, all you have to do is to look through here and when you can see us all in the picture, just squeeze this bulb."

The old butler treated the whole business with the utmost suspicion, and held the Kodak as if it were a bomb. Then, with the camera at an angle of 20 degrees, they all heard the click of the shutter and relaxed.

"Are you going to use that for target practice, sir?" asked Rod as a joke.

"You are right, quite right," Buller replied. "I have ordered a single-lens reflex and my supplier and I have devised a long focus lens attachment. That'll record who is going wrong at 'shoots.' "

Buller and Clemmie escorted the Maclewins to the front door, where the Buller carriage awaited them.

"It's time we went to sea again, Midge," said Buller to Rod on the doorstep. "We're getting slack as landlubbers."

Rod agreed. "A force ten gale in the Bay of Biscay would do us both good."

"And some action would be capital, too."

"I think I can do without that, sir."

And now it seemed likely that they were to experience both, although more than two years had passed since that light-hearted family hide-and-seek in London. In world affairs the Entente Cordiale had brought Britain and France together as mutual allies after centuries of antipathy and intermittent warfare, while Germany became threateningly aggressive and powerful. Japan, the new power in the East, had amazed the world by attacking Russia, the mighty bear, which had for some time been provoking and frustrating her eastern neighbor. And "the gallant little Japs," as English newspapers called them, were winning.

In that smaller world of some 120,000 men, the Royal Navy, there was undeclared war, too—war of a different and highly personal kind—between two famous and popular admirals, "Jackie" Fisher, who had reached the top and was now First Sea Lord, and Lord Charles Beresford—"Charlie B."—under whom both Rod and Buller had served in the bombardment of Alexandria and in the Egyptian War which had followed. Their public quarrel was one of the chief interests of the navy, which was becoming increasingly divided by it into pro-Fisherites and anti-Fisherites—or those in "the Fishpond" and those outside it.

Both men had the good of the navy at heart. Neither admiral could agree on how best to increase its efficiency. Fisher the radical charmer, from a humble background and with no money, was loved by King Edward and Queen Alexandra, by many politicians and newspapermen. Fisher was violent and extreme in his opinions, and charming and witty with those he liked and admired. He was only half joking when he threatened to make widows of the wives of the officers who opposed him, and often ended his indiscreet letters with "BURN THIS! Yours till hell freezes!" He had reached the top through superhuman drive and energy.

Charlie B. was Rod's hero. In earlier days Beresford had taken a special fancy to "Lucky Midge," made him his cox, became his unofficial patron, and recently had persuaded Rod to take a commission and become Lieutenant Roderick Maclewin C.M.G., R.N.

Beresford, from an old and fiery Irish family, had been born rich and titled, and also possessed immense charm and courage. The lower deck loved him to a man. He was as strongly conservative as Fisher was progressive, and was as suspicious of the upstart Fisher, and jealous of his close relationship with the king, as Fisher was jealous of Beresford's wealth and exalted position in society.

Now that Fisher had tirelessly and cleverly maneuvered himself into the First Sea Lord's office in the teeth of Beresford's opposition, the split between the two men was wider than the English Channel.

While Rod's loyalty to Beresford remained as strong as ever, Buller continued to admire both men—whom he had known well for years—and deplored the division in the navy. And now in this October 1904, both Rod and Buller were under Charlie B.'s flag in the Channel Fleet based at Gibraltar. H.M.S. *Lily* was Buller's first cruiser command, and his first command since his promotion to post captain in the summer.

"I truly believe you love this ship more than anything, darling," Clemmie said at Portsmouth when she dined on board at the beginning of the commission. "More than me or the children."

"What rubbish you talk, my dear," Buller replied.

When he turned in late that night, he thought again about what his wife had said. Ever fickle with his affections, at the time believing he was in love with every woman he had taken to bed before and since his marriage, he was forced to agree with his wife that his love for this ship was very deep and steady, and that he might be more loyal to 6,000 tons of the best British steel than to any woman he had ever known.

This man-o'-war deserved her commander's loyalty. Brand-new and straight from her completion and acceptance trials, she had been worked up by Buller in the late summer of 1904, and he had familiarized himself and the ship's company with all the strength and vigor and capacities and vagaries that characterize every fighting ship.

H.M.S. *Lily*, a protected cruiser capable of over 21 knots, bristling with eleven 6-inch guns, supported by 12-pounders and Maxim guns, and with 500 tons of armor plate to protect her against enemy shellfire, had a complement of 475 officers and men. By the time this handsome three-funneled cruiser joined the Channel Fleet at Gibraltar, Buller reckoned that he knew the name of every officer and petty officer, and more than half his ratings.

Among the ship's company were tough Irish Catholics from Liverpool, middle-aged warrant officers from Glasgow with accents he could scarcely comprehend, leading seamen from the shires with no sailoring tradition, able seamen from Devon whose family connections with the sea went back to Queen Elizabeth's day, pimply boys of fifteen just out of training school—good men, not such good men, more than a handful who had served terms in prison or detention.

It was Buller's task to forge them into a happy fighting team, and especially to bring the ship's gunnery to the very highest level—the best in the fleet. Within three months he had almost completed the task.

Among them all, no one was more satisfied to be serving in the *Lily* than the gunnery lieutenant, Rod Maclewin, who had responded enthusiastically to Buller's invitation to serve under him.

At six bells on the morning watch on October 23, only three days after the *Lily's* arrival at Gibraltar to join the second cruiser squadron, the duty signalman on watch intercepted a signal from Beresford's flagship, H.M.S. *Caesar*, to the *Theseus*, squadron flagship: "Weigh anchor and proceed with your division," it ran by signal, "to 42.58 North 9.52 West to intercept and shadow Russian Fleet believed heading for Vigo."

Now every man in the Channel Fleet was aware that the crisis that had been developing over the past forty-eight hours was approaching its climax. War with Russia, a naval engagement with the Russian Fleet, appeared imminent. Ninety-nine years and two days after Admiral Nelson had defeated the combined French and Spanish fleets at Trafalgar, the first major naval battle since that historic occasion might be fought within days.

On board the *Lily* no one had time for speculation. Every captain in the squadron determined to be first to hoist the signal "Ready for sea," and although the boiler had been at long notice, it took time to work up steam pressure, the *Lily* was still taking in stores, and everyone of the ship's company had some task to complete before they could slip their buoys.

Rod made a last round of the guns to ensure that they were ready for firing the moment the ship cleared for action.

"We'll be giving those Russkies a drubbing, sir," one veteran chief gunner remarked as Rod checked the breech mechanism of the forecastle six-inch.

"All right, Guns. And I don't have to tell you to keep the

fire steady and let the rate look after itself.'' Rod swung open the breech and checked the firing pin with the practiced authority of a man who has worked with naval guns since boyhood. "And just you remember that the Russians have got guns with twice the range and ten times the power.'' He put a hand on the shoulder of the warrant officer as he ducked out of the gun shields and laughed. "But don't you fret, Guns. The captain'll be dodging them.''

This Russian Fleet had left the Baltic on October 17, en route to Port Arthur in the Far East, where the Russian Pacific Fleet had suffered several defeats at the hands of the Japanese under Admiral Togo. Admiral Rozhestvensky's orders were to reinforce the Pacific Fleet, raise the siege of Port Arthur, destroy Japan's navy, and recover control of the sea. The Baltic Fleet in crossing the North Sea had blundered in the dark into a number of British trawlers, some of the gunners had panicked and, believing that they were faced by Japanese torpedo boats, had opened fire, sinking a trawler and killing and wounding a number of fishermen.

There had been no attempt to offer aid, and no apology. The fleet sailed on, ignorant of the crisis they had created. Britain's relations with Russia were already strained. Now there were outraged demands for war and the destruction of the fleet by the Royal Navy.

The British fleets were placed on a war footing while the diplomats tried to work out a solution. But as the Channel Fleet's second cruiser squadron cleared Gibraltar harbor, headed by the *Theseus* and with the *Lily* rearmost in the line of sleek gray cruisers, war really did appear imminent.

Two days out from Gibraltar, during the forenoon watch, Rod made his way up the ladder to the *Lily's* bridge. Buller was on twenty-four-hour watch, taking occasional naps on a bunk in the chart room and having his meals sent up. This was an anxious time for Buller, and in all his naval career he had never been so conscious of the weight of his responsibilities—a new captain in a new ship costing £400,000, and the men under his command likely to be tested at any moment in battle.

Rod steadied himself against a particularly heavy roll before entering the bridge. The skies were gray with low scudding clouds, and they were butting into a strong northwesterly wind. The bows dug deeply into the Biscay seas, taking heavy greens over the forecastle and shrugging off the water again in cascades as the bows lifted in preparation for the pitch into the next great roller. Rod's sou'wester and oilskins were dripping as he gained cover inside.

Buller was standing beside the compass binnacle, a tall, heavy figure with his long, blue uniform coat buttoned under his chin above his white scarf, swaying against the heavy movements of his ship as if he were controlled by a gyroscope. For one moment before approaching him, Rod was struck by the thought that for centuries now one or another Buller ancestor with the same full nose and heavy stature had, at one watch or another, in one fighting ship or another—from trim frigate to this ultramodern steel cruiser—been standing like this in responsible command and perhaps sailing toward another action.

Then Rod spoke, voice raised against the sound of the wind, "Permission to stand down. The forward port and starboard six-inch guns can no longer be worked and I've ordered the crews to stand down."

The heavy seas had earlier made the bow six-inch gun station untenable, and the rising seas and heavy roll were now sweeping over the two guns and their shields to port and starboard abaft the bridge.

"So we're down to a broadside of four heavy guns, Mr. Maclewin. Let's hope we don't have to remain for too long in range of the Russian twelve-inchers." He smiled at Rod sardonically and strode to the starboard wing to look aft. In conformity with the *Theseus*, the *Lily* was making only 11 knots, but against this wind and in these seas, she appeared to be moving much faster through the water, the waves sweeping past like a river in full flood. The 12-pounder and six-inch gun crews in heavy oilskins were huddled behind their gun shields, ready ammunition beside their weapons. Two ratings were making their way aft along the upper deck slung to the safety line that had been rigged soon after leaving Gibraltar. Astern, the *Lily's* wake faded into the distance, a white counterreflection of the gray-black smoke streaming from her three funnels.

The *Hermes*, next ahead and six cables distant, plunged and rose again in the seas. Like the *Lily*, she was cleared for action with rails laid and top hamper stowed. The *Doris* and *Endymion* could be seen only as fading silhouettes, and the flagship was no longer visible in the van.

Buller shouted into the wind, "Do you remember at my house—more than two years ago—we agreed what we both needed?"

"A force ten gale in the Bay of Biscay, and you wanted some action, too."

Buller laughed, a deep Buller laugh into the collar of his coat. "Well, we've got the first two."

At that moment the officer-of-the-watch ran from inside the bridge. "Excuse me, sir. Russian Fleet in sight, sir."

He was pointing at a bearing of some 100 degrees, and Rod could just make out four heavy and distant dark shapes heading south, their smoke carried horizontally ahead of them. They were Russia's most modern battleships, 15,000-ton ironclads. They were no more than three miles distant, their twelve-inch turret guns trained fore and aft but capable of turning, training, and blowing them out of the water with a few well-aimed rounds.

Rod moved from the open wing into the shelter of the bridge. Two-year-old memories and amiable conversation with his gunnery lieutenant and everything else were cast aside as flags were hoisted and fluttered out from the *Hermes*, spelling the message repeated from the flagship: "Eight points to port simultaneously." Buller trained his glasses on the Russian ships, and Rod hastened up the ladder to the armored conning tower with its communications to every gun in the ship.

For the rest of that day and through the following stormy night, the British cruisers shadowed the Russian battleships and their accompanying cruisers and torpedo boats at the maximum range at which they could keep in visual contact. The Russian Fleet, which stretched out over several square miles of ocean, kept poor formation, partly because the heavy seas made the going very difficult for the little torpedo boats and partly because the seamanship was weak anyway, even the big ships falling out of station and then taking several hours to recover themselves.

By contrast, and as a challenge and provocation to the Russians, the five British cruisers kept perfect station throughout, from time to time increasing speed, bringing the squadron to port or starboard of the battleships, then allowing them to go ahead while the cruisers spread out astern in line-abreast formation. At one point, shortly before darkness closed about this mixed armada spread out over the Bay of Biscay, Buller was asked by one of his junior lieutenants, "Are we at war with Russia, do you think, sir?"

"Who's to know?" asked Buller in reply. "They won't know until they enter Vigo harbor, if that's where they're heading. And we won't know until someone tells us. The second division of the Russian Fleet, which is reckoned to be four hundred miles to the south, may know that war's been declared, and Lord Beresford may already be fighting them."

"It wouldn't be much of a fight in our case, sir."

Buller agreed. "Even with the worst gunnery in the world and the best from us I'm afraid we wouldn't last for long. All we've got is our speed, and our job is to scout and report."

Lights had appeared at the mastheads of the Russian ships, while the British flagship hoisted the signal to darken ship as nightfall came on, one more move to unnerve the Russians.

That night the weather abated, and during the middle watch the stars appeared in a clearing sky and the temperature fell sharply. Later when Buller awoke after a two-hour rest and looked out at the new day, he was greeted with a sight he would always remember. The sun was rising in a clear sky, but there were icicles, some several feet long, sparkling from the shrouds and davits and yardarms.

With the nearest of the Russian men-o'-war now five miles distant, the fleet was ploughing its way steadily south, the smoke rising from dozens of funnels and forming a great black stain against the cloudless blue sky. Beyond, the coast of northern Spain was in sight, almond green, rising to the snowcapped sierra, and a darker gray smudge marked the city and ancient port of Vigo. Within half an hour every British and Russian sailor would know whether or not his nation was at war.

By noon on that October 26, the admiral commanding the second cruiser squadron had learned from a fishing village down the coast that the crisis between the two countries continued but there had been no declaration. A telegraphed order from Gibraltar instructed the cruisers to keep in touch with the Russians but not to provoke them in any way. While the rest of the squadron sheltered in a bay ten miles distant, the *Lily* was ordered into Vigo to observe the activities of the Russian Fleet and check that the laws of neutrality were strictly followed.

And so, at 3:30 P.M. and beneath a sun that had long since melted every icicle and dried the cruiser's decks, Buller brought his ship into the Spanish port and naval base—past the lighthouse and long mole, exchanging courtesies with the port commandant—and dropped anchor a mere cable's length from the massive flagship *Suvoroff*.

Chapter III

⚓

Battle Flags Hoisted

ADMIRAL LORD CHARLES BERESFORD gave a deep belly laugh and said to Buller, "You would have had a capital scrap on your hands if there'd been war while you were in Vigo harbor. The Russkies would've ignored the neutrality laws, you mark my words. They'd already broken international law by coaling from those German colliers."

"Nothing to it, sir. A couple of 'mouldies' "—as the Royal Navy called torpedoes—"into the *Suvoroff,* and we'd have been out of that harbor like a bat out of hell. And I tell you, sir, you've never seen such unsmart men-o'-war. Those battleships are brand-new, but they already look as if they've been in the Newcastle coal trade for twenty years without refit—coal loose or in sacks all over the upper deck, so that the eight-inch guns couldn't have been worked. Brasswork like a Thames barge's—not a shine anywhere. No nets out. Booms rigged by a party from Bedlam. And the ship's company lounging about and smoking—my commander said they looked more like a bunch of workmen on strike than the crew of a battleship at war.

"Take a look at these, sir." Buller drew from his pocket an envelope of photographs he had taken of the Russian flagship, which showed every detail, every lump of coal in the piles on deck, even the dour expressions on the faces of the ratings lined along the rails and forbidden shore leave.

"These are good. Who took them?"

"I did, sir. Photography's a hobby of mine. I've made a darkroom in the *Lily* and have got an assistant. The camera has a long-focus lens."

Beresford grunted and handed the pictures back. He did not hold with "all this modern mechanical nonsense," as he called everything invented since the steam engine. But he offered Buller a massive cigar from an equally massive silver box on his desk, which aroused Buller's suspicions. It *must* be bad news. They were in the commander-in-chief's day cabin in the *Caesar*, still alongside the mole at Gibraltar but with steam up to be ready for sea in four hours. It could have been the drawing room of Beresford's London mansion, with thick Oriental rugs on the floor, deep armchairs and sofas, carved mahogany tables, desks and glass-fronted bookcases, an imitation fireplace, and paintings and brown photographs of ships and officers of the admiral's past.

Buller nipped off the end of the cigar and severed the band. Beresford's ancient and disgusting bulldog had settled on Buller's feet, and he took the opportunity of thrusting it away as he rose for the matches.

"And what's the diplomatic situation now, sir? Is there going to be war?"

Beresford pointed at a telegram lying on his desk and spoke angrily. "War? Not while that cowardly bounder Fisher's in the admiralty. He's tellin' me not to provoke the Russians any further by shadowin' 'em. I could have blown the lot out of the water in fifteen minutes—should have done, too. Shoot first and ask questions after, that's my motto. Did *they* ask questions before attackin' our innocent fishermen? Pah! And now what d'you think, Buller?" He indicated with a stubby finger a second telegram. "This concerns you."

Buller had been ordered to detach the *Lily* from her squadron as soon as he had completed his observation of the Russian ships in Vigo, and to report to the C-in-C, making best speed to Gibraltar. He had imagined that Beresford wanted to hear his findings personally, but now, as Buller had suggested, it appeared that there was an additional reason.

The admiral handed him the telegram, and Buller read it with a growing sense of outrage. "RELIEVE CAPTAIN BULLER OF HIS COMMAND AND INSTRUCT HIM TO PROCEED TO SINGAPORE IN LINER ORANTES DUE GIBRALTAR OCTOBER 29 REPORT TO C-IN-C CHINA FLEET"

Buller threw the paper onto the Admiral's desk. "But this is monstrous, sir. I have just worked up the *Lily*, she's a smart ship, the gunnery's first-class, I know my officers and men, the commission's run only three months."

Beresford rose from his desk, a stout and ponderous figure now, heavy with twenty years of good living since his courageous and popular actions in the Egyptian War. Buller knew that he could still charm the birds off the trees, but he was always in some rage about some supposed injustice or bungling at the Admiralty. In his florid face, the handsomeness of his prime years was scarcely discernible beneath the heavy flesh and jowls, the onetime flashing blue eyes dimmed by years of self-indulgence. Buller was glad not to be on his staff, whose lives were made hell by his choleric manner.

Now Charlie B.'s voice rose in volume like summer thunder: "I knew your father well, and I met your grandfather once when he was an old man—he could even remember Horatio Nelson. I know you well, Buller, too. You're a good officer, and I don't want to lose you. But while the Admiralty is run by a criminal nincompoop who will ruin the navy in twenty-four months exactly, there's nothin' I can do but command you to obey this order."

Buller rose and prepared to take his leave. "What am I wanted for in the Far East, sir? I don't understand."

"Something about wantin' two good gunnery officers, a senior officer and a junior officer. Anyone special you want to take with you?"

Buller's reply was as swift as the fire of a 12-pounder Maxim. "Yes, sir. Lieutenant Maclewin, sir. He's serving under me in the *Lily*."

Beresford slapped his thigh with the flat of his hand, a

beguiling Irish smile spread over his heavy face, and his personal barometer suddenly soared from "Thunder" to "Fair." "Maclewin—'Lucky Midge'—by Gad, I'm glad of that! 'pon my soul, I haven't even set eyes on the little feller since he was made a lieutenant. Tell him to come and see me before you go—he used to be my talisman, y'know, always brought a feller good luck."

That afternoon, Rod Maclewin was taken to the flagship. It was a brilliant autumn day, Algeciras and the dusty coast of North Africa clearly visible across the strait, the massive Rock of Gibraltar—well named a Pillar of Hercules— standing its eternal guard over this entrance to the Mediterranean.

The meeting between the very senior admiral and the very junior lieutenant was brief but full of affection and reminiscences and inquiries about each other's well-being. Rod knew how disappointed and angry his old patron was at Jackie Fisher's appointment as First Sea Lord. There was no need to refer to this blow, or to express sympathy. Beresford knew where his friends lay and knew also that Rod was one of his stoutest supporters.

"I'm sorry to lose you, Lucky Midge. Without you, if the Russians attack we'll all be at the bottom in fifteen minutes." He laughed deeply at his own fantasy and prodded Rod's shoulder with his fist. "Good-bye and good luck—I don't know what they want you for out east. It'll probably be some wild goose chase organized by that half-wit in Whitehall."

The voyage to Singapore in the *Orantes* was like some dream after the rigors of stormy shipboard life in a cruiser, and passed as quickly as any dream. It was not considered proper for a junior officer to share a first-class cabin with a post captain, but Rod and Buller spent a lot of time in each other's cabins, playing bezique or Mah-Jongg, or just chatting. The ebullient, extroverted Buller went to all the liner's dances, drew the attention of a great number of the women on board—mostly the wives of Indian Army officers, Indian civil servants, and naval officers whose husbands were in the East—flirted with them extravagantly, and, after ensuring that her husband was not a fellow Royal Navy officer, shared a bed with one for three nights as they steamed through that furnace of a passage, the Red Sea.

The upright Rod Maclewin, who was innocent when he married his Rosie in Newcastle-upon-Tyne and had never looked at another woman since, felt himself to be in an alien world among the extravagancies of first class in a luxury liner, and his fellow passengers appeared startled at his "Geordie" accent and quiet shyness.

"It's all right being an officer when I'm at sea," he had once told Rosie. "That's a world I understand and there aren't any class barriers in the wardroom. But posh folk ashore—that's something different."

Like many men from a poor and deprived background who had built a successful life, Rod harbored no grievances against the privileged and rich, and respected the class barriers which he had overcome himself. On the contrary, he was proud of his new position as an officer in the Royal Navy. But that did not make him socially comfortable among what his mother would have called "your betters."

After stopping at Karachi, Bombay, and Madras, the *Orantes* anchored in Singapore roadstead three days before Christmas, and as always both Rod and Buller were thankful for the end of slack times and the prospect of activity.

Both officers had become accustomed to the heat and were as suntanned as any of the other Europeans in the city. At naval H.Q.—a fine, shining white building on the quayside guarded by Royal Marines in matching white uniforms and puttees—their arrival was expected by the duty officer, who sent them off at once to the flagship to see the commander-in-chief.

The admiral was a portly, purplish officer who clearly enjoyed his appointment and had been on the station for six years. He made both officers welcome with a great show of hospitality and large gin slings, which Rod and Buller sipped while enjoying the slow-revolving fan above.

"Well, I hope you get on well with the little Nips, Captain Buller," he began.

Buller responded with a puzzled expression and said, "I'm

sorry, sir, I don't quite understand.''

"The Nips—you know, those clever little fellers—beating the Russkies hollow, they are. You two are joining their navy—didn't Charlie B. tell you?''

"I don't think he knew himself," said Buller.

"Well, when the Baltic Fleet arrives, if it doesn't sink on the way, there's going to be a bit of a ding-dong, what?'' Pacing up and down his day cabin, uttering a high-pitched laugh from time to time, the admiral explained their mission. As experienced gunnery officers, they were to be seconded to the Imperial Japanese Navy, observers under the Anglo-Japanese Treaty. The Japanese welcomed the opportunity of showing off their newly acquired skills to the Navy from which they in turn had learned everything. All the Japanese senior officers, including the commander-in-chief himself, Admiral Heihachiro Togo, had learned most of the finer points of naval warfare in England.

"Our friend Togo's already put out of action most of the Russian Pacific Fleet. When Admiral Rozhestvensky gets here, Togo will be waiting to receive him with open arms—and a samurai sword in his scabbard—eh?'' And he laughed again, relishing the idea of Britain's ally knocking out the Russian Fleet. "It's a long time since there was a fleet action—one hundred years in October. And this'll be the first ironclad battle. We don't want to miss any lessons, eh, Captain Buller—eh, Lieutenant Maclewin?''

They also learned that Captain W.C. Pakenham—"Paks" as everyone called this fearless and eccentric officer—was to be a third observer in the battleship *Asabi*. "I want a full report of everything that you see—and no ducking behind the conning-tower armor.'' His laugh was pitched on a higher note than ever. "And no getting blown up, or you'll answer for it.''

They closed the admiral's cabin door and walked down the passageway. Buller, mimicking the voice and high-pitched laugh, said, "Damn rum fellow, what?''

"Damn rum service, the navy," Rod replied in a quiet voice. "I don't know about you, sir, but I sometimes think every admiral's a bit touched. Even Admiral Beresford.''

"Especially Admiral Beresford.''

• • •

If seniority and long service in the Royal Navy unbalanced the brain, the reason—Buller reckoned—could be the continual shock of unexpected change. One day butting into a force 10 gale in search of a possibly hostile fleet a hundred times your own strength. A week later wallowing in the luxury of an ocean liner in the equatorial sun. And now, in February 1905?

The protected cruiser *Akura* might have been prepared for inspection by the emperor himself. From the shining brass of the tampions and guardrails and compass binnacle to the gleaming holy-stoned teak decks, there was not a speck of dirt anywhere. The ship's company were equally smart in their sennit hats, loose blue jumpers, and bell-bottom trousers.

Surveying the ship for the first time, Rod received the impression that he was joining a British man-o'-war in Portsmouth harbor instead of a Japanese light cruiser in Tokyo Bay. The officers, warrant officers, and men wore uniforms almost identical to Royal Navy uniforms, the ship had been built in a British yard (by Armstrong's of Newcastle-upon-Tyne, Rod was delighted to discover) and was almost identical in specification and appearance to the English *Pelorus* class with four-inch guns and two tall funnels.

It was at first unsettling to note that the faces of these sailors were Oriental in cast, the name of the ship on their hats was in Japanese script, like the ship's name on the stern, and the flag fluttering at the staff was not the White Ensign but the Rising Sun.

Since their first meeting with Admiral Togo on arrival at naval headquarters in Tokyo, Rod and Buller had been treated with the utmost courtesy and given the best accommodations, had learned a few words and phrases of the language, and had come to admire these diligent, enthusiastic people who only fifty years earlier had been shut off from the outside world.

One day they went to sea in the *Akura* for gunnery practice, and Rod and Buller watched with keen, expert, and admiring eyes the four-inch guns straddling the target with the first rounds at 6,000 yards' range. Entering habor again, they met two troopships bound for Korea, the soldiers in their khaki uniforms and packs lining the rails. As the *Akura* slipped past toward her anchorage, the soldiers raised their rifles above their heads and with a roar that caused the scavenging seagulls to veer away in alarm, shouted together, *"Banzai!"*

The *Akura's* captain, Shu-sa Goro Saito, said through the interpreter, "Those men are bound for Mukden," adding with a grim chuckle, "and now the Russians will soon be back in Siberia."

Rod could well believe it, and both he and Buller had already seen ample evidence of the Japanese's singleminded determination to batter into surrender an army larger than France's or Germany's.

On land it had been a terrible and bloody struggle, brought about by Japanese fears that Russia would one day occupy the whole of the Korean peninsula and Manchuria and eventually threaten the Japanese home islands. Over a number of years, Russia had steadily advanced into Chinese territory and independent Korea, breaking treaty obligations to withdraw. A final attempt by Japan to persuade the Russians to withdraw from part of Mukden, southern Manchuria, and parts of northern Korea failed in the face of Russian truculence, and the two nations went to war in February 1904, just a year before the arrival in Tokyo of Rod and Buller as naval observers.

As Togo himself explained at their first meeting, Japanese loss of control of the sea would inevitably lead to defeat. They were in the admiral's day cabin, an austere cabin by contrast with Admiral Beresford's: a rolltop desk (Rod observed), a large, round table for conferences with his staff, a smaller table, a sofa with a folded rug and a blue pillow, some artificial flowers, and a pair of dwarf evergreen trees flanking the fireplace. As evidence of the war they were fighting, there was a painting by Togo's steward of the bombardment of Port Arthur by the fleet, and a Russian shell found on the flagship's bridge after an engagement. Luckily it had been a dud or Admiral Togo would not be talking to them now.

On another wall was a map divided into numbered squares, from the north Russian port of Vladivostok to southwest of Korea. "We have a Special Services Squadron of fast-armed merchantmen constantly searching for the arrival of the Russian Baltic Fleet," Togo explained. "They all have this wonderful Marconi wireless, and if the enemy is sighted they report the square number and course." He looked in turn at Buller and Rod with his penetrating black eyes. They could understand why every Japanese sailor was prepared to lay down his life for this man. "And we shall be ready for them," he continued through the interpreter, "not with so many fighting ships but with greater skill and greater valor."

"And where shall we be waiting, sir, if that is not secret?"

"It is as secret as the shrine of Chohaya. But you shall know because you are our friends, and you will be with us and go into battle at our side."

With a slender bamboo, Admiral Togo pointed to a wide bay on the southern coast of Korea, separated from the sea by a string of numerous small islands and the extensive island of Ko-je-do. "The enemy would give the imperial jewels for this anchorage, for it points at our heart across the Straits of Tsushima. There we shall wait while our scouts learn the strength of the Russian Fleet, and whether it will steer for Vladivostok through this narrow strait or take the Pacific Ocean side of Japan. I believe they will take this short passage, but if they go the long way we shall catch and destroy them just the same.

"Captain Buller, Lieutenant Maclewin, I hope you will take tea with me now. And perhaps we shall be joined by another officer, who is due and with your permission will join you in the *Akura* to observe our great battle."

They had scarcely put their lips to the sweet-scented tea served by the admiral's steward when the marine guard knocked on the cabin door and announced a name in Japanese. It sounded faintly like "Kambull." But the shock to Buller was total when Captain Whitney Campbell U.S.N. was shown in. The American bowed first to Togo and then extended his hand to the two British naval officers.

"I guess I have the advantage over you," said Whitney. "I knew you were with the fleet, and you didn't know I was coming. So now the *Akura* will have to hoist the Stars and Stripes as well as the White Ensign and the Rising Sun."

The bay was called Chin-hei, a magnificent expanse of sheltered water with the rolling Korean landscape to the north, green and rich and cultivated, broken by rivers, dotted with villages. With his binoculars Rod could make out cattle and teams of bullocks in the fields, figures moving about the village tracks, and along the coast the tied-up fleets of small sailing craft, all fishing having been banned for security reasons when the Japanese main fleet had entered the bay.

The *Akura* had been assigned a position close to the island of Niem-po, one of dozens on the seaward side of the anchorage. There was sufficient sea room for the fast little cruiser to steam between Niem-po and the next island to the west, and make the open sea in half an hour. With her role of scout to the scouting squadron itself—the van before the vanguard, as Whitney had described it—the *Akura* had to be first away, and with steam up twenty-four hours a day, the ship's company, more than any other, was aware of the imminence of contact with the enemy.

With more than twenty-five years of service behind him, Rod Maclewin suffered no sense of foreboding. There had been a time, many years earlier, when his nerves had come near to breaking point, and his broken nose and scars were evidence of past violence. But this hardened little veteran was as fearless of battle as he was of a storm at sea. The fine edge of alarm had long since been dulled by overuse. What he was feeling now was homesickness.

"Homesick!" he exclaimed to himself. "This is ridiculous. Me homesick! I spend three quarters of my life away from my Rosie and the children, and I don't remember feeling homesick before." He put his binoculars to his eyes again and ranged over the nearby island. A stream tumbled down the rocky side, splashing white where it was swift-flowing, reflecting the pine trees in the pools. There were heather and bracken, summer green. It could have been Rod's native Northumbria on a late spring morning, babbling burn, Scotch pines and larches, outcrops of granite. He could even catch the same smell blending with the smell of the sea—richly scented bracken and pine . . .

"That must be it. Memories of walks with Rosie across Armstrong Park on Sunday afternoons." He put away his binoculars and watched instead the exchange of signals between the flagship *Mikasa* and the battleship *Asahi*, newly arrived from Kure after battle damage repair, and with Captain Pakenham on board. Beyond the battleships were Admiral Kamimura's eight-inch-gunned armored cruisers, which would fight in the line with the battleships, the fine new twin-funneled *Nisshin* and *Kasuga*, and the even sleeker and faster *Idzumo* and *Iwate*.

As the sun went down over the great anchorage, and the ships of the Battle Fleet became darker silhouettes against the gray water, Buller and Whitney joined Rod on the forecastle, and they sat down for a smoke and talk on chairs brought by a rating.

Whitney said to the sailor in Japanese, "Please ask the steward on duty to bring three sakes from the wardroom." He turned to the two Englishmen and laughed. "We might as well relax. This may be our last night."

"Last night before what?" Buller demanded.

"Before the battle." The American began filling the big briar pipe he was so fond of. He once told them that he had been given it when he was at Annapolis Naval Academy nearly twenty years earlier, and that it had sailed 185,000 miles and twice fallen overboard. "I went over to the *Asahi* as soon as she dropped anchor and had a word with Paks. He said the latest intelligence is that the Russian Fleet left Kua-be near Van Phong on May 14 after coaling from German colliers. I worked out that at ten knots, they should have been entering the Straits of Tsushima in twelve days, and might have been spotted by the southern Japanese patrol twenty-four hours earlier. Now it seems that their economical speed is obviously a knot or two less. But I reckon they'll be sighted tomorrow morning, and we'll engage them before noon.''

Buller raised his glass. ''To victory to the Japanese!'' he said.

Whitney and Rod repeated the toast, startling a couple of ratings fishing from the ship's prow.

''How do you two Limeys feel about it?'' asked Whitney. It was clear that he relished the prospect of any engagement at last after the months of training and waiting. Everything about the American equipped him well for combat: his alertness and eagerness, his determination and belligerence (which they had both seen and suffered from in games of deck tennis and table tennis recently), his keen sense of appreciation and anticipation—all marked him as an exceptional sailor. The seeming innocence and vulnerability of their American rapidly disappeared before Whitney Campbell the professional naval officer. Buller would have felt full confidence in him if he had miraculously replaced Togo himself at the last moment before battle.

Rod as usual allowed Buller to speak first, which was not difficult at any time. ''How do I feel? My ancestors,'' said Buller, ''fought in the Dutch wars, fought against the Spaniards—the Dons they called them—against the French more often than anyone else, they fought your ancestors, Whitney, in 1812 and didn't do very well that time. They fought Chinese pirates and Algerian corsairs. But I reckon that not one of them would believe that a Buller would fight with the Japanese against the Russians.'' He laughed, threw back his sake, and concluded, ''And I think it's a grand prospect.''

Characteristically, Rod was briefer and less emphatic. He had been watching the masthead lights of the other ships fading instead of brightening with the onset of darkness, and had felt the chill of the evening mist. ''What I feel about it,'' he said slowly and in marked contrast to Buller's swashbuckling and highly personal response, ''is that Admiral Rozhestvensky will almost certainly try to break through the

Tsushima Straits, and that if it is foggy tomorrow he might slip through the net and make Vladivostok. And that will be very serious for the Japanese.''

A steward appeared at their side out of the half-light and announced that dinner was served. The three officers rose from their chairs. In background and breeding they could hardly have been more different, Rod from deprived but hard northern stock, Whitney from comfortable East Coast American affluence, Buller from a long line of rich West Country seamen. The contrasts in stature and physique were equally marked, Rod a stocky, lean, upright five foot four, Whitney a whippy and equally lean five foot ten, and Buller a heavy six foot two, a trifle stooping now after so many years of shipboard life, which was unaccommodating to anyone above Whitney's height.

Though they represented two navies and two nations, the three men had much else in common, first among them being their professionalism and their love of the sea. Now one of them had predicted battle on the following day, which must result in a conclusion one way or the other by this time tomorrow. Nor did any of the three doubt that, with their ship's assigned rôle, the *Akura* would be in greater danger of destruction than any other ship in the fleet.

Buller could just make out the time on the wall chronometer in his cabin: 5:25 A.M. The morning watch had little more than half an hour before standing down. ''Or would they?'' Buller asked himself. His ear, fine-tuned from decades of experience, told him that the *Akura* was preparing for sea. There was no doubt of it. Bare feet running in the passageways, on the main deck above, on the upper deck, all over the little steel cruiser, the sound echoed and increased minute by minute to become a continuous riffle. There were harsher sounds, too: the capstan's engine increasing in tempo, the rattle of the anchor chain in the hawsehole, then the deeper beat of the three-cylinder, triple-expansion engines throbbing into life and drowning the voices and orders of warrant officers and officers.

Buller leaped out of his bunk and pulled his uniform on over his pajamas, grabbed his hat and camera, and threw open his cabin door. He was not going to miss one moment of the action. And action it must be, for there could be no other explanation for this sudden activity.

On deck the first sight that attracted Buller's attention was the pall of black smoke rising from more than a hundred funnels. Fires in every boiler had been kept burning night and day, and now the engine-room personnel would be striving to raise steam for the departure for battle. A gusty wind sent spume flicking from the wave tips and fluttered the signal flags hoisted and lowered in hectic conformity with the bustle on the ships' decks. So Rod's fears of thick mist had not been realized.

The ship's purser, an English-speaking graduate from Tokyo University, greeted Buller and paused to talk. "Good morning, captain. I think we shall be fighting today, at last. Admiral Togo has had news of the Russian Fleet."

"Where have they been sighted, Lieutenant Otowa?"

"Square two oh three. That can mean only one thing. Admiral Rozhestvensky is trying to slip through the eastern strait, the one closer to Japan. And now," he added emphatically, striking the rail with his fist, "we shall cut him off and destroy every one of his ships. Every one."

Buller glanced down at the young lieutenant and wondered again at the fanatical confidence of these sailors, remembering at the same time the sullen, defiant expressions on the faces of those Russian sailors lining the *Suvoroff's* decks in Vigo harbor.

A fresh string of flags in the Japanese code was hoisted on the flagship, and Lieutenant Otowa called up to the bridge, evidently asking the signalman to repeat the message. Buller had his binoculars on the flags, but could not interpret them. He had mastered only the basic signals.

The purser turned back to Buller. "It is a message from Admiral Togo to everyone in the fleet. It says, 'We shall soon meet the enemy. The emperor knows that every man will do his duty today.' "

The Nelson touch, thought Buller. And quite right. Carried on the wind, he could hear the sound of cheers from the flagship, and then a band began playing martial airs. One by one the ships' crews echoed the cheers, and Buller became aware of a great surge of enthusiastic loyalty rising above the assembled fleet like the funnel smoke that was carried away in a single cloud on the wind.

In the little *Akura* the clang of the engine-room bell was followed by an accompanying vibration of the steel upper deck. The twin screws were stirring the water at the stern, and the cruiser got under way, with three cheers from her crew—the last to acknowledge the admiral's signal, the first to depart to scout for the fleet.

The island of Nem-po slipped past, no more than three cables distant, the gusts of wind tossing the topmost branches of the pine trees. The cruiser had already built up speed to 16 knots as they passed the eastern end of the big island, Ko-je-do. Beyond lay the open sea, gray and white-splashed in the strong wind. The *Akura* began to dig in her bows, and Buller felt the first sting of water in his face. Briefly a fantasy flashed through his mind: This was H.M.S. *Lily*, scouting ahead of the Channel Fleet in search of the enemy, which his ship would help to defeat in the greatest victory since Trafalgar. Then the image was lost in the *Akura's* bosun piping "Clear Decks for Action Stations!"

Buller had a streak of the romantic in him, although he would have been astonished and even indignant if anyone had told him. In his boyhood and early days as a cadet, his great yearning was for the sound of a shot fired in anger. He must have first heard his father using the phrase—his fine, tough, and resolute father who had become a naval lord, but had the misfortune (as he saw it) of serving his whole life during a period of relative peace and, unlike all his ancestors, had never fought a battle.

A shot fired in anger. Well, Buller mused, as he thrust aside the childish and ridiculous image of commanding the *Lily* in an engagement, he had heard plenty of those, from Alexandria in the extreme north of Africa to Colenso in the south. And now, today, he would certainly hear many more shots . . .

Abruptly casting aside futile dreams of the past and predictions of the immediate future, Buller hastened down to his cabin for his instruments and papers, and then made his way up to the bridge. In this battle he was only an observer, not a fighter.

Whitney Campbell had been told by envious contemporaries in the United States Navy Department that he must have a special pull with the secretary, George von L. Meyer, in order to secure these plum appointments, first to London for the coronation and now to the Japanese Fleet. At a ball in Washington in the fall, an admiral's daughter, intent on ending to her advantage Whitney's long bachelorhood, had told him that he was chosen for his charm and looks. Whitney disliked both assertions equally. He regarded his appearance and navy record as average and no more, and reckoned that he was just lucky. He had a sunny disposition and reckoned that he had been lucky all his life, in his parents, in his parents' choice of private school in New York City, and then Groton, and in his own choice of the navy as a career. When he met someone he wanted to marry and who wanted to marry him, he had no doubt that he would be lucky in this choice, too.

He certainly considered himself lucky to have met Buller outside Buckingham Palace that evening, and to have been assigned to the same Japanese ship as an observer. He liked this tough, unsentimental, gregarious sailor with his vigorous appetite for food and drink, gambling and women, while remaining essentially what Whitney's father used to call "an eighteen-carat good guy."

Whitney had known Rod Maclewin for only a short time but had developed a great liking for him, too—this modest, quiet, and essentially kind man with his battered face, broken nose, and unfamiliar accent.

But above all the American was fascinated by the relationship between these two men of about the same age and utterly different backgrounds. All that they seemed to have in common was a love for the Royal Navy and the sea. That was, it seemed, enough to break through what he had always been told were the impenetrable class barriers in English life. He had believed that the United States Navy was the only truly democratic navy. But if this pair of Limeys was a sample, and it was really true that the close relationship had begun when Rod Maclewin was a gunner rating, then there was evidently a common bond between the wardroom and the lower deck which had survived since the War of Independence and earlier.

Individuals apart and disregarding his advantage in knowing the language, Whitney felt even closer to the Japanese Navy than to the British Navy. Although the American Revolution had occurred 130 years ago now, Whitney was still conscious of the raw newness of his country and his service, and all the more proud of what the navy had achieved in the time—John Paul Jones overcoming the *Serapis* off Flamborough Head, the *Constitution* defeating the *Java* in the War of 1812, the brilliant exploits of the *Essex*, Dewey at Manila Bay.

He saw the Japanese Navy as an even younger service, but already with a fine record in the war against China and in this war against Russia, the victories at Port Arthur, and the running battle against the Russian First Pacific Fleet nine months earlier. Whitney had warmed at once to the enthusiasm of this Oriental navy, and felt much in common with their youthful cause.

As for the Russians, he felt nothing but contempt and loathing for them. Their ships were inferior, their guns and gunnery third-rate, their officers decadent and tyrannical, their ratings barbarous. Before leaving the United States, Whitney had read in the newspapers of Admiral Rozhestvensky's blundering, snaillike passage around Africa, of a mass mutiny while the fleet refitted and refueled in Madagascar, of international rows following the admiral's overstaying his legal period in ports on his passage half around the world, as if he feared arrival at his destination must mean disaster and annihilation.

Now, within a few hours, Whitney and his fellow observers would see the reality. And Whitney shared the general Japanese belief that it would be an annihilating victory.

0915 May 27, 1905. The Japanese light cruiser *Akura* on a course of 124 degrees in the Straits of Tsushima, speed 16 knots, sea choppy, visibility three miles intermittently ten miles, traces of the overnight mist, low, broken cloud, sudden shafts of sunhine like broad searchlight beams playing on the water.

Whitney had climbed up to the cruiser's bridge, lightly armored in lieu of a conning tower and with a steel splinter-proof roof. Aside from the cox at the big wheel, there were present the ship's navigating officer, gunnery officer and first lieutenant, and Captain Saito himself, hands thrust into his greatcoat pockets, a blue woolen scarf wrapped twice around his neck. He nodded in acknowledgment of the American's arrival and resumed his scanning of the hazy horizon.

Whitney asked the first lieutenant in Japanese, "Is there any more news of the enemy?"

"The *Idzumo* has been shadowing the Russian Fleet since seven A.M., sir," the officer replied. "The range is about seventy-eight miles when we last heard."

Like nearly all the Japanese ships, the *Akura* was fitted with modified Marconi wireless. There was a complex pattern of aerial antennae strung between the two masts, and at the rear of the bridge from the wireless room, the stutter of Morse code could be heard above the wind and distant beat of the engines.

A wireless rating, identified by the insignia on his shoulder, emerged from the cabin, saluted the captain, and handed him a sheet of paper. Whitney watched Captain Saito read it and then hand it to the navigating officer with a brief remark. After a calculation at the chart table, the cox was ordered to alter course half a point to starboard.

Captain Saito was a solemn officer who took his duties seriously. But he was smiling as he called out to Whitney, "Well, captain, we have not long to wait now. The enemy is off the southern tip of Tsushima Island. We shall relieve the

Idzumo as soon as we sight the main fleet and continue as the only scout.''

High above, in the foremast's spotting top, two lookouts standing back to back were each scanning the horizon through 180 degrees.

Ninety minutes later, with visibility improved and more consistent, a cry came from one of these lookouts, and, in the classic posture of the lookout since the earliest days of navigation, he pointed to the southeast. Everyone on the bridge and on the upper decks of the cruiser heard the cry, and all now gathered on the starboard side in an effort to catch the first glimpse of the Russian Fleet.

A cloud in the sky was the first evidence of the whereabouts of the Russians, a black and menacing cloud drifting away on the northwest wind. A minute later there was a shout from one of the four-inch starboard gun crew who was standing on the upper surface of the splinter shield. It was taken up by a second voice, and then a third. And suddenly everyone on deck could make out the gray shapes of the Russian vanguard, smoke streaming from their funnels. A fourth, fifth, sixth. And more. As each battleship became distinguishable, it added to the impression that the fleet line had no end, that Russian strength was inexhaustible.

It had taken the fully stretched Japanese Fleet fifteen months to destroy piecemeal the Russian Pacific Fleet. And now they faced this new threat from a fleet headed by four battleships newer and more powerful than anything that Togo could muster.

Through his binoculars Whitney could make out more details of the leading Russian ships, their hulls dark in contrast with the yellow black-tipped funnels, big twelve-inch turret guns fore and aft. Often during maneuvers off the American East Coast, with the ''enemy'' fleet closing in to a range of 6,000 yards, the guns all trained on his ship, Whitney as a young lieutenant had tried to imagine what his feelings would be when war games turned to reality. Would he be awestruck, resolute, afraid?

And now here was reality. The fact that these Russian

ships were not his personal enemy made no difference. He was as much at war and as much in danger as his Japanese shipmates, and Whitney shared their own sensations of awe, resolution, and fear. Fear? It was difficult to associate fear with these small, hard Orientals whose fanatical determination Whitney had wondered at ever since he had joined them. But it was fear—as identifiable as those Russian men-o'-war—that Whitney could feel coursing through his veins like some poison. At the same time, deep in his subconscious, he knew that if this had been an American cruiser steaming into battle under his command, his years of training would have seen to it that his judgment and resolution would not be diminished in the smallest measure.

Now, by God, they were under fire! The *Akura's* gun crews, impotent at this range, were uttering cries of *"Banzai!"* in well-disciplined chorus when Whitney saw a flash from the fore turret of the fifth Russian battleship, followed by another as the second gun fired. Buller was busy with his camera, recording this historic moment. Captain Saito had not missed the evidence either, nor his gunnery officer. "Take cover! Take cover!" sounded over the ship's loudspeaker system. "Enemy firing."

The cries of *"Banzai!"* were silenced, the crews manned the guns, the spectators on deck scuttled below. Captain Saito, an erect, sturdy little figure on the starboard bridge wing, continued to scan the enemy line, 8,000 yards distant now but still with no signs of its rear guard. Whitney stood behind him, searching for more muzzle flashes, counting the seconds—six, seven, eight. Then the whistle of the shell, a brief high-pitched scream, and a sudden gust, like a locomotive sounding its warning as it rushes through a station.

Not 500 yards, not 250 yards, nearer 150 yards away, the shell struck the sea and sent up a pillar of water higher than the cruiser's foremast, much of which crashed down in a soaking wall upon them. The crash of the explosion was sharp and concussive, unlike any Whitney had heard in all his years as a gunnery officer. As he wiped some of the cold seawater from his face, he realized with a shock that it was the first time ever that he had been at the receiving end of a live thirty-five-caliber, twelve-inch shell.

Three seconds later the second shell fell slightly more distantly on the port beam of the *Akura*. But not far away. A mere 250 yards. That Russian gunlayer had accomplished the almost perfect straddle with his two opening shots, and would have been highly commended in firing practice. He had also succeeded in amazing and even shocking Captain Whitney Campbell, and at least in causing some concern to the officers on the cruiser's bridge. In a perfect gunnery world, the third shot should land on or within a few yards of the little cruiser, blowing her out of the water. But Captain Saito had already urgently ordered the cox to give full port rudder, and the ship was heeling hard over with spray from the second shell sweeping like hurricane rain across her decks.

As soon as it was dry enough, Whitney wrote on his pad: "1048 hrs. Russian battleship *Oslyabya* opened fire with two ranging shots, at 8,000 yards. Straddle. Captain orders full port helm in evasion." A touch ruefully, Whitney added in parentheses, "(Gee, what swell shooting! Who'd believe it?)." This was going to be no walkover for the Japanese Fleet, which the whole world had come to believe was invincible.

Chapter IV

⚓

Tsushima

ROD MACLEWIN and Buller had chosen the forecastle rather than the bridge, Rod settling himself on the starboard side of the deck and Buller to port. They were particularly interested in watching the gun crews at work, their rate of fire, the gunlayers' reporting of the range, the delivery rate and quantities of ready ammunition, and the other minutiae of the complex art of sighting, firing, and reloading modern four-inch guns in battle, with a moderate-to-rough sea running and uncertain visibility. The harsh reality of war conditions could never be simulated in time of peace, and the reports and photographs of these two experienced gunnery officers must be of great value to the Royal Navy.

From their position on chairs taken from the wardroom, and wearing ear protectors, they were within a few yards of the two forward four-inch guns as well as the port and starboard guns on the upper deck alongside the first of the cruiser's two slim funnels.

From his side of the ship, Buller was in the better position to observe the Russian line as it came fitfully into sight, recognizing at once the now familiar silhouette of the *Suvoroff* and her three sister ships in the van, and recalling their filthy, coal-strewn decks and general appearance of neglect when he had seen them at Vigo. Now, on the other side of the world, they appeared from this range to be in better order in spite of their 18,000-mile voyage.

Buller had his camera on the fifth ship in the line, the modern, powerful three-funneled *Oslyabya*, at the moment when she opened fire. Judging the range and counting the seconds, he looked up into the clearing sky and saw the first of the twelve-inch shells as a small dot, rapidly enlarging as it plunged down toward the *Akura*. Professionally detached, professionally admiring, Buller was far too preoccupied to consider the 800 pounds of high explosive as any personal threat, and merely wiped the seawater from his face and camera lens irritably and got on with the urgent task of recording the facts and his impressions.

Rod was protected from the full brunt of the shock and the wall of water from the first shell, but was in turn soaked by the explosion of the second. Like Buller and often at his side, Rod had experienced many times the effect of guns fired in anger, and an abdominal bullet wound dating back to 1882 still gave him trouble. But this was his first ship-to-ship engagement. And last night, before falling asleep in his bunk, he had become fascinated with the thought that if Togo intercepted Rozhestvensky, he would be a witness to the first fullscale fleet action of modern times.

Captain Saito's task was to report the progress of the Russian Fleet and to avoid damage. A fight might lead to the *Akura's* speed being affected or her wireless damaged. He must keep his ship out of range so long as the Russian Battle Fleet could be kept within sight. For the next half hour this remained possible. The *Akura* was put into a wide 14-point turn to starboard, which placed her in relative safety and on a parallel course with the Russian line, now at 14,000 yards and, in the suddenly improved light, visible in its entirety—twelve battleships stretching into the distance, armored and light cruisers, and (to be identified only through a powerful glass) a scattering of little torpedo boats.

Above in the wireless cabin, the news was tapped out in swift Morse to Togo: "Russian Fleet 34°07' north 129°40' east, speed 6 knots, course 032. Visibility 9 miles.''

By eleven o'clock the slow-moving fleet had progressed a farther ten miles on the same course, and four more reports had reached Togo, who, directed by the *Akura*, was now hastening southeast in his attempt to intercept Rozhestvensky. The last message had reported visibility down to five miles, the next to three miles.

These dwindling figures told an anxious story to anyone with the smallest knowledge of scouting at sea. The little *Akura* would be obliged to close the range more and more, making herself increasingly, and perhaps fatally, vulnerable to Russian gunfire. Those on deck saw the danger, and the news quickly sped the length of the cruiser and down to the sweating stokers in the engine room until the entire ship's company of 220 men knew that action could be imminent.

The mist and cloud banks cleared intermittently, revealing the Russian ships at near point-blank range, then as swiftly and mercifully closing about the *Akura*, but leaving her with nothing to report.

Whitney spoke to Captain Saito as the damp mist closed about them again and the cruiser steamed blindly along at 15 knots, zigzagging to confuse the Russian gunlayers. ''Can you understand why they don't blow us out of the water?''

''Perhaps they are conserving their ammunition,'' the officer replied wryly. ''Those early shots were against admiral's orders, I am sure, or other ships would have joined in.'' He smiled at Whitney. ''Or perhaps they are glad of our company. It has been a lonely long voyage for them.''

A minute later the *Akura* broke out of the bank, visibility again became almost limitless, and ahead there were clear skies for as far as the eye could see. At once they were subjected to a hail of gunfire at short range: six-inch, Whitney judged, some four-inch as well as quick-firing 12-pounders. After the comparative silence they had enjoyed since the first shelling, the sudden firing and explosion of the shells filled the air with a thundering cacophony of sound and a million splinters, which clanged and rattled against the hull and steel upperworks of the ship.

Whitkey ducked for the protection of the bridge armor,

then raised his head and quickly scanned the Russian line. No gunsmoke, no muzzle flash. Only the bulky, dark silhouettes of the battleships digging their prows into the choppy water and laboring relentlessly north toward the shelter of their Vladivostok base. A light shell struck the forecastle deck almost at the prow, exploding in a dazzle of brilliance and black smoke and leaving a smoking four-foot hole with jagged sides and the useless remains of a capstan.

Where was the gunfire coming from? Puzzled, shocked, and ashamed that he had been so slow, Whitney caught the clue. The nearest forecastle starboard four-inch was firing. Two of the crew had been struck down by the hit, and the rest were firing fast, with the gun at a low elevation and on a west bearing, away from the fleet. A Russian heavy cruiser had closed in, by chance or accident, on the *Akura's* port side and was firing swiftly and steadily at a range of 2,000 yards.

The *Akura* was changing course violently and every few seconds, like a man running from stone-throwing assailants. Luck? Well, it might be on their side. But there would have to be a lot of it.

Whitney saw the big cruiser head on. Now she was attempting to ram. With that sharp ram bow she could cut the *Akura* in two. Forward six-inch guns firing fast salvoes. Black smoke pouring from funnels. Russians visible in the conning tower—just their heads and shoulders. Saying, "We'll have this little devil, for Saint Catherine and the emperor!"

The Japanese gun crews were keeping their nerve, firing at the rate of fourteen rounds a minute. Whitney could see them, and the smoking breeches when they opened them. And the range was so close that even the 3-pounders could join in—pebbles against a wall of steel bearing down on them.

Another heavy shell found its mark. The *Akura* shuddered like a struck dog, and a column of smoke gouted up amidships. There was smoke everywhere, their own and the enemy's. A rating darted by. Whitney had seen him with the captain seconds earlier. He was down the access ladder onto the forecastle. Now shouting at Rod and Buller below, gesticulating and pointing at the nearest hatchway. Smoke obscured them from Whitney, and when it cleared, Rod was making his way through the debris and out of sight. Ordered below by the captain? Whitney waited for similar instructions.

There was no possibility of writing any notes now. He caught a glimpse of the Russian ship's bows, decorated with the imperial coat of arms in brass above the curving ram. The *Akura* was heeling hard over in one more violent turn, slipping so close past the Russian that for several seconds no enemy gun could be depressed low enough to fire and a boarding party would have been more effective. Then they were tossing madly in the big ship's wake. And the shelling began again. Six-inch, at killing range.

The *Akura* gave a great lurch, as if preliminary to capsizing. She did not capsize. There was no end to her agony in sight yet. Instead a six-inch shell landed square on the forecastle below. Whitney saw it hit dead on the hatchway between the guns, tossing them aside like discarded toys. The men, too, what was left of them.

Whitney picked himself up from the corner of the bridge, half concussed, badly bruised. He could feel blood flowing from under his hat, which oddly had not been blown off. Was that left leg broken? No. He felt it, and saw that it was only cut.

But what about Rod and Buller? The *Akura* had two-inch deck armor, no more. If the shell had penetrated to any depth before exploding, they would have had little chance. Whitney dragged himself to his feet. A signalman lay dead on the port wing of the bridge, his head in a pool of blood, one hand still clutching a flag. Whitney could see through the smoke that still poured from the volcano mouth of the shell hole that the lower half of the ladder was misshapen and unusable. It was hot, too. He could feel the heat of the twisted metal as he held it before jumping the last six feet to the deck. The dark shape of Buller's camera with the brass projection—the long-focus lens—lay half in the scuppers.

Whitney had already developed a strong faith in the indestructibility of Buller. He had imagined him collapsing at about eighty-five, at his favorite baccarat table in the Marlborough Club, a bottle of '77 Croft's port and a pile of counters at his side. Not in action. But little Rod was different. Tough he might be, but he also had a vulnerability about him. Whitney did not wish his wife to be widowed and his children made fatherless by some Goddamn Russian gunner. Shucks, no! He needed help, and even Buller might benefit from a hand.

Or was he already too late? Whitney found that the hatchway the two Englishmen had used was unrecognizable. There was another one above the forward boat derricks. The *Akura* took one more hit, somewhere aft, as he raced down the ladder to the thick smoke and confusion below. Water was getting in through some hole below the waterline, too. And there was little light. A rescue party of four men with two stretchers bustled past him as if he did not exist.

You had to hand it to these Japanese, they did not panic easily. A burly warrant officer was organizing a repair party running out a hose. A dozen men, each carrying two shells under their arms, bustled past. Somewhere a hydraulic line must have been severed, paralyzing the ammunition hoists. They were followed by another rescue party, three members of a four-inch gun crew, half stripped of their uniforms by the blast, revealing raw burns but still alive. The next lot appeared dead, and one a mangled corpse, which Whitney wished he had not seen.

Whitney forced his way down the narrow alleyway against the tide of humanity, some uninjured, some wounded, some dead. The smoke and smell were becoming more intense—cordite stink, an acrid, burning smell. There was more shouting, too, and more water. A party of ratings under a sublieutenant was attempting to shore up a collapsing deck pillar. Whitney shouted at the sublieutenant, "Have you seen the two English officers?"

The Japanese officer turned and shook his head, applying himself again to his work. The water was around their knees and rising fast. For a moment Whitney became aware of the fact, which he had not previously considered seriously, that this ship could sink. In fact, unless fate intervened, or the

Russian heavy cruiser ceased fire, this catastrophe seemed inevitable. He could hear the *Akura's* guns still firing, their shells no better than stones against the Russian armor plate.

Farther down the passage, Whitney recognized in the dim light the figure of Sho-sa Kamimura, whose father was in command of the Second Fleet. Whitney had played chess with him in the wardroom the previous evening and had been beaten. "Where are the English officers?" Whitney asked him. The lieutenant commander did not hear him. The water was pouring through the bulkhead door ahead of them, and the officer was giving orders to get it closed quickly.

Whitney repeated his question, holding Kamimura's arm. "Captain Buller and Lieutenant Maclewin? Have you seen them?"

"There are many missing in there," said the Japanese officer, indicating the hell of the main-deck forecastle. "And now it is too late."

Below, the cruiser was divided into waterproof compartments, which could be isolated by closing the doors of the bulkheads that separated them. Kamimura had clearly decided that the leak in the forecastle was serious enough to shut off this forward section of the *Akura* before the water flooded the rest of the ship. And any who were still alive behind the door?

At first for a few seconds only after the firing began, Whitney's mind had felt paralyzed and his body impotent. Now his reactions were as swift at thirty-nine years as they had been the time he had led the baseball team at Annapolis back in '85. Two ratings seized the steel handle from its locker, slipped it through the eye in the threaded door bolt, and were rapidly screwing the closed steel door to secure it.

Whitney shouted at them first in English and then Japanese, "You can't do that! My friends are in there—I know they're in there."

Kamimura's voice echoed in protest, "Do not interfere with my orders, Captain Campbell." Whitney seized hold of the handle from the sailors and began to unscrew it. The Japanese officer waded through the rising waters. "Captain Campbell—no, Captain Campbell."

The sailors were fighting back, too. Whitney threw them roughly aside. Others were coming to help them. Kamimura was shouting, "You will sink the ship—you are mad." There were hands on Whitney, struggling to take the handle from him. But he had unscrewed the last thread, pulled the handle through the eyehole, using it first to knock off the two swing bolts that secured the door so that it was thrown open by the pressure of water.

It was like releasing a dam. The accumulated seawater poured in, knocking over two of the ratings. Whitney struggled against its tide and forced his way through, still holding the vital handle. The faint light revealed nothing, only water and the outline of alleyways, the trunk of one of the four-inch gun mountings, drifting hammocks and a drifting body.

Whitney shouted, "Buller! Maclewin!" the names echoing sepulcherally above the sound of lapping water. The ship quivered again from one more hit. Even down there in the bowels of the forepart of the ship you could hear the intermittent crack of the brave *Akura's* defiance.

It was ten seconds before the cry was answered. "Whitney—give us a hand, old fellow." It came from far forward. Whitney waded toward it. "Jesus, what am I doing?" he kept asking himself. "Disobeying orders, hazarding this ship in battle. I must be out of my mind." His training, his powerful sense of discipline instilled from long service—all were overcome by the instinct to save life, the lives of the once-indestructible Buller and the little lieutenant from someplace in northern England Whitney had never heard of.

He found them in the port chain locker where the blast of the Russian shell had blown them, trapping Rod between the disturbed anchor chain and the side of the ship. Buller was struggling to ease him clear, had been doing so for five minutes. The reinforcement of strength did the trick. Not a word was spoken between the three men. Rod put an arm on each shoulder, and they waded clear of the flat and back toward the bulkhead door, the torrent of water above their thighs and threatening to overwhelm them.

Buller stumbled, caught himself. Another body and debris

ripped past on this full-flood tide. But it sped their pace, taking them through the door. Kamimura had acquired another handle, and his party were steadily winning in their struggle to close the door again. Once through, Buller and Whitney threw their weight against the steel in unison. Whitney had never left hold of his handle and he slipped it through the eye, and the moment the door was held against the flow, he began turning it.

The whole episode had lasted no more than three minutes. Two men had been saved who would otherwise have died—drowned, suffocated, while watching and feeling the steady rise of the water. But many hundreds of gallons of water had flooded out into the midships section during that time. If the *Akura* were now to capsize, with the inevitable loss of many of its crew, Captain Campbell U.S.N., a mere guest by courtesy of the Imperial Japanese Navy, would be to blame and no one else.

Sho-sa Kamimura was shouting at them furiously, "Get away—go! Wait until the captain hears of this."

Whitney said nothing. There was nothing to say. If he had been Kamimura he would have felt the same way, might even have shot this foreigner who disobeyed orders and risked the ship in the heat of battle.

The firing had suddenly ceased. A strange silence had seized the ship, a funereal silence for all the dead. Whitney and Buller got Rod up the steps and onto the upper deck. His leg was bleeding but no bones had been broken, and Whitney decided his own cuts and bruises were not worth medical attention. They were all soaked and cold, in a state of depression and shock. Buller said formally, "Well, thanks. Very decent of you."

Buller recalled Rod's old nickname. " 'Lucky Midge'— that's what Charlie B. called you when you were his cox. A good name to stick with."

And now, as the three men came out into the blaze of daylight again, they were greeted with a sight that caused them at once to forget their ordeal, to forget any fears for the immediate future, and to fill them instead with an awesome sense of being witnesses to a chapter of history.

The *Akura* had been spared further battering. The Russian heavy cruiser had been recalled to her station, and her stern was already five miles distant.

Beyond, the full spread of the Russian Fleet still ploughed north, battle flags hoisted. And far to the north a second black cloud signaled the approach of Togo's fleet, distant smudges on the horizon but already within visual range of the enemy and already impressive in its own massive strength.

Only some maritime miracle could now prevent this clash of arms, dreaded and feared by one side, yearned for with such ardor during the waiting months by the Japanese.

The *Akura's* upperworks were a shambles, steel and wooden fittings alike pockmarked by shell splinters, fragments of boats hanging from their davits, all but two guns out of action, the bridge a mass of twisted steel. A temporary bridge of canvas screens had been rigged at the base of the mainmast, and there Captain Saito stood with his wounded navigating officer, first lieutenant, and the cox at the reserve wheel. Steering was laboriously by hand, speed was down to 3 knots. But the *Akura* was defiantly afloat, leaks repaired or sealed off, and she was moving.

Buller, who had now recovered his camera and found it not fatally damaged, picked his way aft through the wreckage. The dead and wounded had been removed. Their blood, diluted by oil and seawater, ran in the scuppers. This might not be his country's war, but he was experiencing a sense of exhilaration and fulfillment now that—for the first time—he had seen action at sea, like his grandfather, Archibald, at Trafalgar, his great-grandfather, Alastair, at the Battle of the Saints, and like all the numerous naval ancestors from whom he was descended.

Buller focused his camera on Togo's flagship in the van of his fleet. Even at 7,000 yards he could pick out the details of the battleship, her decks cleared, battle flags flying, with Togo's own flag and the Rising Sun at the mast. He was leading his two divisions on a westerly course across the van

of the Russian Fleet, crossing the "T" in the classic naval
maneuver but still out of range. Buller pressed the shutter
bulb.

One by one the Battle Fleet followed the *Mikasa*, the
Shakishima, the *Fuji* and *Asahi*, the *Kasuga* and *Nisshin*, and
the big armored cruisers of the second division, their smoke
drifting in a great cloud toward the enemy fleet like a black
insult thrown into the Russian faces before the work of
destruction began.

At 2:00 P.M. the *Akura* still lay between the two fleets, her
flags bravely flying. The first to engage, her battle was over,
her duty done. The Russians had now formed into a single
line, unevenly spaced, maintaining their north-by-northeast
course, still bent on reaching Vladivostok as if the Japanese
Fleet had never seen or intercepted them. After passing north
of the *Akura* and steaming briefly on an opposite parallel
course with Rozhestvensky, Togo had now ordered a 16-
point turn in succession, a dangerous maneuver but one that
would leave the flagship in the lead and the order unchanged.

Buller watched the evolution, in some anxiety, at a distance of no more than two miles. Not a gun had yet been fired
since the heavy cruiser had ceased firing at the *Akura*, and an
expectant silence lay over the waters of the Tsushima Straits.
But the two fleets were now within range of one another, and
Togo offered the Russians easy target practice as his ships in
turn reversed course at the same point.

Whitney joined Buller on the raised platform just abaft the
Akura's second splinter-peppered funnel. "Dammit, why
don't the Russians open fire?" he exclaimed to Buller.
"They'll never get a chance like this again."

"They have," replied Buller, who had his lens on the
Suvoroff. He had spotted the twin flashes from her forward
twelve-inch guns, firing at the *Mikasa* as she completed her
turn. He watched the fall of shot. "And it's good shooting!"
He saw the twin spouts of water, one just ahead of the
Japanese flagship, the second even closer to her stern, and he
took another photograph.

The Russian fire intensified, from heavy- and medium-caliber shells, so that the sea was soon thrashed into a cauldron of spray from the shell bursts.

"Togo's mad!" Whitney shouted above the roar of the Russian guns. For the next minutes it did indeed look like mass *hari-kari* as the Russian fire intensified and a sudden spark from deep inside the maelstrom of smoke and spume proclaimed another hit on the Japanese ships. Yet one after another, at intervals of some thirty seconds, the Japanese ships emerged from their ordeal, some clearly knocked about but none fatally or even seriously damaged.

The fourth ship to reappear was the great 15,000-ton *Asahi*, a near-sister ship to the *Mikasa*, with black smoke pouring from her twin funnels. She was little more than a mile distant, her twelve-inch guns trained on the enemy. Whitney through his binoculars, and Buller through his long-focus lens, could see the captain and his officers on the bridge. They were all peering keenly toward the enemy. The battleship's deck were cleared, not a soul was to be seen with the exception of a single figure on the upper deck just abaft the first funnel.

"Who in God's name is that?" Whitney shouted. "He must be out of his mind. Why hasn't he been ordered below?"

But even as he asked these questions, Whitney knew who the officer must be—the near-legendary "Paks," the British naval observer who had been sending home dispatches on the activities of the Japanese Fleet since the first days of the war, and had never stepped ashore for fear that the *Asahi* might be called to sea in a hurry.

Pakenham, with a writing tablet on his knee and a pen in his hand, might have been relaxing on some English village green keeping the score of a cricket match instead of noting the finer points of the evolutions and fall of shot at the biggest naval battle since Trafalgar. He was reclining in a cane chair, his feet on a bollard, wearing a high white wing collar and a white drill uniform, his monocle glinting in the sun.

They saw him glance briefly at the stricken *Akura*, raising binoculars to his eyes and lowering them in order to write a few words on his pad. He had identified Buller and Whitney as the mighty *Asahi* slipped past at 12 knots, pushing up a high bow wave. "Paks" gave them a brief wave before continuing his writing.

Now the *Mikasa* opened fire, her guns scarcely elevated for the range of no more than three and a half miles; then the next in line, the three-funneled *Shikishima*, the smaller *Fuji*.

Large- and small-caliber shells were falling close to the *Asahi*, sending up "splashes" of varying height that obscured the battleships for several seconds. Buller caught a glimpse of "Paks" and almost simultaneously saw the flash of a hit on the side of the *Asahi's* hull just below the third six-inch gun embrasure and not fifty feet from the Royal Navy observer. He appeared completely unharmed and unperturbed. Buller had it all recorded on film as evidence.

The last view they had of Captain Pakenham was of him still lying completely relaxed in his chair while the forward turret of the *Asahi* blasted out a salvo in reply. The muzzles were no more than a hundred feet from the officer when they were fired, and the charge smoke swirled in a curtain across the upper deck, concealing him again.

Buller had no doubt that he would survive. "Paks" had been through every engagement of the war in this position. Once, he had been seen to descend below when the fighting was particularly hot, and the Japanese thought that at last he had had enough. But he reappeared a few minutes later in a fresh white uniform, in replacement of the one he had been wearing, which had been sprayed with the blood of some unfortunate gunner.

For the next half hour the Battle of Tsushima—as it came to be called—unfolded in a series of diminishing panoramas before the eyes of the British and American observers. Fate had spared them during their cruiser's ordeal, and fate now offered them this grandstand view from her torn decks: the Japanese battle line increasing speed to 15 knots, far above the maximum speed of the Russians; the excellent initial shooting of the Russian gunners, its rapid falling off as soon as the Japanese began to make hits, a certain sign of demoralization; the Japanese line now "bending" the Russian line as the Japanese closed and headed across the bows of the

Russian vanguard; the concentration of Japanese fire on the enemy divisional leaders, Rozhestvensky's *Suvoroff* and the big, slabsided *Oslyabya*, both of them now raging furnaces; and the sudden capsizing and disappearance of this second flagship at 2:45 P.M.

"I guess that's the beginning of the end," Whitney commented. The battle was now raging fifteen miles away, marked by an awesome cloud of smoke from a hundred funnels, from gunsmoke and the fires burning in the damaged and sinking men-o'-war.

Buller turned to Rod, who had his injured leg up on a hatch cover. He had succeeded in acquiring more writing material and had been covering pages with notes as the battle faded away to the north. "What did you think of the gunnery?" he asked. "I mean the Russian and the Japanese."

"I missed the opening rounds," said Rod. "I thought the Russian shooting was better than we expected at first. But overall the Japanese shooting was much superior. And they had this huge advantage of speed so that they held the initiative all the time."

"I found the fall of shot very confusing," Whitney confessed. "With twelve-inch and six-inch and even twelve-pounders all firing at once, I don't understand how the gunlayers identified their own 'splashes.' "

"I agree," said Buller. "If Togo had opened up the range instead of closing it, and used only his twelve-inch guns, he would have had the Russians at the bottom in half the time."

The *Akura* labored northwest with just enough way on to keep her damaged bows into the rising seas. It would be long after dark before they made their anchorage and their wounded could be got ashore. One man who would never leave his temporary bridge was Captain Saito, who had been generous enough to congratulate them on their escape instead of rebuking them for hazarding his ship. Now Rod turned to the two captains sitting beside him and said, "After what we've just seen, what our navies want are not battleships with a mixed armament of heavy, medium, and smaller-caliber guns, with a speed of fifteen or eighteen knots, like the *Mikasa* or Lord Charles's flagship, *Caesar*, or, Whitney, your latest battleship, the *Ohio*. What we are going to need are battleships with heavy guns only and a speed of over twenty knots.''

Buller and Whitney considered Rod's formula for a moment. Then Buller said, ''I think you may be right, Midge. I think you may be right, and I think that's probably the most important statement you've ever made in all your life.''

The three men laughed. The deep and sustained explosion, louder than any that they had heard at this distance, sounded in their ears. Somewhere in that now far-distant cloud, where thousands of men were fighting for their lives, and many were losing their lives, one more catastrophe had just occurred, no doubt marking the end of more men in a searing sweep of white-hot vapor and a million fragments of white-hot steel.

The two Englishmen and the American looked at one another, and there was no need for them to say, ''This is no time for laughter.'' All three understood and recognized again how fortunate they had been.

Buller reached his hand to an inside pocket of his jacket and withdrew the leather cigar case King Edward VII had once given him, the crown and Buller's name engraved on the silver shield. He offered one to Whitney and said to Rod, ''You ought to try one of these—they are good for the nerves.''

Rod replied, ''Nerves! What do you know about nerves? You haven't a nerve in your body.''

Buller said, ''Oh, you would be surprised.'' And he recalled that burning morning in Natal at the Battle of Colenso when he had looked at his hands and had said, half unbelievingly, ''I am shaking with fear!''

It was a sight Whitney would never forget, a picture he hoped he would one day describe to his grandchildren— inadequately, no doubt, because it almost defied description. It had taken the *Akura* two days and nights to struggle back after her ordeal, the worst-damaged fighting ship in Togo's fleet. When they arrived, steaming at 3 knots to their appointed position, a cheer went up from the men lining the decks of the nearest vessel. The cheers were taken up by other crews, signal guns were fired and bugles sounded in their honor.

The little *Akura* had guided the Japanese Fleet in the last stage of its hunt for the enemy, giving Admiral Togo the opportunity to place his line in the most favorable position for meeting Admiral Rozhestvensky. The outcome of the engagement was spelled out for the *Akura's* company. For as far as the eye could see in this hazy morning light lay the Japanese men-o'-war—battleships and armored cruisers, light cruisers and destroyers—in lines, many bearing the scars of battle, all dressed overall with multicolored signal flags and pennants strung between jack staff and foremast and mainmast and ensign staff, with the Rising Sun flying from the masts and the flagstaff.

The rising sun itself broke through the haze as the *Akura* dropped anchor, marking the occasion, appropriately and momentously, casting its light on the most significant of all the ships present. These were the dreadfully battered captured Russian battleships, the *Orel, Nikolai, Seniavin,* and *Apraksin,* the Japanese flag flying above the Russian flag on the jury-rigged masts of all four vessels, several of which had had to be towed from the scene of battle.

And what of the *Suvoroff,* like the *Orel* one of the most modern battleships in the world, and of Admiral Rozhestvensky and his staff, and the other admirals and senior officers of the Russian Fleet? They were to learn the answers to these questions and many more later that day, when all four observers were summoned to the *Mikasa:* "The admiral would be honored by the presence on board his flagship of all the British and American observers" ran the message.

Admiral Togo appeared drawn from exhaustion and lack of sleep, gray-faced, the lines about his mouth more marked then when they had last seen him. But the black eyes gleamed brighter than ever, and there was an air about the man of satisfaction and fulfillment. He had waited a long time for this moment, when he could proclaim to the world, "The Russian Navy is no more." This was implicit in his bearing

and expression. What he said to Buller and Rod, Whitney and
Captain Pakenham, was: "Thank you for joining me in my
ship." Whitney translated for the other three. "You will see
that we have scored a great victory, and it will be an honor to
me if you report to your navies how we won this last naval
battle of the war. I say last because there can be no more. The
Russians have nothing left. Their fleet was stronger than ours
at the outset. We destroyed it. So they sent another, also more
powerful than ours. And now we have destroyed that."

He smiled at the four men in turn, the immaculate "Paks"
who looked down at the commander-in-chief through his
monocle, at Buller in best white drill that could never match
his fellow captain's, at Rod, who was the same size and build
as Togo, and at Whitney, who asked him in Japanese, "Did
any of the Russian ships escape, sir?"

"I think some cruisers reached Manila, where they will be
interned by your own admirable navy, Captain Campbell.
Another cruiser and two torpedo boats have been reported at
Vladivostok, and one or two vessels of no importance have
reached Shanghai." Togo spread out his hands and smiled.
"And that is all. The others are at the bottom, or where you
can see them here. Not a battleship in Russian hands. Alas,
many Russians are dead, and we do all we can for their
wounded, including Admiral Rozhestvensky, who was rescued from his flagship before she went down and is gravely
wounded."

A steward entered the cabin with two bottles of champagne
and glasses on a silver tray. As he poured out the Mumm's
Extra Dry, Togo remarked, "The fruits of battle, gentlemen.
There were fifty cases in the *Orel's* wardroom. No doubt,"
he added, "they were reserved for the victory celebrations. A
very correct decision." The admiral raised his glass, a smile
on his face. "To the end of the war, gentlemen, which now
cannot be long delayed. And to the end of all wars, with the
suffering and distress they occasion."

Chapter V

⚓

The Countess's Invitation

"DO YOU REMEMBER him at Alexandria—a real fire-eater?" Buller recalled. "Marching into the city as if he owned it, ordering looters to be shot, bodies to be piled up at street corners for immediate collection. If he had met Arabi Pasha with his bodyguard, he would have gone for them with his walking stick, I do declare."

Buller and Rod were on their way to the admiralty in a hansom cab to report to Jackie Fisher, First Sea Lord for nine months now, whose highly charged style and sweeping reforms of the navy were making him new enemies.

"Why is it that there are so many eccentrics among the senior officers in the navy?" asked Rod.

"You should have seen my father-in-law in his heyday," said Buller. "Lord Huntley—he believed that the navy was ruined by steam engines and rifled cannon, that the only action worth a single golden guinea was close action between three-deckers. Died mad of drink five years ago. I was devoted to him. I think the sea drives us all mad in the end—that and a commander's loneliness."

Buller glanced out of the open window. Not much chance of becoming lonely here. They were crossing Parliament

Square in heavy traffic of horse buses, brewers' drays, trademen's vans, carriages, growlers, and hansom cabs. It was the last day of the summer session for the House of Commons, and many of the carriages belonged to Members of Parliament.

The traffic was easier up Whitehall, past Downing Street where Arthur Balfour, the prime minister, would later be leaving Number 10 for Question Time in the House. The cabbie turned left through the Adams screen of the Admiralty and drew up alongside the pillared façade. There was little evidence of change here over the past 150 years, only the elaborate wireless antennae on the roof marking swifter if less reliable means of communication to the country's naval bases than the semaphore of Nelson's day.

The guards clicked to attention and saluted this tall captain and his shorter lieutenant companion, both bronzed from their summer voyage back from the Far East. A messenger took them at once up the side staircase to the First Sea Lord's office.

Fisher rose to meet them, pacing across the floor, arm outstretched. He was wearing an old double-breasted, four-button dark blue suit and a cravat, with a white carnation in his buttonhole. Like Buller, he had put on weight since the Egyptian War in which all three men had fought twenty-three years earlier. As well, there was a heaviness about his chin and eyes, and the dark skin (his enemies claimed his Oriental features originated in his illegitimate birth in Ceylon) had lost the tautness of young middle age, when Buller had known him best. "Why I am ugly," he once wrote, "is one of those puzzles of physiology which are beyond finding out." But there was none of Beresford's high color of self-indulgent living in Fisher's face and figure.

At sixty-four, Fisher was at the height of his powers. He ruled the navy as a dictator with the proverbial rod of iron, disposing of the enemies who sought to oppose his reforms or setting them against one another, shamelessly favoring and promoting those who supported him. He cultivated newspaper proprietors, rising politicians, and all who backed his causes. He wrote letters and memoranda at the speed at which most people speak, and when he spoke the words tumbled out like cartridge cases from a Gatling gun.

In his earliest days, Buller's father, George, had recognized genius in young Fisher and had done him many good turns. In Fisher's eyes ever since, no Buller could do wrong. Now he grasped Buller's hand in both of his. "The greatest moment of my week, Buller! Welcome home. I hear that those Russkies nearly did for you—and for you, Midge. Lucky Midge, that mad Irish dissolute, Beresford, calls you, I believe. Well, young fellow, your luck nearly ran out this time."

"It was a good fight, sir. You would have relished it, knowing how awfully keen on a scrap you are," said Buller with a laugh.

They sat in armchairs about a round table upon which stood an old globe showing half the world unexplored. "I sent you two out there as good gunnery officers and observers. Now I want to hear what you observed before I receive your official report. Official reports tell you nothing. I use them to set fire to my enemies."

Buller indicated that Rod should speak first, recognizing his conciseness of mind and delivery. Rod recounted what they had seen of the Battle of Tsushima, omitting their irrelevant personal ordeal, speaking of the difficulty of spotting the fall of shot and "the splash," with different calibers of guns firing simultaneously and forming a confused pattern for the spotter and gunlayer.

Fisher turned to Buller. "And your conclusion?"

"I think we should build single-caliber-gun battleships, sir. Nothing but twelve-inch guns. Firing in regular salvoes in accordance with Captain Percy Scott's *Excellent* scheme," said Buller, citing the revolutionary theories of this gunnery expert. "But *not* mixed salvoes. Please look at this photograph, sir."

Fisher examined the enlarged print placed in front of him, and Buller pointed out the "splashes" of Russian shells about the *Asahi*, varying from a mere ten feet to as high as the mastheads of the Japanese battleship. "Imagine the spotter's confusion attempting to identify his shells. Then observe Captain Pakenham quite undisturbed by this hit a short distance from him. That six-inch shell might have been a dart for all the damage it inflicted. Only twelve-inch shells sink battleships, sir. That's the first conclusion, and it's confirmed by the Japanese themselves."

Fisher asked sharply, "What do you mean?"

"Before we sailed for home, we had several days in the Admiralty in Tokyo," said Buller. "They were feeling in top form and mighty boastful, too. Their navy had all but won the war. They were going to be the Britannia of the East, build their own navy, and no longer rely on us. Then I was shown in confidence the plans for a battleship of 20,000 tons with twelve twelve-inch guns."

There was silence in the First Sea Lord's office. Fisher stared expressionlessly at Buller with eyes that were as piercing and almost as dark as Admiral Togo's. Then his face suddenly relaxed, and his smile was part mischievous, part confiding, and as warm as the sun in the red Sea when Buller and Rod had sailed through it.

"Our all-big-gun ship—*ours* is not a plan. It will be laid down in two months and be ready for sea in fourteen months. It will have a broadside twice that of any battleship in the world, forward fire three times that of any other battleship, will be turbine-powered, and steam at over twenty-one knots." Fisher slapped his knee as if intending to break it. "That will confound the Germans and the whole world. And the king will name her H.M.S. *Dreadnought*."

Again there was silence. It was a trick of Fisher's to challenge anyone to question what he had stated. Through the open windows came the faint, steady beat of horses' hooves on cobbles, the cry of a newspaper boy in Whitehall, and then the first of twelve notes from Big Ben, indicating noon in the capital.

Rod was indeed impressed, and relieved. This was to be a revolutionary man-o'-war, of that there could be no doubt, and if she was really to be built in a year, a quarter of the usual construction time, the naval world would be thrown back on its heels. But the practical, down-to-earth Rod never allowed himself to be overimpressed; and now, firmly and respectfully, he broke the silence with his Geordie voice which caused heads to turn in a wardroom, for Rod had always declined to make his voice conform and sound ''posh.''

"That is very good news, sir. You will no doubt be accused of making the Royal Navy's Battle Fleet obsolete at a stroke while you are making every foreign Battle Fleet obsolete. But, sir, I admire your courage, if I may say so. However, your *Dreadnought* is not going to be enough. What we also learned from the battle was the critical importance of speed. If the Russians had been capable of a few more knots, they would have laughed all the way to Vladivostok, and we should not have drunk their champagne with Admiral Togo.''

"So what do you propose, Midge?'' Fisher was not menacing, but he expected a good and precise answer. ''Isn't twenty-one knots enough?''

"I propose twenty-five-knot armored cruisers that can scout for the fleet and not be blown out of the water as we nearly were.''

Fisher rose from his chair and walked to his desk. From a drawer he withdrew a roll of heavy paper, spread it out, and asked them to examine it. It was a sketch of rig of a big armored cruiser with four turrets and no secondary armament, an all-big-gun cruiser. Rod bent over the plan and read the numerals "9.2" against the guns.

"Speed twenty-eight knots,'' said Fisher, his voice rising with glee. ''H.M.S. *Unapproachable*, that's what I call her. What do you think, Buller?''

Buller turned a questioning eye on Rod and said doubtfully, "What do you think?''

To gain time Rod glanced down at the plan. She would certainly be the most formidable armored cruiser in the world, and a fine-looking ship with three wide-spaced funnels for her numerous boilers and twin tripod masts. Then he said firmly, "Sir, I don't think this ship is good enough.''

Fisher snapped back, "And why not?"

Rod answered at once. "At the risk of being insubordinate, sir, from what we have seen at Tsushima and what Captain Pakenham observed at the other engagements when fire was opened at 20,000 yards, the nine-point-two-inch gun is obsolete as main armament."

"Do you agree with that, Buller?"

"Yes, sir, I do. It is unprofitable for us to be sent to witness a battle on the other side of the world and then to censor our conclusions to conform with the First Sea Lord's plans."

"Absolutely, totally, and comprehensively right," Fisher bellowed and beat the top of his desk with his fist. " 'The truth is great, and shall prevail,' as Patmore has it. How I miss that fellow! I shall tell our Committee on Designs that we shall have twelve-inch guns. And we shall rename this goliath of an armored cruiser H.M.S. *Buller*."

"That would scarcely be just, sir," said Buller with a deep laugh. "Rod here is the brains of our team. I just watch and take pictures through my new lense."

"H.M.S. *Maclewin* then will be our first," said Fisher, a puckish grin creasing his face. "Our new armored cruisers will be ocean greyhounds with the teeth of tigers. Dreadnought cruisers with twice the armament of today's battleships and ten knots greater speed. They will destroy everything at extreme range, and retire at leisure."

"And our report, sir?" asked Rod, reeling with wonder at the wildness of this admiral, who seemed to combine genius with unfettered power and explosive decision-making.

Fisher took them both by the arm and led them toward the door. "I have had your report. It is all I wish to hear. You approve of my *Dreadnought*, but not of my cruiser. The medium-caliber gun is dead." His voice rose. "And so will you both be dead, burned to charred ashes which I shall order Charlie Beresford to cast upon the waters, if—*if* you divulge one word of this conversation to anyone." He chuckled again as Buller and Rod saluted, and then offered them his hand. In the short distance from his desk, Fisher's expression had changed a dozen times. Now he smiled at them warmly, and they understood why he could charm the birds off the trees, and why the queen and the most beautiful women in the land were in love with this man.

"Buller! Gee, it's swell to hear your voice."

"I can scarcely hear yours," Buller replied. "I don't know why I had this damn telephone thing installed. But it's good to hear that you are in London."

Whitney, speaking from his office in the London United States Embassy, said, "I've been back here for three weeks. Yokohama to Frisco, straight into the transcontinental, spent a couple of days with my folks in Buffalo, and then down to Washington where the Navy Department kept me busy for a week. Then back to your country in the White Star *Baltic*." His familiar laugh came over the wires as a cackle. "We Americans believe in moving fast."

An invitation to Buller for dinner followed. "At the Café Royal. Mostly naval folk and their wives—I hope your Clemmie can make it."

Buller explained that she was in Scotland for the start of the grouse season. "But I'd like to come very much."

The Café Royal's small banqueting room accommodated the twenty-four guests easily, a drawing room and a ladies' room completing their comfort. Buller, wearing white tie and tails and a full row of decorations, looked strikingly handsome in a fully matured way, although, as Clemmie would say forthrightly, "If you lost thirty pounds no one would say you were the worse for it—especially your tailor." Twenty-five years of life in the navy, most of them spent at sea, and the campaigns in which he had fought added to the impression of total and unselfconscious masculinity and strength which he carried about him. A shrewd judge would pronounce, "There is a man who is going far and in war will do well." And might add conditionally: "But not *quite* the brains and balance to get *right* to the top."

Buller recognized most of the men present: the Second Sea Lord, the American Ambassador, Winston Churchill, the First Secretary at the Foreign Office, and the rest mostly naval attachés from Japan, France, Italy, Germany, Holland—but not Count Rudovsky, the Russian naval attaché. A glance at the menu explained this: "A Private Dinner" was headlined alongside a colored drawing of the Rising Sun, "to Celebrate the Victory at Tsushima." The guests of honor, His Excellency the Japanese Ambassador and Princess Hukora.

"It's great you could come." Whitney, looking as fit and bronzed as Buller, greeted him. "I tried for Rod, but he has gone north to his family."

"A great family man is our Rod—and he has a great family." Buller glanced around the room at the numerous women present. "It is time you got yourself a wife and family, Whitney."

The American slapped him on the back. "Time enough before I lose my freedom. Now, who would you care to meet?"

The decision was taken out of the host's hands. The most striking if not the most beautiful woman in the room was making for Buller with a grace and majesty that matched her height. It was the Countess Miranda Reitzberg-Sönderlong, dressed in a cream satin dress caught tight at the waist with a silk sash and a full train. The neckline was provocatively low and square and frilled with lace; her hair was swept up and fastened in coiled plaits on the crown.

Buller bent over her hand as she said with a scarcely discernible German accent, "Ah, the handsome Captain Buller. Sonny tells me that you have been behaving with great gallantry again." She glanced at the D.S.O. on Buller's chest and placed a finger beside it. "And no doubt there will be another medal for your bravery at Tsushima."

"No, countess. Nothing like that. I happened to be on board a small man-o'-war that was fired on by the Russians. I was not fighting the Russians, although I have always been keen to do that. I was observing them."

The countess, standing disconcertingly close to him, smelling subtly and faintly of the essence of lemon, and with her gray eyes almost on a level with his, said in denial, "*Ach,* no. Captain Campbell has told me how close to death you were.''

''And no doubt omitted to tell you that he saved my life, and the life of my fellow officer.'' At that moment Buller spotted Whitney concluding a conversation with the wife of the Italian naval attaché, and called out to him threateningly, ''If you don't stop talking nonsense about my part at Tsushima, I shall tell the newspapers about your successful fight to save our lives.''

Whitney laughed and blushed in an engagingly boyish manner. ''I guess we'll call a truce, Buller.'' He turned to the countess. ''You will have seen, madame, that you are sitting on Captain Buller's right at dinner, and you will be able to ask him all about the great battle.''

''Charming—how charming!''

A minute later the Countess Reitzberg-Sönderlong entered the dining room on Buller's arm, the striking couple attracting the attention of those already present. Buller noticed the count across the table and bowed in his direction before sitting down. He had no doubt that this aristocratic and influential German naval officer was as bellicose as he had been when Buller had first met him. Certainly his claim of ten years ago that Germany would one day have a great navy was being realized and was becoming the first anxious concern of the British Navy and the British Government.

Buller made small talk in halting French to the wife of the French naval attaché on his left as a matter of courtesy, but was mainly taken up by the countess through the long, rich courses of the dinner.

''And your dear, beautiful wife? She is . . .?''

Buller explained about the Glorious Twelfth, the start of the grouse season, and told her he expected to see her when she returned the following week. Later, over some rich *gelée au Curaçao à la Chantilly,* she asked innocently, ''And your conclusions of the battle, Captain Buller? Did you believe when it was over, like so many others, that the smaller guns of Tsushima, the ten-and even the fifteen-centimeter guns, were *unnütz*—quite useless?''

"Are many other people saying that?" asked Buller, stalling and concealing his surprise at her directness and technical knowledge.

"Oh, but everyone. Everyone who knows about navies. I know about navies as well as about people."

Buller's laugh was not altogether spontaneous. "My own experience was that the fifteen-centimeter—the six-inch—Russian shells were extremely effective and blew me down two decks and almost sank the cruiser I was in."

The countess turned the conversation back to social matters and to Buller's family, until Whitney stood up and toasted the Emperor of Japan and the Imperial Japanese Navy in Veuve Clicquot '92. "As you all know, peace negotiations between Japan and Russia have just begun in my country at Portsmouth, New Hampshire. And it is to the magnificent performance and bravery of the Japanese Navy that the world owes for the end of hostilities . . ."

At the end of the evening, Buller escorted the countess—spectacularly stately in a long sable coat—to her carriage drawn up in Regent Street. "Allow me to drop you at your Mayfair house, captain," she offered. And when Buller said how kind but that it would be no trouble to take a hansom cab, she pressed him. "It will be pleasant company for me. Sonny has some beastly late meeting at the embassy."

Inevitably, and as Buller had half expected with a growing sense of curiosity and anxiety, the carriage took them direct to Wilton Crescent in Belgravia, where the count and countess had a rented house. "It is scarcely past midnight, captain, and I insist that you sample a sip of Sonny's famous '62 Napoleon brandy, captured by his father after the Battle of Sedan."

It was a cool evening for August, and a fire was burning in the study where they sat sipping the priceless cognac.

"It is enough reason to go to war, do you not think, Captain Buller?" said the countess, laughing and warming the brandy glass with her large white hands, which had so strongly attracted Buller the first time he had met her. He imagined again their strength and the feel of them against his body.

"The loot in France must indeed be rich," Buller replied. "But I hope that there will be more important reasons for waging war."

The countess laughed again, a laugh as deep and engaging as her voice. "Do not be so serious, dear captain. I am joking only. And I cannot continue longer to call you captain. May I say Archibald?"

It was Buller's turn to laugh. "Indeed you may not, madame. No one has ever called me that, and I do not much like Archy either. People just call me Buller."

She rose to her feet, and when Buller stood up she took his arm and guided him toward the wall beside the curtained window. Although she had held his arm as a formality earlier in the evening, it felt closer and much more intimate in the privacy of this room, and she held him so that his forearm lightly brushed against the softness of her breast.

"Now, Buller. Please look at that photograph." She pointed at a picture of a battleship at full speed, black smoke streaming from the three tall funnels, white bow wave climbing almost to the forecastle. The caption read simply "S.M.S. *Hessen*, März 1905" in Gothic script.

"A very fine battleship," commented Buller. "One of your newest and most powerful."

"Oh, poof, Buller!" she exclaimed. She pronounced it Booler, which he found as attractive as the renewed pressure of her arm. "You know as I do that the *Hessen* is as old as she is new. After Tsushima it will be battleships with nothing but the biggest guns. Boom! all at once. A great broadside—not twenty-eight centimeter and seventeen centimeter and all those little—how do you call them?—popguns. Now only big guns and more speed."

She must have felt the tightening of Buller's muscles and continued, "That is not secret. Sonny says all the world knows, and your navy will have all-big-gun battleships, and our navy, too, and Captain Campbell's navy. All other battleships will go to the scrapyard and we shall all start level. We call battleships *Schlachtschiffe*. Is that not an exciting word?"

Buller, now breathing faster, said, "You sound as if you

are in love with battleships," and laughed.

The countess held up to Buller the brandy glass she was carrying. "Yes, perhaps I am. They are so big and strong, their guns so long and powerful. A toast to the battleship, Buller."

So they drank to these fearful engines of war, and she stood facing him so closely that he could just feel her breasts against his chest as he looked into her gray eyes, which had turned misty as her lips, partly open, assumed a provocative expression. "Why don't you kiss me, my gallant captain—my Buller?"

Many months had passed since Buller had had a woman. He had not slept with Clemmie since last October, ten months ago, and the enforced abstention had made him more than ever sensitive to arousal. The curiosity he had felt earlier toward this tall, statuesque woman was renewed and reinvigorated with this invitation, and the implication of greater intimacy to follow.

Buller moved his head toward the lips very slowly, savoring the anticipation. When a few inches from her, the warmth of her face like the glow of a fire, he paused and they looked into one another's eyes. Buller saw in the cool gray of the pupils a deep hunger. Everything about this woman told the same story of fulfillment of her ambitions and her desires. He knew that even if he had fought against her wishes now he would have succumbed. Everything—her castle on the Rhine above Frankfurt, her schloss in the Harz Mountains, her husband with his title, his close relationship with the German court, his appointment to this plum post in London, even their big Benz motorcar—all had come to her because nothing was allowed to stand between her and what she wished from life.

Now she wanted this Englishman, and she went about it in a manner that was novel to Buller. She eased herself away from their deep kiss and swiftly, and with a skill that showed easy familiarity with the mechanics of buttons and clips and links, began to undress him, her eyes still on his and only darting briefly to check the movements of her hands. Jacket and waistcoat, cummerbund, tie and wing collar, fell to the carpet along with the white dickey.

Buller, fully aware that this was a gesture to demonstrate that she was in command, waited and watched the countess's face and then said quietly, "You are very efficient. And now you can see that you don't have to bother with a vest. I do not wear one. These dinners I find so hot."

"You are hot now, my Buller." She placed her large hands flat against his chest and moved them gently from side to side. How did she know that this was what he had longed for her to do?

"That is very pleasant," said Buller. He was already overwhelmed with lust and almost past speech, and for the present allowed her to keep the initiative. Her breasts were pressed hard against his nakedness, the silk of her dress like cool water in a fever. She kissed him for a long time with her mouth open as if consuming some rich fruit. Then she led them to the door behind the desk, and they passed through into a room lit only by a single gas mantle beside a bed. "Sonny likes to lie here and rest sometimes. Is that not convenient, Buller?"

She began to undress the moment she had quietly closed the door and turned the key, and she did so with amazing speed and lack of self-consciousness. She paused only once and looked at Buller, who had remained standing and watching the revelation of her body—so large but as beautifully proportioned as that of a newly matured girl, her breasts as firm as they were full. "What are you waiting for?" she asked and laughed deeply.

Buller laughed, too, as he took off the rest of his clothes and allowed himself to be drawn swiftly to the bed. For a short time, her hands seized him firmly and gently so that he cried out.

Then suddenly he thrust her aside, pinning her shoulders to the bed. She struggled fiercely as if for her life and pressed her strong knees hard against him. Buller laughed, admiring and savoring her strength, and then quelled it, holding her legs down and apart with his own so that she was pinioned.

She continued to struggle, grunting with the effort and
making her final capitulation the more triumphantly satisfy-
ing for both of them. How she relished her defeat, and the
moment when Buller could spare a hand to range down her
body, raising her lust to a new pitch!

When they came together it was a sudden, swift physical
duologue between two big bodies straining in muscular com-
patibility, and reaching the end like wrestlers surrendering
together: hot and hard and damp and already, as pleasure
slowly faded, sensing a renewed longing, which had to be
fulfilled before they could rise from the bed.

There were beads of sweat across her forehead and above
her upper lip, the fierceness had faded from her eyes, the
scent of lemon was heavy on the air. "Yes, I knew it would
be marvelous with you," she said. "You have a fine body,
Buller." She slapped his stomach harder then he expected.
"Just a little too much fat here."

"Too much good living, too many dinners with beautiful
countesses."

"This one is called Miranda, and do not forget that,
Buller. Buller and Miranda. I think we shall have a strong
affair, my Buller." She pushed him off her and began to
dress, throwing him his clothes.

When they walked back through the study, she paused
again at the photograph of the big battleship. "Now you
know why I like to lie in bed with you. I like my men like
battleships, though I pretend that I can defeat them." She put
a finger against the glass. "*Ach*, these great guns—twenty-
eight centimeters, perhaps thirty-one centimeters or bigger.
And in the future, only big guns and no peashooters. And
now you must go, my big Buller, my battleship."

She kissed him lightly, and Buller let himself out into the
gaslit street and waved to a passing hansom. Inside, he lit a
cigar and on the short journey back to Clarges Street experienced the old familiar guilt of adultery. So, most of his
married men friends did it. So, it did not mean that he loved
his Clemmie less. So, she was not always faithful to him, or
had not been earlier in their marriage. So, London was thick

with mistresses, from the king's Mrs. Keppel down to city clerks who could not afford them.

All the same, the Puritan blood in Buller still flowed. If only it did not, then he would not now be making these futile promises to himself which he knew he would break at the first opportunity, especially with this woman, this Countess Miranda, who offered so much in size and satisfaction.

Chapter VI

⚓

The Young Rebels

WHILE CLEMMIE BULLER was staying at Balmoral in Scotland with the king's grouse-shooting party, and Buller himself was in London on official (and strictly unofficial) business, Rod Maclewin traveled by the Great Northern line to a city that lay between them—Newcastle-upon-Tyne, the home of the Geordies and Rod's home.

After being seriously wounded in the Egyptian War in 1882, Rod had been nursed back to health by his mother with the help of a girl who soon became his wife, Rosie Hamilton. Thanks to Rod's promotion, first to warrant officer and then to lieutenant (one of the very few to get a commission from the lower deck), Rod was able to move his family from the small flat in the tough and poverty-stricken Elswick area, and buy a house in Grosvenor Road, Jesmond.

The little Groom Road house was taken over by Rod and Rosie's married son, Tom, now twenty-two, while their daughters, Sarah and Mary, aged twenty and eighteen, still lived at home together with Rod's mother, Doris, widowed now for some forty-one years. Doris Maclewin, Scots-Presbyterian down to the soles of her feet, had led a hard life, fighting constantly against penury and hunger, and later alleviating the sufferings of her neighbors in Elswick. She was only sixty-five, but the last time Rod had come home on leave, he found to his dismay that she was confined to a wheelchair because of her arthritis.

As Rod walked up the hill from the railway sation, an observer would have noticed little change from the able seaman of the 1880s. His step was brisk and springy, his stance slightly leaning forward as if in eagerness to reach his destination without actually running. He carried now a small imitation-leather case in place of the kitbag of earlier days, and wore the uniform of a lieutenant R.N. instead of the jersey and bell-bottoms of the lower deck.

The most marked contrast between 1880 and 1905 was this sailor's compass course, as he would have called it, northeast by north instead of southwest by west, literally turning his back on the harsh, crowded working-class area of Elswick and toward the newly built terraces of Jesmond with net curtains and aspidistras in the windows, and, for many, a maidservant quartered in the attic bedroom. Like many others, the Maclewins' maid came from the Elswick area the Maclewins had left behind. There were many other first-generation middle-class families in this part of Newcastle: foremen who had made good in the shipyards and foundries; bank clerks and shop assistants whose parents had urged them to leave the arduous and backbreaking factory work and who had somehow scraped together the money for night school for their sons; others of greater intelligence or industry who, with luck on their side, had struggled free from the slavery of working-class life.

Thse families of Grosvenor Gardens, Holly Avenue, Osborne Avenue, and the many other roads of Jesmond were pleased with their new lives, and some of them tended to show it and to conceal their regret for the greater freedom and robust friendliness of crowded Elswick. Rosie Maclewin was not one of them. She missed much of her old life, and even the sounds—the sounds of distress and laughter, of children playing and drunken men singing out of tune. But she also enjoyed the peace of Jesmond and the light and the comforts, especially for her ailing mother-in-law and for her daughters, who were likely to make more refined marriages here.

Rod had come up in the social ranks as he had in the ranks of the Royal Navy to a king's commission. He would not have cared to hear it spoken, but he and Rosie had become middle class. Rod experienced a flicker of pride as he swung open the little iron gate and ascended the steps in diamond-tile pattern (washed by the maid that morning) to the front door. It was set in the diminutive pillared porch, with colored glass in the fanlight around the elaborate script naming the house "Balmoral."

Rosie was there, of course; safely predictable, small like himself, her little face with the fresh complexion and the freckles on her nose, unchanged in his eyes since they married twenty-three years ago. "Oh, Roddy—welcome home." Her soft voice had never lost its Scottish accent. Her arms encircled his neck.

Rod's eldest child, Tom, remembered most vividly the conditions in the slums when he was a young boy, the sufferings of the unemployed, the men on strike or locked out of the workshops and yards, those who were too sick or injured to work, and (the saddest of all) those who were too soaked in liquor to work. Although he had never had to beg at the yard gates, hoping some of the men coming off shift had leftovers from their dinner boxes, he had run and played and fought with these boys—had run barefoot in summer to save shoe leather, had seen the effects of malnutrition, had helped his grandmother organize her street soup kitchens for the most distressed.

Young Tom Maclewin's heart remained with the working people of Elswick, and when the rest of the family moved out to Jesmond, he insisted on remaining behind in the Groom Road house, shocked that his mother and father had shown themselves to be traitors to their class, as he considered it, and to the political radicalism which had become his religion. For Tom Maclewin had rejected the God-fearing Presbyterianism of his parents and as a young laborer in the Armstrong gunshops, had also become a shop steward in the Tyneside branch of his union.

Tom was too fond of his family to cut himself off entirely, and on special occasions would take the route 3 tram from Westmorland Road up to Jesmond Dene. It was a point of honor to him that he always dressed in his working clothes (oil-stained peaked tweed cap, loose collarless shirt, torn waistcoat, kerchief, trousers, and steel-studded boots), which caused net curtains to flutter at the windows of ''Bella Vista,'' ''Borrowdale,'' ''Mon Repos,'' and the rest.

He arrived at ''Balmoral'' with his dark and silent wife, Elsie, for supper at 6:30 on the day his father arrived home. Even as he shook hands (warmly enough) with his father, Tom's eyes flickered from the gleaming black shoes to the white wing collar. To him, these spelled traditional authority and elitism, and only the last strands of family unity and a genuine filial affection prompted him to remember the man beneath the uniform.

''Well, papa, so you won a great victory.''

''And was nearly sunk for it,'' Rod answered, laughing. ''But not *my* victory. I was only a spectator.''

Rosie served out cold ham and tongue, and Sarah and Mary handed around bread and butter and mustard and pickles.

''Did you speak to any of the Russian prisoners?'' Tom asked.

Rod said that he had only seen them from a distance, being ferried ashore. ''And a scruffy lot they were, too. Even scruffier than when I saw them at Vigo earlier.''

''Because they were so beaten and bullied by the officers,'' said Tom in the tones of a fanatic, with which they were all now familiar. ''And shot, some of them. Conditions were so terrible that there was a mutiny at Madagascar among the Bolshevik crews—and there were plenty of them.''

''How do you know all this?'' his father asked.

''We have ways of knowing,'' said Tom darkly, treating the tea as if he had not eaten for a week. His claim was true. The proscribed broadsheet, *The Rebel*, circulated widely among the nation's manual workers, passed secretively from pocket to pocket in workshops and mines. It had recently told of the mutiny of the Russian battleship *Potemkin* in the Black Sea and of the other first rumbles of the 1905 revolution that was to sweep through Russia in a few weeks' time.

At length Rosie said firmly, "Enough of politics now, Tom. And you watch out or you'll be in trouble with the police—mark my words. Now, Roddy, tell us what you did in London." The tea and games that had followed at Buller's London house remained strongly in Rosie's memory, and she wanted to hear more of her husband's friend and family.

Later, after helping his mother upstairs and after Tom had left (leaving nail marks of his boots on the shiny hall linoleum) with his wife, Rod took Rosie out for a walk in the last light of the evening. He was proud of her smartness, dressed in a tailored suit with a long, full skirt and three-quarter-length jacket, a lace-trimmed chiffon blouse, a wide-brimmed straw hat, and buttoned boots on her dainty feet.

They talked of his mother, of the girls and of the boys who were courting them. Because neither wanted the first evening spoiled, Tom was not mentioned. But both experienced the flicker of anxiety and remorse that always followed a visit from their son, who made them feel that they had callously discarded their true class inheritance, that they were more concerned with material self-improvement and bettering themselves socially than in the sufferings and injustices of the class into which they had been born.

They would talk about it later when they had got to know one another again, Rod told himself. It was the same after every long absence at sea. Adjusting back to their old intimate and loving relationship was sometimes awkward, but always a pleasurable process—and no less pleasurable for being essential in their marriage.

But as Rod opened the front iron gate of "Balmoral" for Rosie, an incident that had occurred on Tom's first visit to the house flashed across his mind.

It was a summer evening like this. The carpetlayers had just left—and now Tom was leaving, in a paroxysm of fury, shouting so that all the neighbors were sure to hear: "To know that I am the son of snobs fills me with disgust. I feel dirty, d'you hear? And when the revolution comes, you'll be fighting the workers, I know—the naval brigade, with bayonets fixed. These fancy gutters'll be running in blood—you'll see.''

He was still shouting as he stomped off down Grosvenor Gardens, like any drunkard down Groom Road in rough Elswick. But Tom was not drunk. He had never taken a drop—he kept his money for political party funds. And Rod had reflected miserably, ''He needed a father at home all the time, not a sailor father just sometimes for a few weeks. It's all my doing . . .''

The gate squeaked as he closed it. He would see to that tomorrow. There were always jobs to do about the house when he was on leave. He took Rosie by the arm and led her up the spotless tiled steps to the front door, thinking how simple life was at sea—life run on discipline, the immutability of rank, respect, and routine.

At Wyston Court a few weeks later, Buller sharpened the carving knife before sinking it into the big sirloin—fine West Country beef from his own home farm, hung to perfection. The butler held out the first of five plates, and Buller laid three identical slices on it. Clemmie's plate, then Lucy's, Harry's, young Richard's, and last his own.

''Thank you, Gutteridge. We'll have the Bollinger now. I hope it's well chilled.''

Buller cast his eyes over the family luncheon table before sitting down. His family, his home crew as he thought of them, was like most ship's companies a mixed crew: Clemmie, his second-in-command, steady, loyal, trustworthy, reliable in a crisis, well able to handle the ship on her own, as she had to do for much of the time. Then Lucy, at seventeen a problem, like a brilliant but mercurial chief petty officer, much loved but unpredictable. And Harry, fifteen now, a once promising able-seaman, but for the present a bitter disappointment. And young Richard, a real sailor, eager, willing, the salt of the lower deck.

Buller stood behind his chair for a moment and raised his glass of champagne. ''To you all,'' he said, glancing at them each in turn, Clemmie last, and smiled at her over his glass as they both sipped. It was their first family meal for a year and the last until Christmas, for tomorrow Harry would be returning to Eton, Richard to Mr. Glover's Establishment at Gosport, and in two weeks' time, Lucy would be back at Oxford.

Buller's memory flashed back a generation to his own boyhood, his father arriving from London as he had arrived this morning, his father full of pride in his twin midshipmen sons, and of himself; Cadet Archibald Buller, off to his first year in the *Britannia*. His father's pride, too, in the news he gave them of his promotion to vice-admiral and appointment as Third Naval Lord.

"What a settled lot we were!" he told himself. "Probably no better but more predictable and less discontented."

Harry was saying to Clemmie, "You know, mama, the metal market has been badly hit by this peace treaty between Russia and Japan. Bad for a lot of businesses that were making money in the Far East." Typical of Harry, who would no doubt be a millionaire before he was thirty—Harry, whose refusal to go into the navy had so shocked his father. The City indeed! The Bullers had plenty of money, and the place for a Buller was on the bridge of a man-o'-war, not in a London office.

Buller turned to Richard, who could not hear enough about the Battle of Tsushima. How Buller adored this boy who promised so well! Richard was as puzzled as Buller himself had been shattered by the older boy's rejection of the service that was synonymous with the Royal Navy, the sea, and the Buller name.

"No, the Russian gunfire was very accurate at first, as good as any I've seen," he said.

Lucy was not in the least interested in the war or her father's experiences or anything really except her work, the injustices of a male-dominant world, the suffragette movement and its heroines, like Bessie Rayner Parkes, Dr. Elizabeth Garrett Anderson, and Frances Power Cobbe.

Clemmie and he had worked hard to keep Lucy from going up to Lady Margaret Hall, and had only succumbed in the end to the pleas of the headmistress of Lucy's school, Chel-

tenham Ladies College. In Buller's eyes (and in Clemmie's
for that matter) girls should receive an adequate education in
the three R's, then go to a finishing school in Paris before
their first Season, when, if they were as pretty as Lucy, they
would be deluged with proposals.

Yes, a lot of disappointment. But then the nation had
changed in so many ways since the Good Queen's death—
mostly for the worse, and mostly affecting the young, the
young of all classes. The educated young saying it was quite
right for the people to rise up against the tsar of Russia.
Workmen going on strike for no good reason. Too much
freedom, too little discipline.

"Archy, dear," Clemmie called from the other end of the
table, "should Richard be having all that champagne? He's
jumping in a gymkhana this afternoon."

Buller laughed indulgently. "It'll be a help," he said.
"Bollinger's very good for keeping you airborne."

"Oh, father, really," said Lucy censoriously, and Buller
wondered what had happened to the sense of humor in that
once-lighthearted girl of his.

With both boys gone, Buller was glad when Whitney arrived
the next day to stay for a week. Buller met him at the station
in his new Rolls-Royce and was pleased at the American's
immediate interest in it. "I tossed up whether to buy a Napier
or this," Buller said as they walked around it before setting
off. "But in that Tourist Trophy motor race in the Isle of Man
last Thursday, the Rolls-Royce came in second—almost
won—and the Napier couldn't do better than tenth."

Whitney accepted the offer to drive, and he handled the
big, quiet car with complete confidence, wearing the bor-
rowed goggles of the chauffeur, who sat behind with his
handkerchief over his face.

Ten minutes later Whitney drew up the car on the gravel
sweep before the house. "So this is Wyston Court," he said
in admiration. It was a beautiful early autumn day and the
deep, generous windows were wide open. Wyston Court had
an ancient wisteria with gnarled, twisting trunks growing up
on each side of the porch. The blooms were long since gone,

but the foliage reaching up almost to the roof gave a warm appearance to the front. "Gee, this is really old, Buller. I bet your family has lived here forever."

Gutteridge welcomed them at the door, and a footman took Whitney's big leather portmanteau. "As a matter of fact we've been here only ten years," Buller explained. "My brothers live in the old family home."

Clemmie joined them at that moment. She had evidently been in the greenhouses, for her basket was laden with peaches and as if by design, she was wearing a long, peach-colored silk dress with puffed sleeves and a wide-brimmed straw hat. She had grown into a handsome, mature woman in her eighteen years of marriage, her figure tight and full-bosomed, her face revealing the faintest lines reflecting her expressions, her hair shamelessly turning from corn-colored to gray.

As vivaciously as always, Clemmie Buller greeted her American guest. "Isn't that grand that you could come? It seems so long, Captain Campbell, since we first met when the king was poorly—wasn't that a strange evening?"

Clemmie swept into the hall and handed the basket to the housekeeper. Whitney was admiring a large portrait by Milais. "That is my mother-in-law. Beautiful, wasn't she?" There was a Constable landscape on another wall, and inevitably (there was at least one in every room) a naval engagement in oils, all fire and smoke and floating spars and sailors dying in agony.

Clemmie took Whitney by the arm and led him up the wide staircase. "I shall show you your rooms myself," she said. "I do hope you will be comfortable and stay with us for much longer than a silly old week."

Buller, grateful as always for his good fortune in having Clemmie as a wife, thought, "What a wonderful hostess! If I did not live here, how nice it would be to come to stay!"

The next morning, Clemmie hacked about the estate with Whitney while Buller spent the time with his farm manager and watched the last of a late harvest being threshed by the Clayton and Shuttleworth threshing machine they had bought last year.

At luncheon Lucy behaved with reasonable decorum, to Buller's relief, though she once chipped into the conversation by asking about the women's suffrage campaigns in America.

Whitney answered genially. "I don't know much about it," he replied, "because I don't know that we have one. The women of America have got what they want already. They dominate everything, tell us men what to do, feed us, control our money."

For Lucy this was not a subject that could be taken lightly, and she snapped back, "I mean legally. Most American women don't have a vote, have no legal rights . . ."

Clemmie saw that it was time to rise from the table and firmly put an end to the conversation. "You and Archy are going out on a rough shoot—if you would like that, Captain Campbell?"

Then there was dinner at Weir Park that evening. It was nearly two years since Buller had seen his twin elder brothers, who were serving in the Channel Fleet commanded by Sir Arthur ("old 'ard 'eart") Wilson. Both Guy and Henry, who each commanded a battleship, were high above Buller in the captain's list, and would soon be looking forward to a shore appointment with the possibility of being promoted to flag rank.

The twins had always teased Buller as a boy, and did so now after the first affectionate greetings. Pretending to study Buller's face, Guy said admiringly, "Yes, Henry, you're right—the eyes slit and inscrutable after that service with the Mikado."

"We once had a brother who was an Englishman" sang Henry. And together they broke into a chorus from *H.M.S. Pinafore*, adapting the last line:

> *For he might have been a Roosian,*
> *A French, or Turk, or Proosian*
> *Or perhaps Ital-ian!*
> *But in spite of all temptations*
> *To belong to other nations,*
> *He remains a Japanese-man.*

"Oh dear, will our husbands *ever* grow up?" Guy's wife asked with a sigh. "Come along, Archy we all know how you like your bubbly, and Chambers has got out some '79 Veuve Clicquot."

Buller fully approved and, knowing that he could drink his brothers under the table, saw his way through a bottle before the dinner had reached the roast grouse.

Guy and Henry were firm Beresford men and, like their hero, believed Jackie Fisher was destroying the Royal Navy. In the billiard room after dinner, the twins questioned Buller more seriously about his mission to the Far East and his report to the Admiralty.

"We know you're in the Fishpond, Archy, but is it true that Fisher's going to build battleships that'll make the whole fleet out-of-date? That'd be criminal stupidity—the Germans'll laugh themselves to death, they'll suddenly find themselves level with us."

Buller placed his cigar on the ashtray, took steady aim, and potted an awkward red at the far end of the table. Then he replied, speaking slowly and, for once, seriously, "You two should get it into your heads that I'm not in or out of any Fishpond, as you call it. I hate anything that divides the navy and that's what Charlie B. is doing. He's even got the Prince of Wales on his side, and that's bad because Georgie loves the navy and is usually sensible."

"All right," said Henry soothingly and turned to Whitney. "You saw this battle, too. There couldn't have been much wrong with battleships that could sink a modern fleet of equal size in half a day."

Whitney laughed and said he was not going to get involved in any argument. "All I know is that the Russians would have gone to the bottom in half the time if the Japanese had used only twelve-inch guns. And it's no secret in Washington *and* Tokyo that there are plans there for battleships with *only* heavy guns, and twice as many as any battleship afloat today. Superbattleships."

"And if we don't move fast in the same direction," added

Buller, "our fleet'll be sunk by the Germans in half a day if there's a war."

"I don't trust that man Fisher," said Guy obstinately.

"I agree," said Henry.

"These brothers agree about everything," Whitney told himself. "Especially if it's conformist. The trouble with the British Navy is that it's still living on the memory of Nelson." And as a good Anglophile this American hoped that men like Fisher and Buller would prevail against the tide of reactionaries, or the Japanese and the Germans, to say nothing of his own United States Navy, would soon be knots ahead.

Then they joined the ladies for a game of Mah-Jongg. Buller wanted to play for fifty guineas a time. Clemmie told him not to be foolish, so he asked the butler for a very large brandy and played very badly.

It was two in the morning when they left in the carriage. Buller went to sleep almost at once, and later, when they were getting into bed, Clemmie rebuked him. "Why do you always have to drink so much, Archy? You know you're getting fat, and stupid."

"Not as stupid as my brothers," Buller responded brightly. "They're dear fellows, but Heaven help the navy if they ever get onto the board."

Over the following days Whitney and Clemmie rode in the mornings, leaving Buller to deal with estate business. One evening, they gave a dinner party, and on Saturday they all went to a hunt ball at Longleat. On the way home Whitney said how much he had enjoyed himself. "Your English country life sure is social," he exclaimed as he stretched out in the carriage. "How do you keep this up all the year round? I'll have to get back to sea to recover."

The American had danced hard all evening and, though complaining of exhaustion, seemed to Buller to have genuinely enjoyed himself and to be buoyed up with high spirits. Like any host, Buller was glad to see his guest and old friend so evidently happy. And this made his discovery the following morning all the more surprising.

Lucy was having breakfast alone when Buller came down. She was off to a rally at Bristol and had agreed to sell copies of *Women's Justice*. "Your friend has flown the nest," she told her father.

"What do you mean?"

"The American captain embarked before dawn. Gutteridge told me he got a lift into Cirencester in the milk cart."

"Was there no message? Nothing?"

Lucy shook her head and stood up from the table. "I thought him a rather tiresome fellow," she said. "And *not* well-mannered."

When Clemmie came down, Buller asked her if Whitney had given any warning or notice that he was going to leave before his week was up—and without saying good-bye.

Clemmie turned away to help herself from the assortment of laid-out breakfast dishes. "Oh well, perhaps he had seen enough of us." She appeared to treat the matter lightly and began to talk about the Marquess and Marchioness of Bath, their host and hostess of the evening before.

But Buller could not put the matter out of his head and thought about sending a telegram to the embassy to see if Whitney was all right. Instead, he sought consolation in the fields and woods about his estate. He had always enjoyed shooting, had had a gun since he was eight, and a succession of gundogs, all called Junus, from the same age.

So he whistled up Junus, put a handful of cartridges into the pocket of his old shooting jacket, and set off across country by himself. "Very rum," he kept saying to himself. "Very rum behavior when you're someone's guest." And he had flattered himself that they were chums. Archy Buller was very put out.

"That is very kind of Your Majesty," said Buller, with a slight tilt of the head. "My wife will be honored by your interest. My elder son, unfortunately, is set on becoming a businessman and making a lot of money."

The king exhaled a cloud of blue-gray cigar smoke and

chuckled. "There are worse things he could do with his life, Archy." He broke into one of his long and frequent bouts of coughing.

"But my younger son, Richard, will carry on the tradition. He will be going to Osborne next year under Admiral Fisher's New Scheme for Training."

"He will prosper, I have no doubt," said the king. "It is a good scheme. It is no exaggeration to say that the navy would be in poor health but for our Jackie. He fights the good fight in the face of his enemies." The king leaned forward and continued in a low voice. "He does not know it yet, but there will be a special order in Council shortly to make him an admiral of the fleet. That will bring him satisfaction, I've no doubt. And he needs the money—unlike that rich barbarian, Beresford," he ended, rolling the *r's* of his last words.

The king rose painfully from his leather chair with the aid of his silver-topped stick. He paused for breath, took the big cigar from his mouth, and said, "Come on, Archy, let's take a turn at the tables. It's rate enough for me to get to the Marlborough these days. Nothing but damn boxes and papers and engagements."

Buller proceeded to win 400 guineas from the king, who as always took it in good part and departed reluctantly for Buckingham Palace at 7:30. Buller continued at the baccarat table for another hour, losing the greater part of his winnings, took an ample dinner with two friends, talked over Arthur Balfour's resignation as prime minister and the dread prospect of a Liberal government, and returned to Clarges Street. He was in a cheerful mood, having almost forgotten the snub by Whitney Campbell, and was looking forward to the arrival of his family for Christmas shopping and to his visit to the Admiralty the next morning.

Randolph had placed Buller's usual decanter of Glenfilloch and jug of water beside the fire in his study, and again according to custom when he was alone in London, he read *The Westminster Gazette* and retired.

It was past midnight and he was almost asleep when the telephone rang beside his bed. It was the Countess

Reitzberg-Sönderlong, who was clearly very wide awake and pleased to find him at home.

"So you have deserted your poor family, Buller. Or perhaps you are lonely for them. My husband has been called to Berlin for a few days, too."

Buller listened to her deep, attractive voice with its faint guttural traces, recalling with pleasurable guilt that evening together in the count's study. He found himself saying, "Yes, I would like that very much," to her suggestion that he should call to see her the following evening before dinner. "*Gute nacht.*"

"*Ach, gute nacht, Kapitän Buller*. I am sure you are really fluent in German, as in all things."

"I want you to see my *new*, secret greyhound," said Admiral Fisher, like a young boy showing off his first bicycle. As before, Fisher took from a drawer in his desk a rolled sketch-of-rig plan of the navy's new armored cruiser. He pointed at one of the turrets with a stubby finger. "There! Look there! Twelve-inch guns. That's what you wanted, and that's what the navy will get. And it will confound our enemies. We shall have three of these giant armored cruisers before the Germans have put pen to paper. Twice as many big guns as any *battleship* afloat. Able to catch and blow out of the water any man-o'-war in the world. H.M.S. *Unapproachable.*"

"And her real name, sir?" Buller asked.

"*Invincible*. Invincible by name, invincible at sea."

Buller asked where she was to be built.

"We shall lay her down by Easter. On the Tyne."

"At Elswick, sir? That'll please Lieutenant Maclewin. That's where he lived."

"The little fellow who was with you at Tsushima? There can't be many naval officers who grew up in Elswick."

Buller explained that Rod had been brought up there, his father working in the Armstrong gun shops before he was killed. "And thanks to your liberalizing promotion scheme, he was given his commission two years ago."

Admiral Fisher, always susceptible to flattery, beamed with satisfaction. "That is nothing compared with what is to come. And I shall throttle with my own hands any bigot who opposes me." His deep scowl with lowered eyebrows switched as suddenly to a smile of kindness and concern. "But I have called you here to ask you—ask you what, Buller? You tell me."

"About a new appointment?" Buller laughed. "I will tell you at once in case you should change your mind. I would like, sir, to have back my old command. May I have the *Lily* back? I was working her up into a fine ship and a good company. And I would like Lieutenant Maclewin back as my gunnery officer."

The reply was as swift as an exploding charge after the firing pin has struck. "You shall have both, Buller. In January."

Fisher paced across the window, hands clasped behind his back, and looked out onto the Admiralty yard below. He spoke now in a low, emotional voice. "Because you are your father's son, and I loved him, and because I trust you, I will pass on another great confidence. I am not supposed to know it myself. But I am one from whom no secrets are hid—you will recall that quotation from the Collect for Purity. And I must show surprise when His Majesty informs me. I am shortly to be promoted to admiral of the fleet."

"Well, sir, I am very pleased to hear that. Indeed I am."

"You will see that as a great honor, as I do." Then he turned around, raised his right fist, shouted, "But you do not see why it will confound all *my* enemies, and especially that hollow charlatan, Beresford, who calls himself a sailor, who will never forgive me for snatching the First Sea Lord's appointment from him. For this will give me five *more* years on the active list in order to complete my reforms and build bigger and greater dreadnoughts TO CONFOUND THE NATION'S ENEMIES."

"And your dear wife—when will she be arriving in London?"

"Next week. Next Thursday," Buller spoke gruffly. He did not care to think of Clemmie while he was lying in the arms of this strong and totally fascinating woman.

"I shall have to return to Germany for Christmas, too." She stirred, and her hand moved slowly down his body and held him hard so that he gasped. He had never experienced lust so demandingly as with this woman. When she spoke, saying, "Come, my powerful Captain Buller," he turned and held down her shoulders. They both relished her struggle with all her considerable strength in an attempt to throw him off. The longer and harder she fought, the sweeter the victory, the sharper the ecstasy.

Then they lay, both damp with sweat, their breath slowly returning to normal, the scent of lemon heavy on the still air. She held his hand tightly, her long fingers intertwined with his. "*Ach*, it is nice that you should be in London. Especially just now. In and out of your Admiralty, I am sure, every day. Talking with your friend, Admiral Fisher."

Her deep voice droned on. "Ah, he is a great man, your Admiral Fisher. But no greater than Admiral von Tirpitz. And your Fisher and our Tirpitz all planning their new ships, with my Sonny and you at their side. That is amusing, no? And the ships will no doubt be just the same—all big guns for the battleships. And next, all big guns for the armored cruisers, you'll see."

She turned toward him again, pressing her hand hard against his chest. "You are my all-big-gun battleship, eh—my Buller?"

She drew herself out of bed, standing for a moment without shame or shyness and looking down at him with an amused expression on her face. "My invincible lover." She turned, saying, "Now I must dress for dinner. Oh dear, such dull people. I wish it was with you. Come back later—at midnight, my Buller."

Buller laughed and began to put on his clothes. "You will wear me out, my dear Miranda. And I have to make an early start."

"To Portsmouth, to see your new battleship being built. Have I guessed right?"

Buller laughed but did not reply, saying only "Good-bye" as he left her room.

He dined at his club again and made the mistake of playing bezique afterward. His mind was not fully on the game. For through the haze of physical satisfaction, like the Russian Fleet emerging from the low cloud on that May morning, he could distinguish dangers and difficulties ahead. It was perhaps not surprising that this Miranda was so well informed on the details of design of future men-o'-war. But it was surprising and disturbing that she seemed to know as much as she hinted at. Her low voice echoed in his ears as his opponent declared a double for the second time. What was that she had said? "And next all big guns for the armored cruisers."

And was there—he suddenly remembered with a shock—was there a double meaning to her expression, "My invincible lover"? No, it was not possible that she knew Fisher's secret, not his secret *and* the ship's future name. All the same . . .

"Not your night, Buller," exclaimed his opponent with satisfaction. "I make that 247 guineas you owe me. And on the strength of that, I'll buy a Bollinger."

Later that night, as he walked home up St. James's Street, Buller told himself sternly, "If there has been a leak, it is very serious. And it could be very serious for me if it becomes known that the First Sea Lord has taken me into his confidence, and that I am having an affair with the wife of the German naval attaché at the same time."

Buller, who was by no means a conceited man, prided himself on his steady common sense, and the belief was growing in him that he must watch himself with care. And yet? The memory of the woman's fine, strong body, her large, skilled hands, her passion, and the pace and fury of their lovemaking overwhelmed him, driving out any last guilt or unease that had nagged away at him all evening. Besides, Buller felt a growing fondness far above common lust for this German countess, her teasing ways, her sense of fun and uninhibited appetites.

It was ten minutes before midnight. Buller was at the

corner of Clarges Street and Piccadilly. To the west down Piccadilly lay Wilton Crescent.

Buller turned west, raising his stick for a hansom cab.

Captain Whitney Campbell had never before been in such a puzzling and agonizing situation as he was in the autumn of 1905. "Here I am," he told himself, "almost forty years of age, holding a responsible post in the United States Navy, unmarried and reconciled to it, and now suddenly knocked out cold as Jake Kilrain by John L. Sullivan by love for a woman.

"And, oh God help me, a married woman of my own age, the wife of an honorable and steady friend. And, I truly believe, she is in love with me. It is crazy—Goddamn it, it's crazy!"

It was six weeks since he had last seen her, and there had been no communication at all during that time. Once again, his mind returned to that scene on the track just above the Golden Valley, a horse-drawn narrow boat below making its slow progress along the canal towards Sapperton Tunnel.

Clemmie had drawn up her mare, a lovely bay hunter, sweating freely from a long gallop across the hunting country she knew as well as a captain knows every deck and mess and passageway of his ship. Still stiff from the previous day's ride, Whitney reined in beside her, and they sat silently for a moment, hearing the voice of the boatman calling out to his horse and the laughter of some girls playing among stooks of corn on the other side of the valley.

Whitney, still breathing rapidly from the ride, said, "I love your part of England, Clemmie. It sure is the most beautiful country I've known. New England is beautiful, too, but it doesn't have the soft mellowness of the English countryside."

"You know it's only our rain," said Clemmie, laughing. "And I've been in New England in your fall—and, dear me, the colors. We have nothing like them."

Whitney looked at this stately and beautiful woman sitting side-saddle with the comfort and ease of someone who has ridden confidently all her life.

She turned and smiled at him. "I won't tease anymore by galloping so fast. Silly show-off. I was always being told this when I was a girl. Showing off to my father and all the nursery staff. A spoiled only child." She laughed again and began walking her horse to the track. "Besides, I like talking to you—in fact, I like you very much. You're a 'swell guy.' That's right, isn't it?"

In the short time he had known Clemmie, Whitney had noted with surprise that she would make some totally unexpected observation. Buller himself had once told Whitney that his father-in-law had been one of the most eccentric men in the navy—no, in England. And that was saying something. Nobody could be more sane than his daughter, but the unorthodox speech was no doubt a mild genetic throwback to the late Earl of Huntley.

A few minutes later, they paused beside a stream and got off to allow their horses to drink. It was then that Clemmie had unselfconsciously walked up to Whitney, throwing back her veil, and said, "Will you kiss me, please? While we're like this, more alone than we may ever be again." She smiled at him, but was looking serious and contemplative when she added, "While we're both so hot and smelling as delicious as our horses."

He did as he was asked, amazed at the softness of her lips as they pressed against his and then brushed to and fro across his cheek. Then she stood back, looking at him unwaveringly with her blue eyes, saying, "There must be a lot of foolish women in the world who have missed marrying you."

They were the same height, and Whitney held her eyes, weak with surprise and emotion, conscious of the passion suddenly aroused, and of the smell of leather and horse sweat and crushed bracken where they had broken through to the stream off the bridle path.

Afterward, those smells and the scent of Clemmie's damp skin always prefaced the return once again of the memory of that moment, like turning a page of an album to the one picture you most cherish. Then they had lain close together while their horses grazed, uncaring, Clemmie laughing at the clumsy awkwardness of their undressing.

"Riding clothes were never intended for the boudoir."

Once, Whitney had said protestingly, "But Clemmie
. . ." And she silenced him as swiftly and expertly as she
held his body to her, the scratches of sticks and bracken stalks
against their skin unheeded.

Later, they laughed and chattered all the way back to
Wyston Court, more at ease with one another even than
before. Clemmie referred only once to the passion that had
overcome them by the stream, "May this weather hold," she
said in a heartfelt tone. "Until Archy goes to town on business, the country's all we have."

The reality of what had occurred between them struck
Whitney for the first time as he was dressing for dinner, its
magnitude increased by the certain knowledge that it was not
a passing affair, a sudden thrust of passion. For him it was
not, and that was what made it so serious. And he also felt
with absolute certainty that she, too, felt that there was
something rapidly developed but no less deep between them.

"Now I must leave. There's no doubt of that," he told
himself sharply. "I must get away before the danger creeps
even closer. Never have anything more to do with her again.
No communication—nothing. It never happened, it was all a
schoolboy's dream, I have never been a guest in this house
. . ."

The evening passing like a long-drawn-out gray night-
mare, unreal yet terrifying. When his eyes met Clemmie's he
told himself harshly that there was no recognition. Thank
Heaven, there were four guests, and Buller took the men to
the billiard room immediately after dinner.

The evening broke up early, and Whitney was gone before
full daylight. A sovereign for the astonished housemaid
cleaning the brass, the promise of another if she found him a
means to get to the railway station. No messages, no notes.
No trace of his presence. Wyston Court, and the Buller
family, must accept that he had never been here, never shot
and played billiards with Buller, never ridden beside and
made love to his wife.

At the embassy he had done all that he could to get an immediate transfer back to the United States. The matter had even reached the ambassador, Whitelaw Reid, but he was told that it was out of the question for the time being. He would have to wait for a replacement, the diplomatic consequences of a sudden and premature departure being unacceptable.

From his flat in Chester Street, Whitney led a strictly confined social life, accepting invitations for only small parties of American friends, and official engagements. His anguish at the offense he must have given to his old friend stabbed at him constantly. Typical American boorishness— that's what Buller would be saying. But he believed that it was nothing compared with the devastating effect it would have on Buller if he ever learned the reason for his precipitate departure from his house.

Day by day he struggled to erase Clemmie's image in his memory, and day by day he was increasingly unsuccessful. In his twenties and early thirties, women had come and gone in Whitney's life, some leaving a small mark of remorse or regret. The impression that Clemmie Buller had made on him was deep and ineradicable, and the knowledge that he could never see her again filled him day and night with the darkest depression and sense of hopelessness.

Chapter VII

⚓

Greek Tragedy

ROD WATCHED BULLER unscrew the f/63 Ross lense from the bellows extension of his new Soho focal plane reflex camera. He had been with Buller when he bought the camera from Watsons of High Holborn, selecting in the end this Soho instead of a Graflex, in spite of its relatively large size and weight. Rod had been impressed by Buller's knowledge, which was a match for the salesman's. Buller's photography had become more than an off-watch hobby and had proved useful professionally, too, as it certainly would at the end of this shoot. Rod had seen already the marvelous results the long-focus lense gave when Buller developed the film in the *Lily*.

Now Buller screw on the finely constructed lense, secured his camera to the stand rigged in a corner of the bridge's wing, set the range to infinity, and finally checked the six doubleplate pack on the back of the camera.

The shoot was to be at four miles—just 7,000 yards—and the big canvas target was already in sight on the starboard bow, the old scout towing it rising high in the water and then disappearing from sight into a trough of the swell.

Rod recognized only too well his special responsibilities as chief gunnery officer of the cruiser over and above the normal

arduous duties during a shoot. With the recent appointment
of Lord Charles Beresford as commander-in-chief of the
Mediterranean Fleet, Buller, as a known supporter of Fisher
in the Admiralty, became at once a marked man, his command of the *Lily* in daily jeopardy, the smartness and performance of his ship subjects of the closest and most critical
scrutiny.

As Buller himself had told Rod when the news of Beresford's appointment arrived by telegraph in Malta, "Charlie
B. will need to have some reason for throwing me out, but
it'll only have to be the size of one of those dghaisas." And
from the castle ramparts where Buller and Rod were walking,
Buller pointed at one of the little Maltese rowboats crossing
the harbor below, the Arab at the oars chanting his monoto-
nous dirge.

When Buller had taken up his command again, the ship's
gunnery had lost its edge. Rod had the gun crews practice
three times a day, using .303 rifles secured to the six-inch
guns and telescopic sights. But they were in the lower half of
the results after the first fleet shoot, and Buller had confided
to Rod that he would be on his way back to Britain if
standards did not rise rapidly.

Now, a month later, Rod was aware that at this shoot, his
captain's future was at stake. He placed a hand on the shoulder of the gunnery instructor at the four-foot six-inch Barr
and Stroud rangefinder. "Thank you, Mr. Sparrow, I'll take
the first few minutes, then I'll hand it back to you." The
instructor had a blue insignia on his white sleeve, a crossed
gun over a torpedo beneath a crown.

"Aye aye, sir." The big West Countryman stepped aside
to make room for the chief gunnery officer. "I made it eighty
five hundred yards, sir."

Rod looked into the lenses, rotating the arms of the rangefinder until the two images coincided and became one. The
dial below showed him the range. Rod called out to the
navigating officer, "Eight-two, Jerry. A shade to port,
Jerry—half a point, no more." Then "Steady—steady
now."

The crews at the starboard six-inch guns were making their own adjustments to conform with the range and bearing being communicated to them by the new electric transmitter. The long forty-five-caliber barrels were elevated, live solid shot in the breeches, ready ammunition stacked for immediate use. The captains of guns and crews in their white frocks and trousers had adjusted mufflers over their ears.

Besides the electric transmitter, the ships of the cruiser squadron also had the recently introduced "dotter," invented by the peppery, brilliant Captain Percy Scott. Since the earliest days of gunnery at sea, guns had been fired primitively and at close range by rolling the sights on the target with the ship's movements. This dotter was a simple apparatus comprising a pencil attached to an extension of the gun barrel, a vertical framework, and a handle operating a bicycle chain. This had the enormous advantage of producing a continuous aim for the gunlayer.

The *Lily*, the last cruiser in the Third Squadron to bring her guns to bear on the target, was logging 16 knots and rolling and pitching through 8 to 10 degrees, giving the rating operating the dotter plenty to do. Rod ordered the forward starboard six-inch guns to fire. Now the midships guns and finally the two aft guns. "FIRE! FIRE!" And then the captains of guns were on their own.

Up on the bridge, the concussive effect struck everyone like a physical slap. Veteran sailors compared it with the blow in the face from a wet sail in the old days, when you were aloft and trying to take in a reef in a rising wind. The sound went through the head, more painfully still when a pair of guns was fired in exact synchronization. But everyone abovedecks had a task to perform and was too busy to react to these effects.

Buller for his part was giving all his concentrated attention to his photography. In rapid sequence to match his gunners' pace, he pressed the Bowden cable plunger activating the shutter, drew on the plate tab, steadied his aim through the focusing lens, and when he saw the tall white splashes of his ships's fire near the canvas target, pressed again.

The firing lasted for twelve minutes, every gun discharging no fewer than forty-eight rounds, and two crews succeeded in getting off sixty. Then Rod signaled the ceasefire and everyone relaxed.

Later, when the *Lily* reformed with her squadron and the fleet, Beresford's flagship, H.M.S. *Bulwark,* signaled the score to the *Lily* by semaphore: "Flag to Lily 280 hits. Improvement imperative."

It was not the Third Cruiser Squadron's top score, the *Lancaster* had that honor, but it was better than the 58 percent they had scored on the last shoot. Still, there was no pleasing the c-in-c. This evening, when he had processed his films, Buller would go over the results in detail with Rod and the warrant officer gunner and the captains of guns, assessing the record for the gunlayers' competition he had instituted. With the help of Buller's photographs and really keen practice, Rod was determined to see that his ship would be top scorer in the squadron *and* the fleet. It was possible. It could be done. And Rod would do it.

Three weeks later on March 14, 1906, Lieutenant Roderick Maclewin R.N. became the most successful and admired gunnery officer in the Mediterranean Fleet. In exercises east of Malta, in poor weather and with a heavy sea running, the *Lily* had scored 72 percent hits with her main armament, riddling the tall canvas target—which if it had been a man-o'-war of the *Lily*'s size, would now have been at the bottom. The score was there, on the record board of every ship, clear and incontrovertible: H.M.S. *Lily,* Third Cruiser Squadron, 72%. Second, H.M.S. *Leviathan* (flag), 69% . . .

Rod experienced a greater sense of relief than of triumph, and when congratulated by the cruiser's company had said in reply, "This is not my victory—it is the *Lily*'s, and her captains of guns and gun crews. So three cheers for them."

In meticulous line-ahead with her consorts, *Carnarvon, Lancaster, Leviathan, Suffolk,* and *Vulcan,* the *Lily* cut through the still waters of Grand Harbor, Valetta, and then, with engines a quarter astern, picked up her buoy with a sudden roar from the chains in the hawseholes.

Rod had been a very young man when he had first seen

Malta, from the decks of H.M.S. *Condor*, commander, Lord Charles Beresford. Now Beresford commanded the greatest of Britain's fleets, his flag in the *Bulwark*, which had already anchored ahead of the other battleships, and Rod was a gunnery lieutenant, with the new and special honor of holding the highest score in the fleet.

With the shutting off of the *Lily*'s engines, a silence seemed to fall over Grand Harbor, from Ricasoli Point and Fort St. Elmo to the farthest recesses of the harbor to the south. Then the murmur of chanting and bosuns' voices, distant shouting from the markets and alleyways ashore, the rumble of wheels on cobblestones, made themselves heard.

Rod glanced up at the castle of the Knights of St. John and the white Moorish buildings that rose up tier upon tier like the sides of a shallow cup embracing the waters of Grand Harbor. Throughout its long history from before the days of the crusaders to its capture by the French and recapture by Nelson's navy in 1800, Malta had never known a fleet as powerful as the British Mediterranean Fleet anchored here on this warm March day. The battle practice they had just completed confirmed that these men-o'-war could have blown any foreign fleet out of the water as quickly as Admiral Togo had destroyed Admiral Rozhestvensky's almost a year earlier.

"Mr. Maclewin, there is a signal for you, sir." Rod turned and answered the telegraphist's salute. He took the sheet of buff paper and read: "Admiral Beresford presents his compliments and requests the presence of Lieutenant Maclewin on board his flagship for dinner this day."

One hour after sunset, Rod, resplendent in white mess dress—white jacket with shoulder straps, white waistcoat, and laced trousers, with the ribbons of his decorations a splash of color on his chest—stepped smartly down the ladder to the waiting launch, its copper funnel burnished bright.

News always spread like wildfire through a ship, and only slightly less rapidly through a fleet, and there was not an officer or a rating in Grand Harbor that evening who had not learned of the honor being accorded to Lieutenant Maclewin and of the snub given to his captain in the invitation to dine which had excluded Rod's commanding officer.

Buller himself had been philosophical about the affair. "I am delighted for you, Midge," he had said in the privacy of his cabin. "I flatter myself that it makes more of a chump of Charlie B. than of me. That doesn't matter much. What does matter is that it's one more slice in the great cut that's dividing our navy into two." Then, deciding that Rod should get off to a good start, he had his steward open a bottle of Veuve Clicquot, and they drank to their victory: "To seventy-two percent, Midge!"

The launch chugged swiftly across the smooth waters of Grand Harbor, Rod sitting at the stern, arms folded and conscious of the curious gaze of hundreds of sailors of the fleet relaxing on deck in the cool of the evening. Electric lights sparkled on the upperworks and decks and from the ports of the anchored men-o'-war, and the blinking of signal lamps and the sudden sweep of a searchlight beam across the water gave a golden dreamland effect to the scene.

The *Bulwark* herself, her white paintwork spotless, her brasswork gleaming, her massive hull glowing luminously in this dusk light, was like some fairytale palace, the superstructure and upperworks the towers and pillars. In some way, under these conditions and in this light, the turrets fore and aft with their twin fifty-foot-long, twelve-inch guns and the six-inch secondary armament appeared as no more than decorations.

There was, Rod reflected, some truth and substance in this analogy. The *Bulwark* might be one of the most powerful battleships in the world, a mere four years old, the pride of one of Britain's most admired admirals. But her days were numbered. As Buller had confided to him, the all-big-gun battleship building at Portsmouth launched and named *Dreadnought* by the king only last month, would be steaming on her trials in October. Under Fisher's program, other dreadnoughts would swiftly follow, and the *Bulwark* and every other relatively slow, mixed-battery battleship afloat might as well steer to the nearest scrapyard for all the value they would be.

But for the present no one could deny this battleship her style and spectacle: companion ladder gleaming black with glinting brass treads and rails; bosun at the head piping the admiral's guest on board; Royal Marines guard at attention, trouser creases like knives.

Yes, a fairytale palace, and here in the throne room were the fairytale king and queen, Admiral Lord Charles Beresford and Lady Beresford, the admiral's wife all glinting jewelry and rings and sequins, and heavily made up with rouge, powder, and lipstick; Beresford's decorations and orders across his chest reflecting the light from the chandeliers and table lamps about the cabin.

It was difficult to relate this ornate room of hanging velvet drapes, mahogany tables and sideboards, and desks and bookcases, of silver-framed portraits and seascapes and enlarged photographs of men-o'-war at sea and in harbor, of deep-pile mauve carpet—matching the admiral's cummerbund—with the interior of a ship built for one purpose, to engage and destroy other ships. War seemed as remote as the end of the British Empire.

It was almost as difficult to relate this swollen, dissipated, purple-faced man with the dashing Commander Beresford beside whom Rod had once fought on horseback against a screaming mob in the streets of Alexandria. Now he stepped forward unsteadily, almost tripping over the sleeping bulldog at his feet, right arm outstretched. The voice had changed little, deep, gravelly, and patrician in tone, and the smile was as warm as ever as he said, "Welcome, Lucky Midge. Remember when I first told you you'd be lucky all your life? Keepin' it up—eh? Seventy-two percent!"

Beresford put an arm across the bare shoulders of his wife. "M'dear—remember this youngster? My lucky talisman in the Gippo War of '82."

Rod bowed slightly as he took her hand, his fingers momentarily closing around a hundred thousand pounds' worth of gold, diamond, and emerald rings. "It is very good of you to honor me in this way, madam."

Her laugh was high-pitched and shrill, like a young girl's "Come young man, I'd have been a widow for twenty-five years if it hadn't been for you."

"Widow, my foot—me dear!" exclaimed her husband. "You'd have been hitched up again to some bounder within weeks—a rich young feller, no doubt."

Over the following few minutes, more guests arrived, all captains or commanders from the fleet. The dining cabin was half as big again as any warship's gun room, the silver and glass and linen reviving the analogy of Aladdin's cave in Rod's mind. He had been in numerous admirals' quarters in his time, but none like this, with a steward for every guest and a chief steward to supervise and pour the wine.

Course followed course, and the wine flowed like an ebb tide out of Plymouth harbor. Most of the conversation, of hunting and racing and social scandal, was far above Rod's head, just as he was far below their station in life and their rank in the navy. He listened politely, wondering at the outrage this would cause his son, Tom, if he had been present. Not a word of a professional nature was uttered until the royal toast had been drunk and the ladies had retired, when the port and cigars were passed round.

Then the admiral's voice boomed forth: "I'm damned if I can get used to these Frogs bein' our allies now." He turned to one of his captains, a heavily bearded officer with enormous side-whiskers. "What about you, Arthur? We were both brought up to believe those Frenchies'd be our enemy if it came to war. Now they're nearly at war with the Germans over this Moroccan business, and we're supposed to back 'em up."

"Wouldn't like to fight alongside Frogs, Charlie."

"Don't understand this Entente Cordiale business—I mean to say, we've always been chummy with the Huns. They've provided us with kings and queens, God bless 'em, for two hundred years, and now we're showin' 'em how to build a navy."

There were chuckles all around the table, and everyone took deep drafts of vintage port. "They'll build a good navy so long as they don't take instructions from that Mulatto," Beresford grunted.

There was a moment's silence, which Rod dared to break

by asking, "How do you mean, sir?"

"That Asiatic half-caste in the Admiralty, Midge. The ruination of this fleet and the whole navy." There were mutters of approbation and "Hear, hear!" from around the table. There was not a Fisher man present. "Look at this fleet of mine. In another year there'll be nothing left. 'Wanted in home waters,' the Mulatto says, 'to meet the growin' strength of Germany.' And what about our loss of strength and prestige here? The Med Fleet's always been our premier fleet."

Rod was thankful Buller had not been invited to this dinner. Nothing would have deterred him from speaking his mind. And now, inevitably, they were turning their verbal guns on the new *Dreadnought*. She was not the wonder ship of the world to these officers, not to Lord Charles Beresford. Everyone present except Rod contributed to the chorus of disgusted or alarmed criticism—of her high cost, her relatively thin protection, the fact that she was too big for any existing dock, and above all (and contradictorily and as an unconscious tribute) that she wiped out at one blow the great superiority in numbers of the British Fleet, which had been more powerful than all the foreign fleets of the world.

Admiral Beresford at last turned to Rod. "Well, Midge, you've kept very quiet. What d'you think, eh? You're the only one here who saw Tsushima—you saw what terrible destruction the Japanese secondary guns did to the Russian ships, smashin' all the upperworks, killin' more men than the occasional hit by a heavy shell. What would you like to be servin' in in your next battle, this *Bulwark* or the newfangled *Dreadnought*?"

There was a pause of no longer than a few seconds, but long enough for Beresford to add impatiently, "Well, out with it, man—out with it!"

"Truthfully, sir," said Rod, recognizing at once that he was risking his special relationship with this powerful admiral, and even his career, and also that it must be in the navy's interests to speak out. "Truthfully, sir, I would choose to be serving in the *Dreadnought*. It is my belief that it was Admiral Togo's superior speed and the hits he made with his heavy guns that did for Admiral Rozhestvensky.''

''And that's what you reported to the Mulatto when you got back—eh?'' The color was even higher in Beresford's face, his voice threatening and low.

''I reported what I had seen, sir. I would have failed in my duty had I done anything else.''

Silence. Not an officer moved, not to reach for his glass or to put his cigar to his lips. Rod's eyes were on Beresford, who returned his gaze coldly, then glanced about the table: ''Gentlemen, we shall join the ladies.''

The imperial Yacht *Hohenzollern* had been built for the kaiser to a specification in size and grandeur slightly but identifiably superior to the royal yacht *Victoria and Albert* belonging to his English uncle. Just as the German emperor had taken up yacht racing, putting more and more money and skill into it until the king (then still Prince of Wales) had been soundly defeated and had tired of the sport, so the *Hohenzollern* had to be superior in every department to the British contemporary.

Emperor Wilhelm II could not bear to be second at anything. His army was, without question, the greatest in the world. The fact that his Imperial Navy was smaller than his uncle's provided the driving urge for accelerating its growth until it was great enough to challenge the Royal Navy in battle.

The *Hohenzollern*, lying anchored here in the Piraeus, was the most distinctive and beautiful vessel to be seen in the crowded harbor, with her high, all-white hull, twin funnels, and three masts steeply raked. She was a fitting centerpiece for the surrounding rocky mountains, scattered with thorn scrub and pines, the white buildings stretching toward the wide valley holding Athens itself and the flat-topped rock of the Acropolis.

At noon on this June day, it was burning hot, a scarcely perceptible offshore breeze carrying the smell of pitch and dung and strong coffee and grilling souvlakias. Fishing vessels swarmed everywhere, like insects against the deep blue of the Aegean. The *Lily* eased herself gently through them,

Buller on the bridge very much in command and very strongly aware that his seamanship must be faultless. The kaiser himself would no doubt be watching with a critical eye the arrival of the English man-o'-war.

The *Lily* anchored three cables from the *Hohenzollern*, and at once fired in turn a salute of twelve guns for the port superintendent, and eighteen guns for the emperor. The yacht replied, and a signal broke out from her mast: "His Imperial Majesty invites on board at 5:00 P.M. the captain of the English cruiser."

Buller turned to Rod and his navigating officer. "Well, it's my turn this time, Midge. I hope I'm not asked what I think of the *Dreadnought*!"

"Have you met the kaiser before, sir?"

"Yes, years ago. If it wasn't for that dashed waxed mustache, he'd look like the Prince of Wales. Very courteous, very brainy, don't you know? But something's wrong somewhere—like that withered arm of his."

There was much more Buller could have recalled about the emperor of Germany who was so like his uncle, Edward VII: the warm sympathy of his manner, the deep interest he appeared to have in anyone talking to him, the liveliness of his inquiring mind, as well as the less attractive aspects, such as the inflexibility of his beliefs and the fierce and arrogant response on hearing anything that displeased him or cut across his beliefs. If Buller was allowed one word only to describe him, it must be "imperial."

All this Buller had observed on his first meeting. Now on this occasion, he noted it again, the regal manner unchanged. And why should it be? Since that occasion at the German embassy four years earlier, this man's every wish had continued to be granted by those who served him, adulation had continued to pour upon him like a deluge at every private and public occasion, and the sycophants who served him had grown rather than diminished in number.

And there at his elbow was the most sycophantic of all the kaiser's toadies—Count Sonny Reitzberg-Sönderlong, "the leech," now a Fregattenkapitän and Chief A.D.C. to His

Imperial Majesty, resplendent in white mess dress.

Buller bowed from the waist, just enough to show respect, but, for his own satisfaction, not as deeply as he customarily bowed to King Edward: "Your Imperial Majesty."

The kaiser offered his good right hand. "Captain Buller—a friend of my uncle is a friend of mine," he said, his English with the same German weight on the *r's* as the king's.

Buller turned his eyes slowly, slowly enough to indicate reluctance, to the figure at his side. The three saber scars across Sonny's cheek were purple in the intense heat. A slight nod. "My pleasure, Count Reitzberg-Sönderlong." Did he know that his wife was his mistress, Buller mused, and that their lovemaking had been especially ardent and violent? And where was she now?

"*My* pleasure, Captain Buller."

"And where is Captain Campbell of the United States Navy?" the kaiser asked, demonstrating his remarkable memory for names and occasions. "Perhaps it is as well he is not here, for I would tease him about those terrible new battleships of his. I warned him it would be disastrous to superimpose heavy guns immediately above heavy guns—and now all the world knows the *New Jersey* class are a disaster—twenty-five million dollars wasted. Ah, Captain Buller, all naval constructors should visit Kaiser Wilhelm for advice before drawing up new designs." He chuckled, but he meant it.

They sat under the awning and drank chilled hock from the Metternich vineyard on the Rhine and talked of naval matters, and—bombastically—of German naval plans. Buller had heard of the recent German Third Naval Bill, intended to close further the gap between the strength of the two navies. "And I think you may be surprised when you see the size and armament of our new all-big-gun ships, our *dreadnought-schiffe*. And of our new armored cruisers." The kaiser laughed and looked at Buller through his held-up wineglass. "And, my friend, we have one more singular advantage, a human one. We do not quarrel about *dreadnoughtschiffe* in

Germany—we just build them. Is that right, Sonny?''

"Yes, Your Majesty—indeed yes, Your Majesty,'' Sonny echoed.

When the last of the second bottle was poured out by the wine steward, Buller recognized that it was time for him to depart, at the kaiser's convenience.

But the kaiser, turning in his chair toward his A.D.C., said to Buller, ''And Captain Buller, we have another surprise for you, not a great fighting ship this time, but a great lady, whom you have met before.''

As if waiting in the wings for her entrance cue, Countess Miranda drifted through the open doors onto the quarterdeck where they were sitting, dressed in a wasp-waisted white muslin dress that flared out below her knees and was lace-trimmed at neck, wrists, and hem. She wore a straw hat turned up at the back and trimmed in ribbons.

Buller smiled at her and waited for her to pronounce his name ''Booler,'' which always amused and aroused him. "My dear Captain Buller, how enchanting and surprising!''

Buller bowed toward her, and she continued in her deep, melodious voice, ''Here we are all alone in this terrible, dirty, smelly place, and in comes your smart, clean, beautiful cruiser. How the drains *smell* wherever you anchor in the Mediterranean! Except in your Malta, of course.''

Count Sonny exclaimed in a shocked voice, ''My dear, really!'' But the kaiser was chuckling indulgently, and Miranda turned to him, dropping a hint of a curtsy. ''I know you agree, Willy dear. Only the Nordic races understand cleanliness.''

She took a glass of hock, and they wandered to the starboard rails and watched the lights appearing like stars at nightfall in Athens. Buller was pleased to see that his ship looked splendidly impressive in the half-light. The *Lily*, under his orders given earlier, was dressed overall with signal flags and pennants, from the ''E'' at the jack staff to the figure ''3'' at the ensign staff, and the whole range of color was swept every few seconds by two searchlights.

At Buller's side, Miranda said, ''You must be proud of your command, Buller. She is your first big ship, yes?''

"Yes, and I hope you may perhaps all dine with my officers and me. I will speak to His Majesty."

"Ah, alas!" said the Countess. "Tomorrow at dawn we depart for Constantinople. And—oh, *how* it will smell there! Much worse. But will you show me your ship now—before dinner? I will ask Willy."

The imperial launch cut swiftly across the harbor waters. Buller knew his ship's company well enough to understand how they would admire him for his *coup*, his "capture" of this beautiful and statuesque woman. "Trust our Buller not to let a chance slip—cor! and what a smasher." "All 'e needs is five minutes to get 'is leg over!" That's what they would be saying on the lower deck. And there was the faintest smirk discernible on the face of the officer-of-the-watch as he welcomed them on board.

Buller took Miranda up the ladder to the bridge, helping her with her long dress past minor obstructions, and showed her the navigational equipment and encouraged her to work out the distance from the *Hohenzollern* through the Barr and Stroud.

"Six hundred yards," she said, reading off the dial, and then lowered her voice. "Please, now may I see your cabin? There is not very much time."

She meant it! Until this moment, Buller had innocently supposed she really wished to see his ship and perhaps show off her stylish beauty and dress to the British sailors. He talked to her lightly and informatively as they walked aft on the upper deck, his mind racing ahead. She wants her little victory—to make love to an English captain in an English warship. What could be more improper conduct for a captain R.N.? But who could know? *And now, in any case, there is no escape, no turning back, even if I wished to.*

Scenes from their lovemaking in the Wilton Crescent house came back excitingly into his mind as he opened the door to his day cabin. "Not as grand as your quarters in the *Hohenzollern*, I'm sure," he aid.

She turned and smiled, her eyes dropping to his hand as he turned the key. "And through here? Ah, your dear little bedroom. And here you sleep, all by your dear self, while

your men swing to and fro in their hammocks side by side.''
She simulated the motion with her hands.

''Hammocks are very comfortable,'' said Buller in a voice
as steady as he could make it. ''I slept in them for years.''

''But not good for two.'' She kept her eyes provocatively
upon him as she swiftly unbuttoned her long kid boots and
undressed as if she had waited impatiently all evening to
show off her fine body, talking continuously in a low voice.
''But this should be good enough for two. Come, Buller,
what are you waiting for, eh? You know you are as wanton as
I am. Perhaps you are thinking of rules and regulations and
being sent to the Tower of London . . . That is better . . .
Now we must have our little fight, our struggle, because we
always enjoy that. But not too loudly because decks have
ears. *Mein Gott,* what a noise we sometimes made in London!''

Buller silenced her with a hand across her mouth and
forced her slowly back with his strong right arm, almost but
not quite hurting her. Then they were so swift and violent that
through her moans she whispered, ''Too fast, too fast—but
oh, oh, one more thrust like that!''

A minute passed in silence. Buller breathed in her lemon
fragrance. Then she dressed as quickly as she had undressed.
She always does, Buller noted in wonder.

He led the way to the door, turning to admire her recovered
calm and dignity. Only an inevitable heightening of the color
in her cheeks told of the speed and passion of the past
minutes. ''It's terrible,'' he said. ''Now I shan't see you for
months.''

She patted his cheek as she passed. ''But that was nice, my
dear Buller, my own dear dreadnought battleship. And we
can be thinking about the next time. I have made love to the
British Navy! Think of that! All that was missing was more
time, and a great storm. I would like to make love to you in a
great storm at sea.''

Buller laughed and closed the night cabin door behind him.
''But I am always on the bridge in a storm.''

''Then I shall make love to you on the bridge in a storm—
you'll see.''

Buller saw her into the launch and saluted her formally.

There was a note from Countess Miranda the next morning. It had been delivered during the middle watch, and Buller read it at breakfast in his cabin after he had watched the *Hohenzollern* slip out of the Piraeus like a beautiful white ghost, leaving a light trail of smoke on the still air. Her handwriting was, appropriately, round and bold. "Thank you for a lovely exciting evening, my dear Buller. I am arranging for you to stay with us at our schloss later in the year—we have good boar hunting. And good wine and good beds. Bless you always—*Auf Wiedersehen!*"

Buller especially liked the word "arranging." He had no doubt that she would, too, whatever his professional commitments might be. She would "arrange" the German Admiralty if need be. She would get her way.

The pinprick of remorse and guilt he sometimes felt in England after committing adultery was quite absent here, so far from home and comforted by the old sailor's belief that you left your marriage vows behind at Gibraltar.

Buller felt in excellent form as he went up to the bridge for a brief word with the officer-of-the-watch before dealing with the paperwork in his day cabin. "All well? No trouble in the night?"

In the Piraeus it was not unusual for young Greeks to swim out or row out with muffled oars on the off chance of getting on board and stealing from a cabin. "No, sir. All quiet. And the mail will be here in two hours. The train arrived from Trieste at five A.M."

"Good." Their orders were to rejoin their squadron off Crete when the fleet mail arrived overland from London. They would be clear of Greek territorial waters by noon.

There were a dozen letters for Buller, one from Richard (always a good correspondent in spite of his youth), another from his lawyers, two from the farm manager (they would be tiresome), a camera catalog, and two from Clemmie.

In the privacy of his cabin, he opened his wife's letters first. She had never let him down in all the years they had been separated, sometimes by 12,000 miles. The first was

full of domestic detail, which he always enjoyed and encouraged her to write, and village gossip related by her personal
maid while she was doing her hair in the morning, or by the
housekeeper while she made arrangements for the weekend.
Buller liked to imagine her walking up and down the hall with
Mrs. Benjamin. ''Yes, we'll put the Nicolsons in the blue
rooms . . .'' The news of Lucy was predictable and disap-
pointing, of Richard funny and encouraging.

The second letter, he saw, was postmarked London and
only two days later. He was opening it, thinking that it was
unusual for her to write twice in one week, and that it was also
unusual—as he unfolded it—for her to write only one sheet.

Yes, it was very brief, just a dozen lines under the Clarges
Street, W., address.

Dear Archy

I have heard on completely reliable authority that you
are having an affair with a German countess. All London knows it, and I am humiliated wherever I go. We
both know how often it has happened in the past. This
time I am not forgiving you and have today seen Rem-
ington and Sullivan about a divorce.

They are communicating with your countess, who
will be cited as ''the other woman.''

> *Your inconsolable wife,*
> *Clementine*

Buller read the letter through twice again, slowly, subconsciously noting the absence of a comma after his name, the
poor formation of her signature, which had blotted as if she
had rushed it before folding the letter, although the rest of the
writing was steady, the unchanged careful writing of a
woman who still wrote the rounded hand of her schooldays.

Then he became aware that his own hand was shaking so
that it was difficult to read the letter a third time without
laying it flat upon his desk. He was also aware that the
knuckles of his left hand clutching the arm of his chair were

white, and that his teeth were clenched so tightly that they ached.

At the back of his disciplined mind a voice was saying, "Steady now! You must think about this in an ordered manner." So, in turn, he speculated that this was a hoax letter, that she had written it in a fit of pique, perhaps when she was tired or rather drunk, that in any case she did not mean it, or that he could rapidly persuade her from this drastic course.

But another part of his mind was already racing ahead. What would a divorce mean? He would rarely see his children, Wyston Court would have to go, his promotion to flag rank would certainly be delayed, might never come, he would have to offer his resignation as an A.D.C. to the king, he would be excluded from any public royal occasions, his enjoyable and valuable relationship with Georgie, Prince of Wales, would be put at risk . . . The damage, in countless ways, would be considerable, quite apart from the misery and humiliation and the real grief at the loss of a wife who had been his first love, who had borne all his children, had been his friend and companion for almost twenty years.

There was a knock on the cabin door. It was a leading seaman dispatched by the officer-of-the-watch to remind him that he wished to address the ship's company before raising anchor. "The bosun's piped 'Clear the Lower Deck,' sir, and everyone is present."

"I'll be two minutes." Buller pushed aside the other unopened letters on his desk, reflecting on the ironical sequence of the three he had opened that morning, lying side by side in uneasy companionship: the bold note from his mistress under the black, embossed "Imperial Yacht Hohenzollern," the happy, chatty letter from Clemmie under "Wyston Court, Gloucestershire," and the brief, deadly note from Clarges Street, all three linked by the chain of cause and effect, and bound by the weakness of his character and the strength of his lust.

"Oh God, Clemmie!" he said in anguish before rising from his desk, rolling it shut and locking it.

• • •

Eight bells sounded on the *Lily*, marking the end of the last
dogwatch. They were five miles southeast of Milos, course
173, speed 11 knots. Ahead of them lay the Sea of Crete, and
in half an hour the *Lily* would alter course to southeast by east
to steam well clear of the north coast of that island toward her
rendezvous. The sea was calm with a touch of phosphores-
cence, and on this moonless night the only risk the cruiser ran
was from unlit Greek or Cretan fishing vessels. Buller had
ordered a lookout in the fore spotting top to reduce this risk.
So warm was the night that even up there the lookout required
no coat.

The officer-of-the-watch and the navigating officer had
been on the bridge since the *Lily* had cleared Piraeus, and
there had been no need for Buller's presence. But he had not
been below since they had weighed anchor, and had not
touched the food brought up by his steward. At some time, he
knew, he would have to return to his cabin, to the bunk on
which he had made love to Miranda, and to the desk contain-
ing those letters. But not yet.

The customary sounds of watch changing, of voices greet-
ing, of exchanged ribaldries and harmless insults, the
whisper of bare feet on wooden decks, all faded, and the
watch settled down for the last four hours before midnight.

"Well, sir, good to be at sea again."

Buller turned and saw the stocky figure of Rod leaning on
the rail a few feet away. "It's always good to be at sea,
Midge. It's saved my sanity more than once. And I don't like
these hot Mediterranean ports."

"If you don't mind my saying so, sir, you didn't look too
good earlier on."

"I wasn't feeling too good, either."

Rod said, "Why don't you turn in? You're not needed
here, and you could do with the rest."

Buller remained silent and filled in time by raising his
glasses toward the last fading lights of a Milos fishing port.
He was thinking, *It would do no good to tell him and why
should I bother him with my messy life? And, yet, it would be
a singular relief to talk about it, and he is both an old, close
friend and yet so distant from my sort of private life that he*

might understand it better than my other naval friends or
fellow club members.

Buller spoke quietly. "Actually, I've had some rather bad
news." He paused and Rod said nothing. "I've just heard my
wife is divorcing me."

"Lady Clementine? Oh, I'm sorry. That *is* bad news."

Yes, he had been right. It was reassuring to hear those
supportive words spoken in Midge's familiar Geordie accent.
Very comforting.

"And the awful thing is, I think I deserve it. D'you
understand what I mean, Midge?"

"Well, yes. You mean you're the guilty party. I can
understand it, and not understand it."

Buller remembered that honest-looking, freckle-faced
Rosie Maclewin, Rod's wife, taking tea in Clarges Street, a
bit out of her depth but poised and calm. The thought that
either she or Rod might look at anyone else, or indulge in
Buller's sexual cravings, was as remote as that last flickering
light on Milos, which disappeared just before Buller lowered
his glasses. How much simpler life was for Rod Maclewin
without the temptations that came with wealth and security
and easy everything—women, horses, houses, gambling,
and drinking!

Or was it that he was nicer, more loyal, more content,
more self-disciplined? Yes, that was closer to the truth. And
with Rod, whether under Boer Mauser fire, or going down in
a fatally damaged man-o'-war, or standing now in the darkness as the ship slipped through the waters of the Sea of
Crete, with Rod Maclewin you spoke the truth.

"Yes, I am guilty all right. And not for the first time,
Midge, as you can well believe. Perhaps this time I have gone
too far, been indiscreet and stupid."

They were interrupted by a passing chief petty officer, who
bade them good night. Then Rod asked, "Is she the lady who
came on board last night, sir?"

Buller laughed bitterly. "Trust you to be on target, Midge.
The seventy-two percent man. I expect everyone knew. Was
there much talk in the wardroom?"

"A wee bit, yes." He paused. "But a bit more in the gun

room. The lower deck called her 'a fine wench'—begging your pardon. Do you mind if I say one thing, sir?''

"Of course not, that's why I'm telling you all this, which must be very tedious for you.''

"Your married life has nothing to do with me and I am very sorry about your distress. Perhaps you can repair things when you get home. But please remember . . .''

Rod hesitated, and Buller said impatiently, "Go on.''

"Well, the countess—she's not like some other women, Englishwomen. She is German, and I believe is very close to the kaiser and the German Admiralty. And you. You're English and very close to the royal family and to the British Admiralty and to the navy's most confidential plans. And many people believe that a naval war between us will break out before long.''

Buller felt a sudden surge of anger rising in him, as it used to do easily—far too easily—when he was younger. He wanted to say, "Are you accusing me of treason? What sort of man d'you think I am? Exchanging secrets for a woman?''

But he knew at once, as he fought to restrain himself from uttering words he must at once regret, that his friend was doing no more than counseling caution. And expressed, as Rod had put it, his position was not an easy one, and his relationship with Countess Reitzberg-Sönderlong could be easily misunderstood if it were to be widely known.

"Yes,'' Buller said. "I do understand what you mean, Midge. And thank you for the advice, and for listening to my moans.'' He turned his back on the sea and said, "Good night, Midge. You turn in in good time, too.'' And Buller made his way quickly down to his cabin.

Chapter VIII

⚓

"A wetsheet and a flowing sea."

"I DON'T THINK I've been so deuced low in all my life," said Buller. His old friend, confidant, and fellow club member said he was sorry and ordered the Marlborough Club's standard panacea for life's woes, a bottle of Mumm's Extra Dry, very cool. Captain Mark Holly R.N., who had shared the cadets' training course in the *Britannia* with Buller back in the late '70s, was six feet seven inches tall, and at the club was known, inevitably, as "Lofty" Holly. Five years earlier he had inherited a vast brewery fortune from his father and had taken up ocean yacht racing. That he could afford this expensive hobby surprised no one, but that he had become very proficient surprised all his friends, because as a young man, when the navy still had masts and yards, he had never been able to belay a cleat and fell out of the rigging so frequently that he was at one stage forbidden the ratlines.

Holly accepted with good-hearted tolerance and patience the crosses he bore in life, and was one of Buller's best-natured and most generous friends. Buller knew that he could unburden himself of his double troubles and be sure of a sympathetic ear.

"I'm surprised at your wife suddenly suing you," Holly said now, nodding at the wine steward to top up their glasses. "I mean to say, it's not as if it's the first time, if you see what I mean. And most wives learn to get over a spot of philandering, and aren't always innocent themselves. As for your professional troubles, I'd just keep your head down for a while. Jackie'll look after you."

As he had feared, Buller had been relieved of his command shortly after an incident off Crete. He had judged it wise to seek shelter in a fishing habor after three of the *Lily's* boats had been stove-in during a sudden and ferocious storm. The result was that the rendezvous with the Third Cruiser Squadron had been delayed by twenty-four hours.

A curt signal had ordered him to report home, traveling overland—and with a broken heart—by the Orient Express from Constantinople. He never even saw Beresford.

On this, his first morning in London, he had already been to see his lawyers. There the news was as bad as Buller had feared. The divorce petition was being pursued, Miranda would be served personally with a copy of it, the proceedings would be immensely complicated, long-drawn-out and expensive, and his wife's lawyers had the testimony of a servant at the Wilton Crescent house that she had heard and seen signs of intimacy between Buller and the countess.

Now, late in the afternoon, he was due at the Second Sea Lord's office at the Admiralty to discuss his future. Lunch had been a mournful affair, and it was only after the arrival of Holly that he had been offered any sort of consolation.

Buller succeeded in forgetting his troubles for long enough to ask Holly about his sailing. "Well, you know what next week is," Holly answered cheerfully. "Next week is Cowes Week. Isn't that grand? And I'm going to thrash everyone, including the Germans of course, in my new cutter."

Buller left the Marlborough before tea without even a glance in the direction of the gaming rooms, and walked in the hot summer sun down the Mall toward the Admiralty. In Trafalgar Square newspaper boys were selling early editions of the evening papers, calling out the headlines, which were repeated on the posters: "King to Visit Kaiser in Germany." Perhaps that would lead to an easing of tension between the two countries. Buller's low periods never lasted for very long. Besides being cheerfully optimistic in his view of the world and his own life, his mercurial spirit could spin from very low to high in no time. Now he felt better pleased with himself after a modest lunch with only a shared bottle of champagne after it and not a sovereign lost at backgammon. Tonight he would telephone Clemmie and see if he couldn't make her see sense.

The sentry recognized him when he strode into the main entrance to the Admiralty, and, like the good officer he was, Buller remembered his name and said, "Good afternoon, Bates. I trust your wife is better?"

"Thank you, sir, quite well again now."

Buller approached the Second Sea Lord's office wondering fatalistically about his future. Beresford himself might be out of favor with Fisher and the other Lords Commissioners of the Admiralty, but he was a powerful and popular officer, and it was a serious business for a ship's commander to be relieved in midcommission.

Admiral Sir Charles Drury rose from his desk as Buller walked into his office, a good sign for a start. Then he greeted Buller warmly, asked about his journey, and invited him to call at any time if he wanted another ship. "But for the present, Jackie wants a word with you and I'll come with you."

Fisher, in a well-pressed but well-worn gray suit and matching cravat, was at his most puckish and lively. "Where were you when we launched the *Dreadnought*, Buller? Ah, what a day! The king said to me . . ." The words came tumbling from his full lips in a not-completely-dry torrent, accompanied by gestures and slaps on the shoulder. "I tell you, Buller, she's already the most famous ship in the world before she's been to sea. Like the Word of God, she 'is quick, and powerful, and sharper than any two-edged sword,' as the New Testament has it. Personally, I'm an Old Testament man. What about you, Buller?'' He did not wait for a reply. "Yes, the world no longer speaks of battleships, it speaks of dreadnoughts. All else is finished. And, Buller, talking of the end of things, I'm sorry to hear about your marriage."

Fisher turned to the other officers present, rapidly introducing Buller to Captain Philip Dumas, the naval attaché in Berlin, and Captain Charles Ottley, director of Naval Intelligence, whom Buller knew well. "This is personal and confidential," Fisher addressed them all, "and I'll make a dunghill of the home of anyone who splits. Captain Buller here is in trouble with his wife because he appears to be having an affair with another woman—Sonny Reitzberg-Sönderlong's wife, no less. Now, I know the Bullers, knew his father well—a great man—and they've all been great patriots."

After these two seemingly disconnected statements, Fisher turned his back and stared silently down at the Admiralty yard below. Buller could hear the sound of hooves on the stone setts, but could not see the hansom cabs draw up at the entrance. He was utterly confused by the line Fisher was taking and where the conversation was leading them.

After half a minute's silence, Fisher repeated in a low voice, "Yes, great patriots. And Archy Buller is even putting his marriage at risk for the sake of his country. If the Good Lord will forgive me for mildly distorting the psalm, 'Out of the mouths of very babes and countesses hast thou ordained strength because of thine enemies, that thou mightest still the enemy . . .' "

Was he being ironical? Buller wondered. Who could tell with this strange man? Fisher's intense brown eyes concentrated hypnotically on him. "Captain Buller, your liaison with the countess must be exploited to the full, that's why I've brought you home—I expect you thought that odious Beresford had sacked you. Dumas here is doing great work through the usual attaché's channels. He has already discovered invaluable information about the first German dreadnoughts. It is with the 'invincible greyhounds' that I wish you to concern yourself. I want you in your well-acted infatuation with this woman to allow yourself, after a manly struggle, to let it be known that you have seen the plans of H.M.S. *Invincible*, and that she will have a displacement of more than 15,000 tons, a speed of twenty-four knots, and an all-big-gun armament of no fewer than eight nine-point-two-inch guns. *Formidable!* as the Frogs say."

"There's a measure of our confidence in you," said Captain Ottley.

Admiral Drury added with a note of humor in his voice, "That's the queerest appointment I've ever authorized."

Buller felt like a gunlayer who has received a near-miss from the enemy and is now concentrating on synchronizing his rangefinder again, with difficulty. "That's all very well, sir. But how do you suggest I go about it?"

Fisher broke into a high-pitched laugh that was cut off as swiftly as it had begun. "There are certain tasks upon which it is not seemly or even possible to give advice. I would have guessed that you were the last officer requiring such advice. However, we can provide the propellant if you will discharge the weapon."

With his head reeling with similes and quotations, Buller was instructed to take up yachting, the count's favourite hobby since the kaiser had become enthused, find a berth in the cutter class at Cowes in a week's time, see as much of his countess as could be engineered in order to ensure that he was invited to Kiel Week Regatta.

"Captain Ottley has discovered the likely activities and movements of the Reitzberg-Sönderlongs after Cowes Week. They have, as is their custom, rented a lodge by the sea near Wismar, and on August eighteenth there is an important meeting at the German Admiralty in Berlin, attended by the kaiser, who will by then have completed his talks with the king and the foreign secretary at Cronberg, and will certainly require the presence of the count."

Buller said, a touch sardonically, "You have worked out my fate in the finest detail, sir."

"I trust that the experience will not be all painful," Fisher retorted and then added more solemnly, "I am sorry about the continued deception of your wife. Most painful for you both. You will have to console yourself with the knowledge that one day she will learn the truth and recognize the sacrifice you have made for the navy and for your country.

"For the present, and as token compensation, I offer you one of His Majesty's finest Havanas, presented to me after the launching of the *Dreadnought*—and every one a twelve-inch gun, at least in size if not in power."

"Clemmie dear, I just wish that you would let me see you and we could talk." From Clarges Street Buller spoke to his wife in Gloucestershire by trunk-call telephone that crackled and faded.

"There is nothing to say and I do not wish to see you, Archy." In spite of the interference, he could not mistake the coolness of her voice. If only by some magic as miraculous as this telephone she had been able to hear Jackie Fisher talking to him two hours earlier! And now he was prohibited from offering her this alibi. Patriotism, that was it! Would she ever know, as Jackie Fisher predicted? Or would they be divorced before he could explain?

"You may use the London house—for your affairs no doubt—until you go to sea again. And you are to inform me through my lawyers when that is. Soon, I hope. And you are not to come here. The estate is running perfectly well. I am sorry that it has come to this, Archy. But it is your own doing."

And with that she hung up the receiver.

Buller was incapable from inexperience of facing personal problems of this nature. His relations with his father and mother, his two brothers and their wives, had been uncomplicated and friendly. He had always got on well with people—fellow officers, their wives and families, the lower deck, servants at home. His marriage had been without serious drama or crises. He had sometimes approved and sometimes disapproved of his children, but he had been away at sea for much of the time, uninvolved in their troubles.

And now? Now everything had suddenly become bewilderingly complicated. He was being variously judged, as a patriot making a great personal sacrifice, as a philanderer neglectful of his wife, and (by Rod) as a fellow officer and friend treading on dangerous ground with a German mistress.

Buller had never been much good at self-judgment. He was only aware of the irony of his position and aware, too, of the disturbing and arousing memory of Miranda, Countess Reitzberg-Sönderlong—the scent of her, the strength of her, and the passion of their lovemaking.

There did not seem to be anything he could do. So he laughed to himself, a touch sardonically, and wished again that he was away at sea, as Clemmie wished him to be, facing clear-cut decisions confidently in the vigorous and healthy climate of spume and high winds.

In the hall Randolph handed him his silver-banded walking stick with his initials and crest. "I shall dine at my club tonight," Buller said. "Don't wait up for me—I'll no doubt be late."

Holly was there, which was a stroke of good fortune. He would ask about joining him at Cowes right away. And Buller would not be restricting himself on this evening to the austerity regimen which he had applied at lunchtime.

Holly was equally glad to see him again. "Why, yes, of course. That'll be grand. Didn't know you enjoyed Cowes. Thought you were a shooting man. Shall we have a bottle of that very excellent '84 Veuve Clicquot?"

> *Behold at last,*
> *Each tall and tapering mast . . . .*
> *And everywhere*
> *The slender, graceful spars*
> *Poise aloft in the air.*

Where had he heard that? The *Britannia*, Buller guessed. There was not much poetry at Weir Park when he was a boy. Probably the English master. No, it came back to him now. It was the Chaplain during the Dartmouth Regatta. And it was even more appropriate at Cowes on this beautiful early August morning.

Buller steadied himself against the *Magnolia's* mainmast, one arm through the halyards, focused the lense until the *Hildesheim* stood tall and clear and central, and activated the shutter. The German cutter looked so beautiful and triumphant as she crossed the line off Cowes, spinnaker bellying to starboard, main boom to port, the crew bunched astern now instead of lying flat on the weather side of the steeply sloping deck.

The count's cutter had led from the starting gun, hoisted her jackyard topsail seconds before she crossed the line. Rounding the nab for the last time, the *Hildesheim* had been seriously challenged again by the *Magnolia*, Holly's crew being very nippy at setting up the starboard preventer and easing off the foresheets, and quicker than the German crew at getting the spinnaker full hauled out on the tack. For a moment it seemed as if the English boat might snatch the lead. But with the wind dead astern, the *Hildesheim* confirmed her reputation for exceptional speed, and the gap widened to three lengths—120 feet according to Buller's reading as he pressed the shutter plunger again.

Buller wiped the lense and hoped that the spume would not ruin his picture. He would have the print professionally lettered ''Fregattenkapitän Count Reitzberg-Sönderlong's *Hildesheim* winning the Emperor of Germany's Cup, Cowes, 1906.'' He could see Sonny showing it proudly to the kaiser, to prove how well he had kept the German flag flying in the emperor's absence.

Meanwhile, they would all have to endure the mock-modest boasting, the patronizing gestures and remarks, of the count and his three fellow officers. They did not have to wait for long. The other four cutters in the race crossed the line close together, 24,000 square feet of bellying canvas between them and looking magnificent, and soon Holly's pinnace had picked them up and was heading for the Royal Yacht Squadron pier.

Goodwood and Henley over, Cowes Week was at its height, this most extravagant and spectacular culmination of the social season, attracting great numbers of steam yachts, ocean-racing yachts, cruisers and cutters and launches, from the 160-ton *Brynhild* to an exquisite miniature replica of the royal yacht *Victoria and Albert*, built at untold expense for the Duke and Duchess of Suffolk's six-year-old and heir. The lawns and terraces of the squadron were a sea of men's white caps, wide-brimmed elaborate hats, and parasols as the cream of society of Britain, France, Germany, Russia, and the United States strolled about in groups, members and their guests, recognizing and being recognized, nodding and exchanging chatter and laughter. Among those whom Buller instantly identified were his two brothers and their wives, the Prince and Princess Louis of Battenberg, the Prince and Princess Liechtenstein, the Prince and Princess of Wales, the Dundonalds and the Cathcarts, and Lord Dunraven, the owner of the famous *Valkyrie*. Soon the King and Queen Alexandra would disembark from the royal yacht and receive their guests, the King and Queen of Spain, who had now arrived in their royal yacht, *Giralda*.

Before they disembarked from his dinghy, Holly said, "I'm sorry we didn't pip the Hun, though it might have been bad for relations if we had."

"That was exactly why the king gave up racing them," Bulle replied. "Bad if they beat you, worse still if you beat them. But you did a grand job, old boy."

Buller, between photographing sessions, had been impressed at the skillful way Holly had handled the big boat in conjunction with his professional captain. It was a very different Holly from the awkward, clumsy young midshipman who had done that world cruise under canvas with Buller in the *Bacchante* twenty-four years ago. The amiable buffoon who had scarcely been able to splice a rope had today shown the sailing and social world what a fine yachtsman he had become.

There were words of congratulation and sympathy as they stepped ashore. Lord Dunraven said that he couldn't have done better himself. The Prince of Wales, in reefer jacket and white yachting trousers and shoes, moved toward the tall figure of Holly through the crowd until he saw that he was accompanied by Buller. Then he turned sharply and walked away—his first "cut," Buller noted ruefully, and from a friend who had sailed the world with them both in the *Bacchante*. Now Georgie, Prince of Wales, dare not be seen in the company of an officer being sued for divorce.

Buller was still smarting from this rebuff when he noticed Miranda leaving the clubhouse to greet Sonny when he came ashore after his victory. "Dearest Buller, I saw you photographing the finish. You are so good, and so generous."

"I hope it makes a good picture, but conditions were not up to much," Buller said. He walked beside her for a few steps and then added, "I think under the circumstances we should not be seen together too often in public. I will explain why."

"Come on board the *Hildesheim* tonight, late," she said quickly. "There will be only a few friends and you must tell me what has happened."

Buller hastily rejoined Holly for lunch with his wife and Guy and Henry and their wives. Later he would take the plates to a professional photographer he knew in Cowes for developing and printing.

"I am so sorry the emperor could not be here this year," said Buller. It was just before midnight in the modest-sized but extravagantly comfortable main saloon of the *Hildesheim*, where Count Sonny and the countess were entertaining a number of their friends, the most successful German yachtsmen, and the Marquess of Ormonde, the commodore of the Royal Yacht Squadron and his wife. Apart from the Battenbergs and Holly, who were the only other English people present, Buller recognized nobody, until with a shock he saw again Georgie, Prince of Wales, in the far corner.

The talk was almost exclusively concerned with yachting, and terms such as "*Fieren und holen*" and "*An den Wind Kneife,*" and "Bear away," and "We were on starboard!" could be heard on all sides. Intermittently the sharp click of heels like the crack of a starting gun marked another German introduction.

"We are sorry, too, about His Majesty's absence. But"—Miranda shrugged her fine shoulders—"you know how it is, 'affairs of state,' I think you say in English." She lowered her voice, dropping her formal social tone. "But tell me what is happening, Buller. Today I had a letter from some lawyers, in Gray's Inn I think it was. They were writing about your wife. I did not understand everything and sent it to my lawyers in Frankfurt. It said something like 'You, as the woman named, will shortly be served personally with a copy of the divorce petition with a notarily certified translation into German by the British Consul in Hanover . . .' "

"I *am* so sorry," said Buller, experiencing a rush of anxiety he would never have felt in his professional life. "Please take no notice of it. My wife is very precipitate and not always well advised. It will blow over, I am sure."

He judged that this was the right moment to withdraw from under his arm the rolled enlargement, which he had just received, of the *Hildesheim* crossing the line in that morning's cutter race. It had been beautifully printed on matte, slightly gray paper and showed every detail of the *Hildesheim's* rigging. He pointed to the caption printed in white at the base of the photograph.

"I will have it framed tomorrow and you can give it to Sonny."

"No—I cannot wait. I must show it to him now. He will be thrilled." And she took it from him and turned to find her husband. She was soon surrounded by friends admiring the picture.

Buller had already been celebrating the *Magnolia's* fine showing in the cutter race with Holly and his men, and with a full glass in his hand now felt bold enough to make his way across the saloon toward the prince. The Grand Duke of Saxe-Weimar-Eisenach and his wife and Count Albert Rechberget-Rothenöwen were busily paying court to the heir to Britian's throne.

Buller bided his time, flirting mildly with an Austrian countess and the wife of another A.D.C. to the kaiser. He had thought over carefully the matter of Georgie's apparent hostility to him when he had been cold sober early in the evening: It was a bold, even an impertinent thing that he proposed to do now, but Bullers by family tradition had never restrained themselves if they had something important to say.

When the Battenbergs moved away, and there was a lull in the conversation behind him, Buller excused himself from his company and turned to the Prince.

"Georgie, may I have a word with you?"

At first the prince did not turn his head, but Buller persisted. "Come on, Georgie, you can't treat me like this."

"Like what, Buller?" There was no warmth in his blue eyes when he looked at him. He was smoking a cigarette in a silver-tipped holder. His constant smoking had faintly stained his graying beard and his mustache. But he was a good-looking middle-aged man, and Buller knew as well as anyone that he was by nature kindly and loyal to his friends, a loving if severe father to his sons, and himself a father-worshipper.

"Come, Georgie—you know you cut me earlier today, and that's no way to treat me. We've been friends for twenty-five years."

The Prince of Wales moved toward the mock fireplace near to which they were standing in order to speak confidentially. "You're right, Buller, I owe you an explanation. It is not the company you are keeping, old man. It is the *close* company. I have been told that you are seeing a great deal of our hostess tonight." He spoke earnestly and in a low voice, the ash on his cigarette growing long before it fell to the carpet. "Seeing too much of her for propriety. But what is worse, and dangerous, your wife minds dreadfully, and Count Sonny does not seem to mind at all. Why is that? Think about it, Buller—as an old friend, as you say."

"Yes, Georgie, but . . ."

"The von Reichsbergs are coming over to talk to me, so I must speak quickly. One more warning, Buller, on a quite different subject, and speaking as a naval officer now, I am very concerned at your close association with Jackie Fisher. That is downright *bad* company. He is splitting the navy in two, and I love my navy as much as I love my country.''

Buller replied more sharply than he would have done if he had been stone sober. ''But it is Charlie B. who is smashing the navy, Georgie, with his envy and hatred—you ask your father, he worships Jackie.'' Buller had to silence himself as the prince's eyes turned toward the von Reichsbergs, and the expression on his face changed from one of severity to a formal smile.

With a slight bow and a muttered ''Your Royal Highness,'' Buller withdrew. Behind him, Holly was being congratulated by Miranda. ''Such a good race, dear captain,'' she was saying, looking up at Holly, who was forced to stoop in the low-ceilinged saloon. ''I think Sonny was quite lucky to win over those last meters.'' She turned to Buller, who caught a whiff of lemon, noted the tiny beads of sweat on her upper lip, and at once experienced the rising sense of possessive intimacy and warm lust he always felt when she was close to him.

''Captain Holly tells me that he is coming to our Kiel Week, that is such good news, yes? He had an invitation to stay at the Kaiserlicher Yacht Club—not so grand and old as your wonderful Royal Yacht Squadron. But it is nice.''

Holly said to Buller, ''Why don't you come, too? It's grand sport sailing to the Kiel Canal across the North Sea. Perhaps a night at Heligoland.''

''Yes—you must, Captain Buller. And of course you must stay with us. Sonny would be so pleased. And you could take so beautiful photographs like your beautiful picture of the *Hildesheim* and make all the nice owners happy.''

''So kind,'' said Buller, bending over her hand.

At 3:00 A.M. when he returned at last to his room in the squadron, Buller reflected on the curious sequence of events, starting with a spasm of desire for this woman, which had led him toward a future loaded with danger, to his relationship with his friends on the one hand, his wife and family on the other hand, and—an additional and true hazard—with real danger to himself.

The questions rattled like halyards against a mast in a brisk

Solent breeze: Was the count encouraging his wife's relationship and, if so, for what reason? Was Jackie Fisher confident that he, Buller, would give away nothing and learn everything? Was Miranda's passion contrived or as warm and genuine as it seemed to be?

As for himself, Buller felt an even stronger affection for this robust and amusing and uncompromisingly attractive German woman, was confident that she felt the same about him, and that if there was an ulterior motive in her relationship, he would see to it that she gained nothing of value from him.

After being towed the full sixty-one-mile length of the Kaiser Wilhelm Canal from the North Sea to the Baltic, Holly and Buller were thankful when the lock gates at the eastern entrance opened and the crew could hoist sail. The sails at once filled, and the *Magnolia* left the 197-foot-wide waterway behind. Ahead of them were the broad waters of the Kieler Hafen, dotted with the innumerable sun-white sails of pleasure yachts. From the seaside village of Wik to the south, and north to the fortified town of Friedrichsort where Kiel harbor narrowed before opening up like a funnel into the Baltic, holidaymakers were swimming and playing or lying on the sandy shores.

A mile ahead of the *Magnolia's* bowsprit the eastern shore was wooded, the horizon broken by undulating hills. Holstein cattle grazed in the meadows, the farms appeared prosperous, and the whole scene on this warm August afternoon appeared calm and idyllic.

The cox put the wheel over, Holly's captain called out, "Ready about!" Around went the bows as the *Magnolia* headed south up the fjord toward the inner harbor. At the same time, from the north a dark shape made its appearance on this peaceful scene between the forts at Friedrichsort, a man-o'-war making for the naval base at Kiel at the head of the harbor.

"That's one of the *Braunschweig* class," Holly said. "Germany's latest. Very smart she looks, too."

The battleship's tall ram bows were cutting through the smooth waters of the Kieler Hafen at no more than 5 knots but with a stately grandeur that defied any mere sailing vessel to impede her progress, the forward eleven-inch gun turret rising to the massive armored conning tower, the bridge, the searchlight platforms, and spotting tops on the foremast together forming the impression of some great Gothic edifice steaming implacably toward them.

Five minutes later the battleship slipped past them at no more than a cable's length from the cutter, the black cross on white of the admiral's flag at her masthead, her crew in white drill at the rails. Buller kept his large binoculars trained on her, moving the lense in turn after a pause from superstructure to a 6.7-inch turret, to a gun embrasure, to one of the 24-pounders, to the mainmast searchlight platform, and finally to the aft eleven-inch turret, lingering on the armored shield area, where the two heavy guns emerged and provided calculable evidence of the barrels' maximum elevation.

The admiral himself, members of his staff, and his flag captain could be seen looking down at them. When Holly ordered, "Give them a cheer, lads!" the German officers responded with a smart salute, and groups of the crew gave a return cheer.

Then the battleship was past, black smoke from her funnels carrying away to the east on the wind, while two naval tugs approached her on either beam ready to tow her the last mile toward the forbidden waters of the naval base.

'I'm awfully pleased you haven't brought that damn great camera with you," Holly remarked. "You couldn't have resisted taking snaps of her. And then they'd have had you in irons before you could click the shutter."

Buller laughed and replaced his binoculars into their case. "When I showed these to Jackie Fisher, he quoted his favorite Bret Harte 'The same with intent to deceive.' "

"What on earth did the old man mean?"

Buller gave the black case a pat. "I'll show you later. But I have in fact recorded everything worth seeing today. And

I've had the lense on that, too," he said, pointing toward the torpedo-boat harbor nestling against the west shore near Wik. It was filled with lean little 300- to 400-ton twin-funneled boats lying side by side like cigars in a box, each capable of sinking a battleship with one of its deadly mouldies. Through his lenses he could just make out the numerals "S114," "S115," and "S116" on the diminutive sterns of the three nearest vessels.

Nothing could have been in greater contrast with the black, sinister lines of torpedo boats than the landing stages, the sloping lawns, the blazing beds of roses and chrysanthemums, and the flag-bedecked front of the Kaiserlicher Yacht Club, which the *Magnolia* was now approaching. The scene was quite as spectacular as that at Cowes, the steam yachts and pinnaces, the towering masts of the great cutters and ocean-racing schooners bearing the flags of many nations, and the colorful crowds sitting beneath shade on the lawns and on the club's verandahs. Indeed, many of the boats—the *Meteor*, the new British Admiralty yacht, *Enchantress*, the *Valkyrie III*, the *Shamrock III*, the American *Theseus*, *Columbia*, and *Reliance*—had also been at Cowes. So had many of the people, all rich and many aristocratic or regal, parading about slowly like mannequins at some spectacular fashion show, and all with their eyes on the beautiful *Magnolia* as her crew handed down her sails.

The *Magnolia* picked up the buoy to which she was directed, and her crew swung out the dinghy that was stowed amidships in the cutter and unlashed the oars and oarlocks. "Come along, Buller," Holly called out. "If your countess is there, she's not going to go astern and out of sight."

Buller laughed and lowered his binoculars. "She's there all right." It was not difficult to pick out Countess Reitzberg-Sönderlong in a crowd, and for confirmation she had waved a handkerchief at the *Magnolia* and made her way across the lawns toward one of the landing stages to meet them.

After lunch with Miranda and the count and three others, a

lunch which had included the famous local Kieler Sprotten, Schleswig-Holstein raspberries, and an enormous stuffed pig, Buller had seen a figure he had never expected to find here for Kiel Week. It was Whitney Campbell, there was no doubt of it. He had taken off his white cap to talk to a woman and was wearing a double-breasted blazer, white trousers, and white yachting shoes, standard dress for the occasion. It was his full head of red hair that indisputably identified him. In addition, the inevitable pipe clutched unlit in his hand at once singled him out from the other men. Then the American turned his head as if Buller's glance had acted as an unseen signal. Their eyes met for a second, then Whitney turned away and resumed his conversation.

"What is it, Buller?" the countess asked.

"Excuse me," Buller said, rising from his seat. His reaction had been decisive and immediate, and now he stood beside Whitney until the woman to whom he was talking in fluent German turned her eyes toward him, and Whitney was forced to follow her.

Buller bowed toward the woman and apologized for interrupting. "This is grand, Whitney. I haven't seen you since you did your Houdini disappearing act! Are you with the *Reliance* or one of the other American boats?"

Whitney's expression was as cold as his voice, even in the formal spoken apology for his behavior at Wyston Court. The American was clearly harboring some grudge, and Buller, as always, became impatient with any mystery.

"Well, what in blazes was the matter?" Buller asked. "Did our cook poison you?" His laugh had no humor in it.

"No, it wasn't your cook." Whitney reached for the half-empty glass on the table beside them and began to turn away. "Not your cook, Goddamn it. Now why don't you return to your beautiful countess?" The voice had a hard edge, which Buller did not like. His anger was rapidly replacing his earlier curiosity. If he had been in a less public place he would have seized the American's shoulders and asked him what he meant, instead of returning to his party.

"What is the matter, dear Buller?" the countess asked.

"You look quite *unwohl*. I have seen before that man you were talking to—where was it? What did he say that upset you?"

"Never mind," said Buller. "Let's go to see what races we have tomorrow. I haven't had the program yet." Count Sonny was in the highest spirits, a bottle of German champagne at his side, from which he restlessly topped up his glass after every sip. "Comet *mit* Theseus *kollidieren . . .*" he was saying with a renewed burst of laughter as Buller entered the room.

The count at once switched to English. "Ah, Captain Buller, I was telling our friends here about our race this morning, and how at the last minute my *Hildesheim* lost two of her opponents. You saw what happened, of course? And I hope you took one of your beautiful photographs."

From the cockpit of the *Magnolia* Buller had watched the last-minute maneuvering of the seven great cutters as they bore away and jibed and described circles just behind the starting line. The *Magnolia's* skipper was shouting "Lee O!" and the cutter was rattling into the wind's eye, foresheets flapping like machine-gun fire, and then swung around onto the other tack.

A cable's length distant, two English boats and the American cutter *Theseus* were taking fearful risks in their efforts to avoid one another, to avoid breaking the rules, and to reach exactly the starting line in the thirty final seconds. Buller heard a distant voice shouting, "Break out the staysail," heard the crack that was an echo of the starting gun. The American boat bore away and passed under the stern of the two English cutters, heeling lee rail under as she tore through the foaming white tracks.

At that critical moment, a French boat, the *Comet*, passed too close across the bows of the American cutter, which had the right-of-way. There was another sharp crack, and this time it was the American bowsprit breaking like a match and at the same time making a shambles of the other boat's rigging. As Sonny had been recounting with vast pleasure,

Comet had indeed collided with *Theseus.* Soon after the start, the other three cutters showed themselves to be outclassed by the *Hildesheim* and Holly's *Magnolia,* so that the race, as at Cowes, had narrowed down to a close contest, which the German boat had won by half a length. The champagne was therefore flowing generously in the count's rented villa, where he was celebrating with a number of German naval friends and their wives and the defeated Englishmen after the long day's racing.

"As to photographs," Buller answered the count's question, "I was told that photography in the Kieler Hafen by foreigners is frowned upon because of the ships and naval facilities and forts."

"Ah, poof to that! I would see that there was no trouble for so distinguished a guest." The count turned and indicated the photograph Buller had taken of the *Hildesheim* winning at Cowes. It had been framed and hung in a prominent position on the wall. "It would have been so pleasant to have a companion to your masterpiece. But I shall take this to Berlin tomorrow. The kaiser will be so admiring and proud, especially when he hears who took the picture."

Holly had been reluctant to attend this celebration at all, suspecting rightly that he would be subjected again to a barrage of insincere sympathy and patronizing praise for his effort. Buller watched his friend's face as Count Sonny took him by the arm and led him away to a quiet corner, where Buller guessed he was going to be told how he could have won if only . . .

At the same time, an arm slipped gently under his and propelled him toward the open verandah doors. "Dear Buller, I hope you will enjoy your little holiday with us," Miranda said. "These tiresome people will soon go, and my husband leaves tomorrow."

The count and countess's rented villa was set back a quarter mile from the sandy beach of the Kieler Bucht, separated from the high-tide mark by sand dunes and saltings rich with bird life. The sharp, salt smell of the Baltic and the gentle wash of breaking waves drifted up from the shore in the last light of the day.

Buller said, "Dear Miranda, I really must ask you this. I have meant to ask you before. But doesn't Sonny mind us being alone here with only the servants? He seems strangely unjealous. I mean . . ."

Miranda placed a finger over Buller's mouth. "There is no worry. You need say nothing. Sonny is very kind and understanding and for years now is not interested in—how should I say not to shock you?—in the bed." She sighed and shrugged her shoulders. "It is sad but true."

Buller remained silent because he did not know how to respond to this astonishing revelation. It seemed scarcely credible that the tall, hard, handsome Count Sonny Reitzberg-Sönderlong, great naval officer, Chief A.D.C. to the kaiser, renowned for his sporting prowess, and with this handsome, stately wife, was no more than a eunuch.

Buller remembered the lawyer's letter Miranda had received and asked her if Sonny knew about this, too. "Yes, of course I showed it to him, and the divorce petition served on me by the British Consul in Hanover. I have no secrets from Sonny. We are husband and wife and close friends, as you can see. Yes, he has seen it and has instructed our lawyers to reply. He has also told them to answer not too definitely— how do you say? To procrastinate. Your wife will see sense, I am sure, and this silly divorce nonsense will fade away—like the daylight here." She gave a slight shiver and turned to lead him inside. "It is no longer so warm for my bare arms."

Holly had been told that the count's chauffeur would drive him back to the Kaiserlicher Yacht Club at any time, and now he was anxious to leave. "I only came because you were so keen, old man," he told Buller, "so I'll go after I've paid my respects to your beautiful countess and her odious husband."

"Will you come with me first?" Buller asked. "I've something I want to give you to take back to England."

In his bedroom overlooking the sand dunes and the sea, Buller unlocked the leather Gladstone bag he took from the wardrobe. His black binoculars case with his initials and family crest embossed on it was at the bottom under some papers.

"You're going to need those if you're boar hunting with the count," Holly said. "You don't want me to take those back with me."

"No, but I want you to take back something else— something smaller. Servants are always packing or unpacking luggage, and I don't want any accidental or nonaccidental discovery of this."

Holly watched in amazement as Buller slipped off the lense in one half of the binoculars, unscrewed a minute butterfly nut inside, and slipped out a small roll of film. He put it in an envelope, sealed it, and gave it to Holly. " 'The same with intent to deceive,' as I told you, old man. Look after that carefully. And as soon as you get to London, take it direct to Charles Ottley. He'll be expecting it. The photographs include all the forts, the details of that new battleship, the torpedo-boat harbor, the ammunition depot just north of Neumühlen, and the imperial dockyard, though that's rather distant."

Holly laughed. "So that's why you've suddenly taken up yachting! You're a real card, Buller. Where did you buy this?" He picked up the binoculars and peered through the eyepieces. "I can't see anything through the right lense."

Buller explained the working of the photobinoculars, the optical viewfinder in the left half, which was in effect a monocular with a 200-mm. lense, and a similar-strength lense in the right half with the shutter and film in the eypiece behind. Focusing was done by adjusting the milled wheel between the eypieces, which, like the whole unit, were indistinguishable from an orthodox pair of marine binoculars.

"Ross made something like this back in the early 1890s," Buller said. "It was called 'The Photoscope,' and quite a lot of people bought it, more for fun as a toy than anything else. It soon went out of fashion. It was my idea to revive it for more serious purposes, and the research scientist at Ross and I worked this one out, with a telephoto lense which gives very good center definition. It was made in secret in conjunction with the D.N.I. Only Ottley and Fisher know about it, so keep mum.''

Holly put the envelope into his inside pocket, and they returned to the party. Five minutes later he had left. When the other guests had also departed, Miranda excused herself, and Buller and Count Sonny were left alone, smoking their cigars over a nightcap. The count seemed to Buller to be unusually effusive and still in high spirits.

''Now I have just five days of business in Berlin, you understand, Captain Buller. And then I join you at our schloss in the Unterharz. You have brought your own gun, yes? Ah, good. The boar, I hear, are very fine this year. Then we can shoot during the day and talk 'navy' in the evenings. As you say in English, 'That will be good sport.' ''

Neumünster, Segeberg, Oldesloe, Hamburg, over the great Elbe River at midnight, the change of note from the wheels as the train crossed the wide bridge and then south into the Lüneburger Heide. ''It is so dull, Buller. Nothing to see for so long, so we travel by night, and then we have the day for me to show you the schloss and the gardens, and we can go riding into the forest.''

Now, lying together in the comfortable bed—too large and grand to be called a bunk—as the train rattled south across north Germany, Buller said teasingly, ''You are a terrible liar, Miranda. You only wanted to travel by night so that you could say we had made love in a train. First my ship, and then a train, and—''

''You forget the storm, that we will do one day,'' she said. ''But you must admit it is especially nice with the rhythm.'' She played her fingers in time with the click of the wheels across his stomach, and then turned and fell heavily upon him, pinning him down by the shoulders as he had so often held her, provoking him to throw her off and make love again. He pretended to use all his strength, grunted and failed, and she cried out in triumph.

In the early evening, under instructions from the count, Miranda had taken him around the dockyards and base head-quarters at Kiel with the Imperial German Navy's inspector-general, who happened to be the kaiser's brother, Admiral Prince Heinrich of Prussia. The courtesy shown was almost excessive, but the tour was swiftly conducted, and Buller noticed that more sensitive areas like the torpedo department and the yard where the first submarines—the *Unterseeboote*—were being completed were omitted from the itinerary.

Buller was allowed to inspect another yard, where a light cruiser was being fitted out. "That is the *Königsberg*," the admiral announced. "Not large, but very, very fast—too fast for me to tell you, Captain Buller," Prince Heinrich added with a laugh.

Buller noticed that one of the largest building slips, with a length that he guessed was over 500 feet, was empty, though with stacked material beside it suggesting that a large war-ship's keel was soon to be laid. But he said nothing, and they were soon back in Prince Heinrich's office, where they drank schnapps until it was time to leave for the train. Half a dozen compartments had been reserved in their name, for the vast quantity of luggage the count and countess carried with them everywhere and for their personal servants.

Clickety-click, clickety-click went the wheels. Lüneburg, Uelzen, Eschede, Celle on the River Aller . . . Buller stretched an arm from the bed and drew back a corner of the curtain. There was a trace of light in the sky to the east. Miranda was asleep, and he slipped out of bed and put on his dressing gown. For the sake of respectability it was suitable, he decided, to be awakened in his own bed. Besides, he needed an hour or two of sleep himself.

"Yes, it was a good meeting," said the count. "And very important for us. It is time for the decisions, yes?"

They were keeping their voices low. Distantly and far below in the valley that stretched away to the southwest, they could hear the beaters and the intermittent whines and yapping of the short-haired pointers that were working their way toward them.

"You mean shipbuilding decisions, Sonny?" asked Buller. "Yes, the *Dreadnought* has—we have a saying—'set the cat among the pigeons.' I had hoped that the king and your emperor would discuss an end to this lunatic arms race. We are both strong enough at sea and neither of us wants war."

"It was a good meeting at Cronberg, Willie told me. He has a great affection for his uncle," said Sonny. "But you must understand that the *Dreadnought* is a great provocation. Everyone must now build *dreadnoughtschiffe*, and the Imperial German Navy cannot be left behind. We have our empire, our great merchant fleet, our trade as well as our pride—all have to be protected."

Buller, lying close alongside the count on soft grass behind a ridge of granite that made a natural hide, caught a glimpse of figures moving between the trees below. Clearly, there were boar between them and this hide above, but the dogs appeared to have temporarily lost the scent beside the tumbling river. Immediately in front of Buller and the count there was open, rock-strewn, steeply sloping land stretching to the pinewoods flanking the river.

When the count said, "It will take time," Buller at first thought he was referring to the period it took to build a battleship. But Sonny's mind was now on the boars. "They must not press too hard or they will turn and pass so fast through the beaters and the dogs that nothing will stop them." He shifted his position and squinted down the sights of his Mannlicher.

There was a brief silence between the two men. Buller wondered how long it had been since Sonny had ceased to cohabit with Miranda. Or was it, he suddenly conjectured, that he had lost interest only in his wife and had a mistress, perhaps in Berlin, where he was often alone and where there were so many kept women? Perhaps he and Miranda had a mutual agreement not to mind or interfere in one another's affairs?

Sonny turned his head. "Yes, it will be a little time yet," he repeated. "Tell me, Prince Heinrich gave you a good tour at Kiel?"

"He was most courteous and informative," said Buller.

"Did he show you the empty slip—the big one?"

"No, but I couldn't help seeing it."

Sonny spoke knowingly, "Ah, Captain Buller, that will soon be occupied."

"I imagine so. You have few empty slips—so do we. That is the consequence of this arms race."

"In that slip there will be—I tell you this in confidence but soon all the world will know—there will be our greatest and fastest armored cruiser. Beside it, the *Gneisenau* and *Scharnhorst* will be like Kieler Sprotten. And all big guns, Captain Buller. A dreadnought armored cruiser. What do you say to that?"

Before Buller could answer, the count, with his binoculars to his eyes, put a hand on his arm and pointed. Three hundred yards below, a shape had emerged from the cover of the woods, gray against the dark trunks of the trees. The boar had been caught momentarily in a difficult position by the dogs, which were closing in on three sides. His only means of escape was across the open land climbing steeply above him. The only cover was a spinney of small trees, shrubs, and tight bramble.

The big animal suddenly made up its mind, accelerated at surprising speed, and headed for the thicket, no doubt believing from his low viewpoint that it was a great deal larger than it was.

"Now you see, this will be interesting," said the count urgently.

Buller tightened the butt of his 7-mm. Mauser against his shoulder and at the same time made his body relax. He had a fine 180-degree view down the side of the valley.

The boar was heading straight for the thicket, head down, a big beast of at least 250 pounds, its feet sending up a small cloud of dust. The animal crashed into the undergrowth as if it did not exist. Buller heard the impact clearly, saw the top branches of the trees and shrubs quiver. Then the boar emerged into the open, clearly shocked at this sudden second exposure, hesitated again, and began running to the left, seeking the woods again.

The boar was at eighty yards, and in a second the range would rapidly open. Buller and the count made the decision to fire at the same moment, so close that their guns fired together made only a single loud crack. The boar, tusks high in the air, leaped in a scurry of dust to a height of three or four feet, uttered a single squeal to echo the guns' single report, and fell heavily to the ground. The slope carried it another twenty feet toward the trees, and then it lay still.

The beaters and dogs emerged together from the safety of the wood, the dogs yelping, the men running. The count turned to Buller, saber scars bright purple from the heat and excitement, and smiled. "*Ach*, so—that was good shooting, yes? I think perhaps we both hit. Anyway, I must say so, for you are my guest." He laughed and stood up. "Now let us examine our victim."

Later in the morning a wagonette took them down the mountainside on the track, which at length joined a road. Parked there, with refreshments laid out beside it, was Sonny's new silver nine-liter Mercedes 60. Buller sank gratefully into a canvas chair and was offered champagne by a manservant.

"You have not yet answered my question." The count sat down beside him after handing his gun to the chauffeur. Buller looked at him with a puzzled expression. "You remember—before that boar entered our sights? Was it not like an interesting conversation on the bridge that is interrupted by the enemy being sighted, and then comes the tiresome business of sinking him—like our boar."

Buller laughed and raised his glass. "*Prosit!*" He echoed Sonny's toast. "Yes, I remember. You asked me what I said to your announcement. I have to say I am surprised that you told me, but not surprised at the news. If we are to have nothing but all-big-gun battleships, then it follows that we have all-big-gun cruisers. We are facing the same situation.''

"And your dreadnought armored cruiser will soon be laid down, too," said the count, his voice clipped and decisive. "On the Tyne River. You see, Captain Buller, we have our knowledge of your plans as you know something of ours because I tell you." He leaned closer to Buller and said in a low voice, "We also happen to know that your *Invincible* (you see we even know its name already) will have nothing but nine-point-two-inch guns—no seven-point-five- or six-inch peashooters like the *Black Prince* and your other new armored cruisers."

Buller turned his head sharply, spilling half his champagne. "And how did . . . ?" He won time by wiping his trousers until, a second later, the servant dabbed them with a white cloth and refilled his glass. Then Buller turned with a smile to the count, who had relaxed deeply into his chair and was looking at him with a smile of undisguised satisfaction on his face.

Buller spoke first and succeeded in achieving a light note. "As the advocates say, 'I have nothing further to add, m'lud, and rest my case."

Sonny laughed, holding out his glass for a refill. "We both rest our cases, Captain Buller. Neither of us wishes to say too much. We both have our intelligence departments for this work, yes? So for now—let us give a toast to our monarchs and to our navies, for both are great and strong, and may they never quarrel."

From the wide open windows there came the sound of the wind brushing the treetops, the distant hooting of an owl, and faint scurries of movement in the forest. A three-quarter moon spread a soft, luminous light over the Harz Mountain slopes and peaks: a perfect late summer night in this most beautiful part of Germany.

Lying close against Miranda's hot body, Buller listened as her breathing steadied and she fell into a deep sleep. Gazing sleepily into the eye of the moon, he blessed his good fortune

that he had carried out his mission through the offices of
Count Reitzberg-Sönderlong rather than through this woman
beside him—this woman who fascinated him and filled his
need for tenderness and relief for his new and deep sense of
deprivation, as well as for his abiding lust.

Chapter IX

⚓

Lightning Strike?

BY THE SUMMER OF 1908, dreadnought madness had seized the world. Germany led the way with eight dreadnought battleships and two dreadnought armored cruisers (soon to be called battle cruisers) under construction. Besides the British *Dreadnought* herself, now in commission and the envy of every navy, Britain had laid down six more dreadnoughts and three *Invincible* class dreadnought battle cruisers. The United States Navy had four dreadnoughts nearly ready and was about to lay down four more. Japan, France, Austria, Russia, Spain, even the near-bankrupt South American rival republics of Chile and the Argentine, had ordered them or had them under construction. Brazil was soon to order the biggest battleship in the world.

Everyone had suddenly decided that to be seen by your neighbor as a military power you had to have dreadnoughts, the more the better and never mind if you could not afford them. Soon Greece and Turkey would be ordering them in preparation for the coming struggle.

But the first league battleship race remained for the time being between the German and British Empires. Britain

continued to claim that Germany already had the most powerful army in the world, and any attempt to wrest the rule of the
waves from Britannia, who depended on sea trade for her
livelihood, was aggressive and provocative. The German
Reichstag passed a new Navy Bill increasing from three to
four the number of dreadnoughts to be laid down each year,
which would give the Germany Navy thirty-seven by 1915
and over fifty by 1919. In the early 1890s, the German Navy
was a handful of coast-defense vessels.

Britain countered with a "two keels to one" policy in the
winter of 1907-1908, supported by almost every newspaper
in the country and by the king, who increasingly believed that
his nephew, the kaiser, was going mad. The kaiser countered
with an interview in which he said, "You English are mad,
mad as March hares." He even wrote a private letter, nine
pages long, to the British First Lord of the Admiralty, attempting to justify German construction of his vast armada.

The British First Lord, Lord Tweedmouth, was so excited
and flattered by this private communication from the German
emperor that he told everyone about it, including the king,
who wrote to the kaiser rebuking him for this offense against
protocol. Lord Tweedmouth was, in fact, really going mad
and soon died.

His enemies claimed that Jackie Fisher, the First Sea Lord
and the professional head of the navy, was mad, too. Beresford said so loudly to anyone who would listen, but many
people thought Beresford was even madder. When Fisher
proposed to King Edward that the Royal Navy should make a
preemptive surprise mass attack on the German Fleet while it
was in harbor, the king replied, laughing, "Fisher, you must
be mad!"

But Fisher was not mad. Those who knew him intimately
recognized that he was preparing his beloved navy for the
inevitable war. In a famous speech at the Lord Mayor's
Banquet in November 1907, he reassured his anxious audience that the navy was all-powerful still, and that "you may
sleep quiet in your beds."

Fisher did not take his own advice. He did not sleep quiet
in his bed. He sometimes worked twenty hours a day. His

worries included not only the number of German dreadnoughts being built but their size and power. Captain Dumas
and several spies responsible to Captain Ottley continued to
feed Fisher with information. For example, Fisher knew that
the first German dreadnought had been laid down shortly
before the *Dreadnought* herself went to sea, that she was
have been armed with only eight big guns, but that her design
was changed when the *Dreadnought's* armament was revealed as ten twelve-inch guns. It took a year, Fisher
learned, before the German ship could be redesigned to carry
twelve heavy guns.

Fisher also learned, incidentally and from the other side of
the Atlantic, that the United States Navy had been quick off
the mark with its first dreadnoughts, laying them down even
before the British battleship and sitting all the guns on the
center line so that they could be fired on either broadside.

British relations with America, however, remained cordial
as relations with Germany deteriorated year by year, and
Fisher's continuing lack of information about the first German dreadnought battle cruisers irritated and worried him.
He knew that Buller had planted the ''secret'' that the British
''ocean greyhounds'' were being armed with 9.2-inch guns
when, under the most strict security, twelve-inch guns were
being fitted. These fired a shell almost twice as heavy up to a
range half as far again as the smaller gun. The Germans were
being equally successful in guarding the size and armament
of their first battle cruiser. All Buller had learned was that she
was to be built at Kiel, a fact which Captain Dumas would no
doubt soon have reported anyway.

In Washington the secretary of the navy and the chief of
Naval Intelligence were also becoming concerned about the
sudden growth of naval rivalry in Europe at the same time as
the Japanese were embarking on a large program of construction themselves. At a meeting in the Navy Department on
Friday, June 26, 1908, it was decided to strengthen the
intelligence services in Berlin, replacing the elderly naval
attaché, who had held the post as a sinecure for some years,
with a younger and more experienced officer. A list of twelve
candidates was prepared by the Intelligence Department. It

included Captain Whitney Campbell, who was finally selected for his earlier and successful record in London, and for his fluency in German and other foreign languages.

Whitney had held a sea appointment for eighteen months as captain of the old cruiser *Brooklyn*, which was due for a major refit and reconstruction. The ship was steaming at ten knots from San Juan, Puerto Rico, to the Brooklyn Navy Yard when he received the signal confirming the appointment. He regarded the news with mixed feelings, professional and personal, which he expressed in a letter he wrote in his cabin that evening:

My beloved Clemmie,

I have to tell you that I shall be in London shortly on official business en route to Berlin. I find it hard to describe my feelings, which I think you understand anyway. It is so long, and for such a fleeting moment, since I last saw you before escaping from my guilt, that your beautiful face has become like a fading gravure portrait in my mind. I would throw away my career, join a leper colony, become a pauper, for a renewed sight of you and to hear a renewed echo of your voice and feel again your hands against my face.

It will at once be an intensification of agony and a joy to be at least in the same country as you, but you know that if I saw you I would certainly again dishonor myself and you by risking breaking up your family and your life with Archy. I know he has been foolish himself, but unlike my abiding love for you—the first and only real love in my life—Archy's passion I am sure is a fleeting thing that will soon pass. So I beg of you again to drop these divorce proceedings, forgive him and accept him back, for your sake, for your children's sake, for Archy's sake, and for me.

I shall be careful not to go about in London for the few days I shall be in the city, and it is selfish of me even to tell you I shall be in England. But I also feel it would smack of deceit to keep the knowledge private.

If you love me at all, I beg you to repair your marriage, but also sometimes to remember that I shall love you always.

Whitney signed his name, did not read the letter through, and at once called for his secretary to collect the envelope along with a number of official documents in case he should be tempted to destroy it.

Captain Campbell sailed from Boston to England, arriving in the liner *Tudor Prince* at Liverpool on July 27, 1908. London was full of political strife centering around the new Liberal premier since April, Herbert Asquith, the imminent North Sea Convention, naval rearmament, and the king's visit again to Cronberg for further discussions with the kaiser. By chance, Whitney was scheduled to arrive in Germany on the same day as the king, August 11. His host was not quite as lustrous as the king's. But he felt that he was getting off to a good start in his appointment by being invited to Schloss Kroonbach by Fregattenkapitän Count Reitzberg-Sönderlong, the Kaiser's Chief Naval A.D.C. "To shoot boar, drink wine, and talk over naval matters," as an informal note with the formal invitation defined the visit.

"It is so very good that you could come, Captain Campbell." The countess held out her hand, and Whitney bent over it. "And I am so glad that the day is nice."

The valet unstrapped Whitney's luggage from the carrier and took it inside the open double doors of the schloss. "Frau Heinleen will tell you where to take that," Miranda called out after him.

"What a beautiful place!" said Whitney in German. Schloss Kroonbach, where Buller had stayed two years earlier, was set at the head of a deep valley. A thousand feet below, a stream, which rapidly became a swift-flowing river, tumbled southward, sounding out a steady rumble from its cataracts and waterfalls. On all sides the forest-clad hills rose one above the other. "If we were standing here a thousand years ago, it would look the same," he observed.

"I am glad that you like our country, Captain Campbell,

and that you will be here for some time. It is so *höflich* that you speak our language so beautifully, too.'' She led Whitney toward the front door, her arm in his and laughing at his description of someone who had shared his carriage in the train. ''Here you will find we have a small house party. This is our custom after the rigors of Kiel Week. The men take out their frustration at not winning in the races by shooting boar.'' Several shots rang out from deep in the valley, the reports echoing against the rock faces. ''Listen to that—there is more bacon for the pantry.''

''They are meeting their wives for a picnic, but I think we have a quiet lunch here.'' The countess indicated the rounded figure of Frau Heinleen standing in the hall a few yards away. ''Please take Herr Kapitän Campbell to his room. We shall have some champagne on the terrace in ten minutes.''

Whitney followed the woman and the valet with his bags down several corridors. The schloss was enormous and laid out in a complex pattern which offered all its many rooms a fine view over the mountains. The housekeeper hesitated at the beginning of one corridor, apologized, and walked back two doors, jingling a ring of keys. She inserted one in the lock of a door, found it already unlocked, apologized again, and showed Whitney into his room. ''The maid will be here shortly to unpack for you.''

By now it was no surprise to Whitney that the room was spacious, beautifully decorated and furnished, and had its own balcony. It smelled pungently of wood, from the floor and paneled walls and, more resinously, from the nearest pine trees, which were only yards from the building.

''Maybe I'm going to enjoy this assignment,'' he told himself. He filled and lit his pipe, walked out onto the balcony, grateful for the clean, scented air after the sulphurous, long train ride.

He never much cared for the European custom of having one's bags unpacked, and he began to take out his clothes, unfolding his uniforms and suits with the speed and efficiency of a sailor who has always looked after himself, usually in a confined space. He opened the big fitted pine wardrobe and was surprised to see it already more than half full with suits and uniforms not unlike his own. The drawers below were full, too, with unfamiliar and untidily arranged socks, underwear, and shirts. Then for the first time he saw there were brushes, combs, and an open stud box on the dressing table.

Whitney had often stayed in houses where he had been given a room normally occupied by a member of the household who had not cleared all his possessions. But as he stood in puzzlement beside the open wardrobe, sucking at his pipe, he knew that this could not be the case at Schloss Kroonbach. The housekeeper had given him the wrong room, a fact she could have suspected when she found the door unlocked.

The owner of these clothes, probably out shooting, was also a naval officer. With a mixed feeling of guilt and curiosity, Whitney ran his hand along the hangers. Yes, British Navy—monkey jacket, ball dress with epaulettes and four rings on the sleeve, heavy yachting jacket, dinner jacket, morning coat. The hangers were scattered about in an unsailorlike way, and below, the dozen pairs of shoes, from white yachting shoes to heavy boots, were scattered about and not even in pairs. Among them was a Gladstone bag, its top open, the strap and a black binoculars case and bundles of papers hanging half out.

Always curious about the small domestic ways of his fellowmen, Whitney bent down to a wicker hamper lying beside the Gladstone. It had a stout brass lock on it, but the top lifted at once. It was a beautifully made hamper with leather-and-brass corners, from one of those smart shops in Bond Street, Whitney guessed, and was no doubt fitted inside with silver cutlery embossed with the owner's name and coat of arms, leather flasks, sets of bone-china plates, a corkscrew, a bottle each of claret and champagne, half a dozen cut-glass tumblers, all safely and economically held by leather straps to the sides, the lid, or the base. He had lunched from a case like this at Ascot one year, and very satisfactory it had been—ham and smoked salmon, a bottle of Krug, strawberries . . .

Whitney glanced inside. It contained, after all, none of these luxuries—no crockery, no china, and the only glass was in the finely ground lenses of a camera, which was secured along the whole length of the hamper, as purposeful as a .300 Mauser rifle.

Whitney bent down for a closer look and raised the heavy velvet cloth that half concealed what was below: a square black box—matte black—a carrying strap, an empty plate container on one side, two short brass rails on the top on which the cameraman could slip a viewing monocular, and, extending eighteen inches or more from the case, a brass cylinder, the telephoto lense, with a knurled focus-adjusting wheel. To confirm the lense power of this beautiful example of the cameramakers' craft were the small embossed numerals "840" followed by the letters "mm."

Engraved on the camera's body was the name "Carl Zeiss Jena." Some three inches from the barrel of the lense there was a spring-loaded button secured to the inside of the lined wickerwork. There was a faint line in the shape of a square that was almost invisible in the half-light of the wardrobe. At the base was a single three-inch brass hinge like a miniature gunport lid before a cannon's barrel in a sailing man-o'-war.

Whitney closed the basket gently and backed out of the wardrobe. There could be no doubt of the sinister implications of what he had found. But was it by chance that he had made this discovery, or had it been arranged that he should be taken to this already occupied room? He guessed that he would probably never know. But when the housekeeper returned a minute later, knocking on the door and entering at Whitney's *"Ja, eintreten!"* her embarrassment and dismay appeared genuine enough.

With effusive apologies, much rattling of her keys, and with the excuse that she had been employed for only a week at the schloss and still did not know her way about properly, she escorted Whitney back into the corridor. Before leaving, Whitney's eye was caught again by the silver brushes on the dressing table. The engraved coat of arms was faintly familiar, the "A.B." initials set his mind whirring to a medley of shock, wonder, dismay, and speculation. The coincidence, at first judged outrageous, at once became positive and acceptable. The days ahead, which had always seemed likely to be interesting, had suddenly been lifted to a new level of potential excitement and possible danger. "What, for heck's sake, is Archy Buller up to?"

"*Danke*, Frau Heinleen!" And he was alone again, in his correct room this time, with as wonderful and panoramic a view as the last and a wardrobe that was quite empty. He washed rapidly, ran a comb through his thick red hair, and stuffing his extinguished pipe into his pocket, went in search of his hostess.

The shooting party returned, looking like a platoon of irregulars, shortly before six o'clock, the guests in two small open charabancs, gun cases secured to the side running boards, followed by the beaters in breeches and old jackets and Tyrolean hats, sharing a wagonette with the dogs, and lastly a wagon featuring three boars like enemy dead strung by their feet upside down across a rigged wooden framework, their blood dripping onto the straw spread on the floor.

The guests, led by Sonny, climbed down from the charabancs, the women as mud-splashed in their high boots, long tweed skirts, and tight-fitting jackets as the men in their breeches and shooting jackets. They were all talking—in French and English as well as German—and laughing, boasting lightheartedly to the countess of their exploits, near-misses, and triumphs.

Whitney for the present kept in the background, feeling excluded as a new guest but fascinated by the countess's display as a hostess. *How at ease they all seemed!* Whitney thought. And how conscious of their superior class, how entitled they all felt to the privileges they were enjoying—as they had enjoyed them all their lives!

Could it last forever like this? Would these people always be rich and relaxed and carefree, shooting boar and drinking champagne and flirting in this paradise of a setting? While hundreds of thousands of underpaid riveters and gunsmiths, steelworkers and blacksmiths, joiners and template workers, in the shipyards and gun shops of dozens of shipyards around the world, strove to build more and yet more 20,000-ton dreadnought battleships and cruisers?

The servants were unstrapping the guns and handing them with a click of the heels and a slight bow to their owners. Others were taking down the boar corpses, one old fellow pretending to pick his teeth on the end of a tusk amidst laughter from his mates. A guest was taking a photograph of the scene with a folding camera.

On the train from Hamburg that morning, Whitney had read an article in the *Berliner Zeitung* which claimed that war was inevitable (a war Germany did not want) unless England ceased dictating to Germany the acceptable size of her navy. And Buller's concealed camera? And that fine model of the battleship *Preussen* in the hall of the schloss, and the photographs of guns and admirals and battleships on the walls of the corridors . . . ? On all sides you could see the portents if you were not blinded by the glitter, and hear the more threatening sounds if you were not deafened by the chatter and laughter and the rattle of sporting rifles.

There was Buller. Unsurprisingly, he was talking to a highly attractive young fair-haired woman. He was holding his gun case in one hand, and Whitney recalled the charm of his manner, the open friendliness of his conversation, as he watched him walk with the woman at his side toward the countess, with another unusually tall man on her other side.

Whitney bided his time and just before Buller entered the front doors, called out his name. Buller swung around, at first a puzzled and then an uncertain expression on his face. Clearly, he was as surprised to find him here as Whitney had been to learn that Buller was a fellow guest. There was a note of caution in Buller's voice as he said, "Well, this is a pleasant surprise. I didn't even know you were in Europe— let alone in Sonny's schloss."

Whitney said in a low voice, "I want to talk to you privately as soon as possible—it's important." Then, raising his voice, "It's great to see you, too. I'm over here as naval attaché—what do you think of that?"

The count, the last to enter the house, was just behind

them, and Buller turned toward him but continued to address Whitney. "You won't get any secrets out of our host, I'll tell you that, Whitney. He gives you plenty of vintage champagne but absolutely no dreadnought intelligence."

Sonny joined in their laughter. "I tell you all I know, Captain Buller. The rest you will no doubt find out by your own devices. Now I think a schnapps to warm—how do you say?—'the cockles of our heart.' Then baths to warm ourselves more. Then I hope we have an enchanting evening, yes?"

Before they separated on their way to their rooms, Buller called to the tall man he had been accompanying earlier. "Holly, come and meet an old American friend of mine. Whitney, this is Captain Mark Holly. We once sailed halfway around the world and back when we were youngsters. Now we just sail up and down the Solent and the Kieler Hafen. Or Holly does, while I sit in a launch and watch."

"Buller's taken to umpiring this year," said Holly. "None of this hauling on the sheets and other labors." He patted Buller's stomach. "That's why he's getting so fat."

It was not until close to midnight that Whitney saw Buller make some excuse to his partner at the bridge table and leave the *salon* after a quick glance in Whitney's direction. Out on the terrace, which stretched beyond the width of the schloss on both sides, Whitney stood still for a moment to allow his eyes to adjust to the darkness. There was a moon behind broken clouds, and when it suddenly shone, Whitney caught sight of a figure in the shadows of some pines nearby. He gave a low whistle and heard in reply the first bars of "Rule Britannia."

Buller laughed when Whitney was beside him. "I see you're getting the hang of being a naval attaché in Germany. Are you wearing your false beard?"

"This isn't any gosh-darned laughing matter," said Whitney. He told Buller of his discovery in his room. "I don't care what you're up to—none of my business," Whitney said as they strolled deeper into the woods. "But it's sure crazy that

I was wrongly given your room out of the twenty or thirty in the schloss. And it's even crazier that the wardrobe was in such a mess, your bag had things falling out, and I only had to lift the lid of your hamper to find your camera.''

"You're not dreaming, old man?''

"Certain sure, as I'm talking to you now.''

"I'll tell you something more curious still,'' said Buller. "When I left to go out shooting, the wardrobe was shipshape and locked. And the Gladstone and hamper were locked, too. And everything was the same when I went up to change this evening. What happened in between and after you left?''

"Were they after your film?''

"It'll be interesting if they were,'' said Buller enigmatically.

They emerged from the pines onto a track and walked down it, Buller lighting a cigar and Whitney his pipe.

Whitney said, "I'm not going to ask anything about what you're doing with that darn great telephoto camera. I know you're hot stuff with cameras, and I guess you were photographing the racing.''

"Something like that. But now we're here and you're not being so damn rude to me like last time we met, let me ask you the question again: Why did you suddenly leave my house without telling Clemmie or me?''

"Because I had fallen in love with her.''

"And had she fallen in love with you?''

"I didn't know. It was all so darn quick. I just felt I had to get away before anything terrible happened.''

Buller stopped and took a long puff from his cigar. "Did you sleep together?''

Whitney said unhesitatingly, "Yes, we did.''

Buller considered this and then said, "Well, you weren't the first. We haven't always been faithful to one another. It's the same with most of our friends. That's why it was a bit of a blow when she said she wanted to divorce me because of my affair with our hostess.'' Whitney saw that Buller was looking at him steadily as he asked, "It wasn't because she had fallen for you and wanted to be married to you instead of me?''

"I've never seen her since I left your house."

"That doesn't answer my question."

Whitney said carefully, "We've written to one another, and I believe she is fond of me. But I swear to you that I have done everything I can to persuade her to drop the divorce. I've told her that it's madness, and that your affair with the countess is just a passing passion."

Buller said, "How the deuce do you know? I could say the same about your affair with Clemmie. And now that I know, it makes a great deal of difference to the divorce proceedings—you'll understand that, and if you don't my lawyers will." He laughed and put an arm on Whitney's shoulder. " 'Put the man at ease, quartermaster.' No, it's all right. I think things can be patched up between Clemmie and me. And it's grand of you to tell me all this and be so frank. We'd better get back before everyone goes to bed—and to their own bed here. People behave much more correctly in Germany. Or most of them do."

Whitney's second day at Schloss Kroonbach began stormily with low clouds clinging to the mountain slopes and peaks. A shooting party had been arranged by the count for 11:00 A.M., but the rain was sheeting down, and it was not until after lunch—and after a morning spent mainly in the salon talking and playing bridge—that it was fit to go out, although the ladies decided to remain behind.

The men with their rifles—the French Consul-General from Hanover, a Russian general, Grand Duke Roland, the thirty-six-year-old Ernst, Duke of Saxe-Altenburg, two German admirals, Grand Admiral Prince Henrich of Prussia, and several others besides Holly, Buller, and Whitney—assembled in the drive and climbed into the charabanc when it arrived.

The women remained in the porch, for it was cold as well as damp, laughing and chattering among themselves and calling out to their husbands in several languages: "What brave fellows!" "Off to war go our brave men!" and *"Que c'est magnifique!"* All the men were well-protected against bad weather in long leather coats, some fur-trimmed around the collar, heavy boots; Holly and most of the others in Tyrolean hats, Buller and Whitney in heavy trilbys. Most of them were taking the expedition lightly, not expecting much luck under these conditions and participating only because the count had been so insistent that they should get out into the mountain air. He was having a conference with the head beater and organizing the party into two groups, while farther down the drive the pointers were howling with impatience for the chase.

Whitney, Buller, the two German admirals, and the Frenchman were the first off the charabanc. Count Sonny stepped down, too, to give them instructions on the route they should follow: skirt a bluff and then work obliquely down the valley side through scattered rock, pine, and birch. "In one hour we will meet you by the river," the count concluded his orders. "We will be coming down the other way, but nearly parallel with you to avoid the risks. The dogs will work in two packs with the beaters from the river up. You understand it all, yes?"

They set off in a drizzle, rifles tucked under their arms, and binoculars at the ready. For a time Buller and Whitney walked together, talking quietly and laughing about the count's organization, which they both admitted was highly efficient and decisive. From far below and a considerable distance came the first sounds of the dogs, who would be spreading out with the beaters, progressing slowly up from the valley floor.

The sun came out and like a giant searchlight at once revealed peaks and slopes previously lost in the cloud and driving drizzle, and reflected a dazzling glitter from the birch leaves all about them.

"It sure is pretty," said Whitney. "I wish I'd brought my box Brownie camera."

"Here, try these," said Buller and laughed. "You've uncovered my secrets already. And you might get a photograph of a boar if you're nippy."

Buller handed the American the distinctive black binoculars case. "You focus with this lense, just like any binoculars, and you press the shutter here.'' Buller indicated a small brass button between the lenses. ''Then if you have time, it's roll film, so you can wind on to the next exposure and 'shoot' again. They're not very powerful, but I've had some good pictures of deer in Scotland as well as yachts—and interesting objects near Kiel.''

Whitney slung the strap around his shoulders, and they drew apart in conformity with Sonny's instructions, Whitney walking and scrambling along the side of the valley while Buller climbed down toward the base of the valley.

It had suddenly become very hot, and Whitney wished he had not followed the count's instructions to be prepared for rain and cold. For twenty more minutes, breaking through bracken and thickets and clambering over rocky outcrops, he continued, catching glimpses of others of their party advancing below his level. The sound of the pointers was now much much louder, and Whitney throught he saw two of them working along the bank of a pool before disappearing into the forest again. The experienced Count Sonny had devised a most effective tactical scheme. It looked to Whitney—whose first boar hunt this was—that if there was game down there, the beaters could not fail to drive it toward one or the other of the two parties.

There was a faint rumble of thunder. Whitney looked up. Black clouds were piling up from the southwest. A gust of wind stirred the branches of the trees overhead, sending down showers of water. A second clap of thunder sounded out, much louder than the first, and big drops of rain began to fall. Whitney, who had opened the buttons of his leather coat, now secured the collar. Visibility had suddenly closed right down, and the rain began to fall in torrents.

'' 'Man's best-laid plans . . .' '' Whitney quoted to himself. ''Poor old Sonny! And poor old us.''

He pulled his trilby down half over his ears and lay down on a rock under a tall pine tree, listening to the rain beating on the bracken and bouncing off the rocks, while the storm wind bent the younger birches almost flat. A streak of forked lightning flashed across the sky, revealing to Whitney the

valley as he had last seen it before the storm shut it off from
his vision, but now with the trees and undergrowth in a frenzy
whipped up by the violent gusts of wind. A third thunderclap,
even louder than the last and seemingly immediately above
the pine tops, crashed out.

Whitney lay on his gun in misery and some apprehension.
He remembered Buller's binoculars and was reaching around
to pull the case under his coat for some sort of protection
when there was another crack. Whitney was at that split
second reminding himself of the folly of lying immediately at
the base of a tree in a thunderstorm, so that when he felt the
pain, stunning, stabbing, incredible in its exquisite agony, he
believed at once that he had been fatally injured, not by an
assassin's bullet but by a bolt of lightning.

Whitney's belief was as positive and as brief as the time it
took for the 7-mm., 220-grain round-nosed bullet to enter his
back, graze past his spine at the eleventh vertebra, and pass
through the right side of his heart. It smashed a rib before
leaving his body and ricocheting off the rock on which he had
been lying, thrusting deep into the wet, sandy soil thirty yards
farther away.

The sodden, dispirited party waited in a group on the forest
track for twenty minutes. In a lull in the storm, they had
shouted agreement to call off the shoot, and in ones or twos
had made their way back up the valley. The rain had stopped
by the time they had gathered together. From below they
heard the whistles of the beaters and an occasional yelp from
a pointer.

Buller waited another five minutes for Whitney under the
shelter of an overhanging rock, and then set off down the
valley again, calling his name, until he heard the voice of the
count shouting for him to return. The charabanc had arrived.
Sonny, like a corps commander in a retreat, was rallying his
men, cracking out orders in German. When Buller joined him
on the track, the count asked where he had last seen Whitney.
When Buller told him, he replied, "He must have gone back
to the schloss on his own. What a foolish American!" He

laughed sharply. "And a gunnery officer, not a navigation officer—eh?"

Buller did not join in the laughter. He remembered that Whitney had been lost the first time he had met him near Buckingham Palace. But the American was no fool. He would never have attempted, without some strong reason—or strong fear?—the five-mile slog back to the schloss in the midst of an appalling thunderstorm.

"I think we should go and search for him," Buller told the Count. "He could have sprained his ankle, slipped on a rock, or met some other accident. Even been struck by lightning."

The count, displeased at having to follow another's suggestion, agreed to organize the beaters into a search party. He remained behind himself, sending the rest of them back to the schloss in the charabanc.

There was a knock on Buller's door. He was in his dressing gown, resting after a hot bath. Miranda came in, carrying his binoculars case. He sprang up, "Thank God, he's back."

Miranda dropped the case onto the bed and came close to Buller, speaking quietly. "Yes, he is back, my poor Buller. But your friend is dead."

Buller realized later that he had been half prepared for the news, that he had been experiencing a sense of unease ever since he had learned from Whitney that his possessions had been rifled, his telephoto Zeiss discovered, the single exposed plate in the camera body removed.

"Our men found him under a tree," Miranda continued. "They thought at first he had been killed by the lightning. But no. His gun was a little way off and had been fired once. The bullet had passed through his body. They said it was an accident of the storm—perhaps he fell and his gun fired."

Miranda was very close, her eyes on him, her lemon scent heavy in his nostrils. Buller said, "You don't believe that cock-and-bull story, do you?"

She continued to stare at him, scarcely a foot away, breathing heavily, and then slowly shook her head. His eyes fell to the bed and the black binoculars case with his initials in gold upon it. Then she said, very quietly, "It was you the bullet was meant for, Buller. And I think they will try again. You must dress at once and leave. I have told your friend, who must go with you. I will tell Sonny that you are dining out with some English friends in Hildesheim. That is what I have told my chauffeur, who will have my Opel ready with your bags strapped on."

Miranda kissed him briefly. "Please make no public accusations about the death of Captain Campbell. The doctor and our men will confirm it was an accident no matter what is said. Good-bye, my Buller."

Buller turned away and began to pack, his sudden sharp sense of purpose at conflict in his mind with shock at the loss of his friend, anger at the perpetrator of the crime, and already a sense of sad deprival at the loss of his lover. Would he ever hear again his name spoken by her—the beguiling, arousing, yet laughable "Booler"?

Chapter X

⚓

A Matter of Gun
Caliber

"OF COURSE IT was murder, sir," Buller said. "There can be no doubt of it."

Jackie Fisher stared across the cloth-covered table at Buller unblinkingly. "And they really meant to shoot *you*," he said. "I'm sorry about Captain Campbell but very glad it was not you. The murderer's time will come. 'Whoso sheddeth man's blood, by man shall his blood be shed.' Genesis Nine. So they had found out what you were up to."

"They thought they had. Captain Ottley had warned me about the German Navy's newly formed S.N. Department of the Intelligence Division in Berlin. And I think they were making things easy for me so that they could catch me afterward."

Holly and Buller explained how they had made arrangements for Buller to act as one of the British umpires for the cutter race during Kiel Week just before their eventful and fatal visit to Count Reitzberg-Sönderlong's schloss. Four launches were positioned at the turns in the Kieler Hafen, the most southerly being in the center of the harbor off the university building and no more than 400 yards from the imperial dockyard.

"I was assigned to this launch with the German and French umpires," Buller recounted. "There was a crew of three, and we were there for most of the day. I could see that the slips were all occupied by men-o'-war under construction and there were others launched and fitting out in the dockyard. You couldn't mistake the *Blücher*. She was twice the size of any of the others, but it would have needed a good telescope to make out any detail."

"And you had one."

"Not for anyone to see, sir. The umpires were told not to use binoculars close to the dockyards. But I had my hamper with a bottle of Krug and some smoked salmon and excellent German wurst."

Buller lifted the hamper onto the table, inserted the key into the brass lock, and opened it, revealing the beautiful dark camera and extended lense nestling at the bottom. "Only the Germans could build such a brilliant camera," he said. "Eight-hundred-millimeter Zeiss. I bought it in London through Ross's agents. The only one in the country. My 'chippies' from the *Lily* built it into the Fortnum and Mason hamper."

Buller demonstrated how the hinged flap could be let down when the camera was aimed onto the correct bearing, activating the shutter simultaneously.

It had been a gusty day with an occasional driving drizzle, the third day of the Regatta, with the cutter race occupying three hours in the afternoon. Before embarking in the Yacht Club's launch, Buller had stopped down the lense to the lowest f/4.2, setting the speed at a fiftieth of a second, the range at infinity on the long lense. He had felt little hope of any success. The other races to follow—the six meter and nine meter—used a different course and one that was more distant from the dockyards.

The opportunity for taking the picture occurred when the last of the cutters, close-hauled on the port, had doubled the buoy and the umpires' duty on this station had ceased. Buller had opened his hamper, drawn out the bottle of champagne and glasses resting on the heavy velvet cloth, turned the end of the hamper slightly so that it pointed toward the dockyard fitting-out basin, closed the top, and swiftly, while his fellow umpires were exclaiming at his resourcefulness in bringing refreshment, lowered the flap with the remote-control release. There had been no more than the faintest click.

"Bonne santé!" "Prosit!" "Your good health!"

Glasses were raised. The seven cutters, close-bunched, were fast disappearing up the Kaiser Hafen before the wind, spinnakers spread and filled out like vast white balloons. Buller remembered saying to himself fatalistically, "Either it has worked or I've wasted my time!" He would not know for some weeks—not, as it had worked out, until now, here in Fisher's office in only a few minutes.

"The trouble was that I had only one shot," Buller recounted. "It was like trying to sink a ship with one gun and one round. There was a bad moment when one of the club's servants insisted on carrying my hamper when we returned to the Kaiserlicher. But I managed to recover it, drew out the plate when I was changing, handed the plate between the pages of a book to Captain Holly, and replaced it with a fine shot of Sonny's cutter."

Holly took over the account. "We had agreed that we had to get rid of the plate at once and that there was less risk in sending it through the post than having it with us. So I posted it to Captain Dumas in Berlin at his private address. And, as you know, Captain Dumas sent it in the diplomatic bag to London."

Fisher smiled mischievously across the table at them. He enjoyed a mystery and enjoyed even more the role of the magician. He turned now to his secretary and said, "Be good enough to show in Captain Ottley."

Ottley entered the First Sea Lord's office with his assistant, who carried under his arm a board measuring some three by two feet.

"Hey presto!" Fisher called out loudly. "Reveal all to our gallant friends, Charles." He turned back to Buller and Holly. "You gentlemen will recall Longfellow's helmsman answering his own question: 'Learn the secret of the sea? /

Only those who brave its dangers/Comprehend its mystery!'
And there we have it, gentlemen, the secret of the sea.''

Buller stared in amazement at the huge enlargement the
Admiralty's photographic department had made from the
plate he had exposed back in mid-August on a damp afternoon in the Kaiser Hafen from a launch hove-to in choppy
water.

His aim had not been completely on target. But it did not
matter. Only the center of the negative had been enlarged, but
that had been enough. On the left were some wharves and
out-of-use cranes, several railway trucks, some steel buildings beyond. Then the curving ram bows of the *Blücher,* her
forecastle piled with equipment and a small crane, the boiler
of her engine at about the same height as several workmen
standing near to it.

There were more figures working on the bridge and
superstructure, and part of the foremast had already been
stepped. But it was the installed turret just forward of the
bridge that Buller bent over and examined carefully. From it
projected two gun barrels, one elevated some 20 degrees, the
other horizontal with the littered deck.

Between the two funnels was a similar turret, a third just
aft of the second funnel. Aft of the mainmast and almost out
of Buller's photograph was a fourth turret, though the guns
had not yet been fitted. Even in this condition, ioncomplete,
swarming with "dockies" and their equipment and material,
unpainted and rust-streaked in parts, the *Blücher* appeared as
a swift yet solid-looking and aggressive ship, about 500 feet
long, Buller guessed. Two years earlier her keel plate had not
been laid. Now, so great was the urgency, she would soon be
ready for sea.

Buller turned to Fisher and said, "Well, sir, she looks a
fine ship and I'm amazed at the detail my camera has caught.
She's a dreadnought armored cruiser, all right. And those
midships turrets must be repeated on the starboard side. So
that makes twelve heavy guns." He turned to Holly and then
to Captain Ottley, and said solemnly, "And the *Invincible*
carries only eight heavy guns."

Fisher could withhold himself no longer. Like a broadside from one of his dreadnoughts, he burst out, "You fool, Archy Buller! You ignoramus, you jackanapes, you scum scraped from the galley deck. Look again. Look at the *size* of those guns—compare the length of the barrel, allowing for what you can't see behind the turret armor, with that man standing there"—and he placed a stubby finger on the spot—"say he's five feet six inches tall. Oh, preserve me from fools! Scrap the lot! You tell 'em, Charles."

As suddenly exasperated at the need to say more as he had earlier exploded with the urgent need to talk, Fisher lapsed into silence.

Captain Ottley, a calm, precise man, took over from his master, quietly explaining that the Intelligence Department identification experts had completed the most minute calculations proving that the guns were 8.2-inch or twenty-one centimeters, forty-five calibers, an improved version of the same gun fitted to earlier German armored cruisers. "A superior though slightly smaller gun than our nine point two-inch."

Fisher returned to the table, now calm, even avuncular, and placed his arms across the shoulders of Holly and Buller. "Now do you see?" he asked. "Now do you see how we have outwitted and outgunned the enemy before the first battle? Admiral von Tirpitz and the kaiser learned that we were going to build all-big-gun armored cruisers, our greyhounds of the sea, our *Invincibles*. Then they learned that they were to carry as many as eight big guns. Then that the size was nine point two-inch. So next, they redesign the *Blücher*, wasting a year, and give it twelve big guns. But not so big as our big guns because our big guns are twelve-inch. The weight of our broadside 6,800 pounds. The weight of the *Blücher's* 2,500 pounds."

The First Sea Lord raised his arms, spread them wide in a gesture of explosive annihilation. "And we shall BLOW OUT OF THE WATER this puny *Blücher* the first time we get her within our range."

Then he put a hand on the Zeiss in the hamper and, with his

saturnine face creased into a triumphant smile, said to Buller, "Now you may take out your camera and fill all the space with bottles of champagne and enjoy a great celebration party. Good day, gentlemen."

From Weir Park Buller wrote a letter to his wife at Wyston Court seven miles away:

My dear Clemmie,

I am sending this by hand so that you get it this afternoon. It is very important that I should see you and talk to you. On my side, it will not be an acrimonious meeting, nor shall I ask anything of you.

I returned from Germany three days ago and shall be taking up a new appointment shortly.

It will be better if none of the children are present.

He signed it "Your loving husband," sealed the envelope, and gave instructions for it to be taken at once.

Both his brothers and their wives and children were away, and Weir Park was silent and empty without them. Buller walked out onto the front terrace and strolled up and down for the exercise, hands clasped behind his back, as generations of Bullers had walked—often with a limp—over the years, thinking about their last voyage, their last action, considering ways to improve the performance of their ships and their men in peace and in war, recalling past campaigns, contemplating the naval careers of their sons and heirs, sparing a thought or two for their wives who were always there to welcome them home at the end of a long commission.

Certainly his own circumstances were different from those of any earlier Bullers. All his fighting had been on land for the reason that there had, so far in his career, been no enemy at sea—no enemy of any importance for 103 years. What he had achieved for his navy and his country recently had been of a shady and highly confidential nature, for which there could be no public acknowledgment. Buller, being the least vainglorious of men, felt no resentment about that. Any resentment that he felt on this dour August day in 1908 was directed at himself. Other Bullers had, no doubt, experienced marital problems, but none had got into the mess he was in: a mistress in Germany who amused him, stimulated him, and aroused him more than any woman in his life; and a wife whom he genuinely and deeply loved, who had, besides, been his friend and companion for so long, the mother of his children, admired as a hostess and friend by so many.

And now, for the present, he was denied both these women and felt angry with himself for falling into this deprived situation, and angry for minding so much.

Buller kicked a stone, feeling like a recalcitrant cadet instead of a forty-two-year-old Post Captain R.N., a Companion of the Victorian Order, a member of the Distinguished Service Order, owner of a considerable estate and fortune, a friend of the king and many of the highest in the land—and without a woman in his life.

He glanced about him, down the terraces to fields and river, the deer park beyond with the little stone church built by his ancestor, Admiral Gordon Buller, and then he entered the wide-open double doors of the great house. His temper was not improved when he became aware that he was working out subconsciously how soon he might hear from Clemmie. He called out to a passing parlormaid, who paused and dropped a brief curtsy. "Maude, will you ask Chambers to bring me a bottle of champagne."

Buller was into his second glass and staring moodily at the eight-foot-long oil painting that dominated the wall above the fireplace in the library. It depicted the Battle of the Nile at its height, with the French flagship blowing up, its glare illuminating a night scene of dreadful destruction and mayhem, with mastless men-o'-war firing at worse-crippled vessels at point-blank range, and the sea littered with debris, corpses, and wounded clinging to masts and rigging.

Chambers entered after a knock. Buller thought that he had come to replenish his glass and even picked it up to drain it first. Instead, the butler said, "Lady Clementine Buller wishes to talk to you upon the telephone, sir."

• • •

Buller and Clemmie touched cheeks like acquaintances observing public manners and then looked at one another shyly. It was three years since they had last met. Buller thought she looked five years older and said that she looked ten years younger. She had lost a lot of weight, and there was a gauntness about her which he had never seen before. Her hair, always a beautiful feature, had turned all gray, but it was not this which made her appear older than her years. It was her eyes, which had always reflected fulfillment and contentment, liveliness and happiness, and now showed uncertainty and anxiety.

Buller was almost overwhelmed by the flood strength of his feelings for his wife. Mercifully, he did not have to define what he saw. This was done for him. "I'm sorry, Archy. I always used to take such a lot of trouble to make myself look nice and welcoming for you when you got back from sea."

"You look grand, darling."

"No, Archy. You know that's not true. I'm in a terrible mess. Full of guilt and shock. Come on, let's sit down."

Clemmie led her husband into the little round garden room, which caught the last of the sun. There were vines growing around the windows, and a view over the rolling Cotswold uplands.

Minutes passed before it became clear to Buller that his wife knew nothing of Whitney's death. The German authorities were evidently keeping it quiet until after an inquest, no doubt with suitable witnesses, and confidential notification to the United States Embassy in Berlin. How could he bring himself now to add to the burden of her worries? And what were these caused by?

The answer to the second question came after a few minutes, in an enigmatic and roundabout way. She said, "Why couldn't he have told me earlier, Archy? Surely he could trust *me?* And he must have known what I was going through."

"There is something serious happening which I don't understand, Clemmie," Buller replied. "Who do you mean?"

"Admiral Fisher asked me to come up to town yesterday," she said. "You must know what he told me."

Buller shook his head, completely mystified.

"He said how grieved he was that our marriage had broken up and began quoting the Old Testament—you know, from First Samuel, 'As saith the proverb of the ancients, Wickedness proceedeth from the wicked.' Then added quickly, 'But not from the good, and Archy Buller is a good man.' Is the old man going mad, Archy?"

Buller said, "No, he's always been like that. He can quote the whole of the Old Testament and most of the New. And a great deal else besides. But what's Samuel got to do with me?"

Clemmie described quickly her talk at 16 Queen Anne's Gate, Fisher's residence. He had told her that Buller had been on a special assignment since his return from the Russo-Japanese War—highly secret intelligence work, penetrating German naval policy and construction, that this had required the cultivation of close relations with a number of people, one of them especially a German woman of great beauty and importance.

"He said your affair with the countess was contrived entirely in the line of duty, and that you were appalled when it led to my suing you for divorce."

"You know I was appalled, Clemmie," said Buller. "That's true."

"He also said that the affair was at an end because your special commission was at an end—and that it had almost ended in your murder. Is that right, Archy?"

Buller, experiencing a tug of conscience as powerful as a battleship's straining anchor cable, nodded, taking a cigar from his case to cover his confusion. What *was* the right thing to say, the right thing to do, under these impossible circumstances? he thought to himself. If he found himself leading a cruiser squadron into a minefield, he would know how to deal with the crisis better than with this dilemma.

"My poor darling—I am sorry." Clemmie rose from her chair and put her arms around his neck. "If only I had known. Everyone said you were besotted with that wretched German woman and would never come back to me."

"What else did Jackie Fisher say?"

"He gave me orders as if I was some midshipman. He told me to drop my divorce proceedings forthwith, give you love—'This thou perceiv'st, which makes thy love more strong' from some Shakespeare sonnet. And to offer you condolences because you had lost a good friend.'' She looked at Buller with a slight touch of resentment in her smile. "I suppose she did become a good friend if you had to be together so much."

Oh God! thought Buller, *what am I to do? What am I to say?* And then, inevitably, his naval training came to his rescue. In some old manual he had read in the *Britannia* as a cadet—what was it?—Should a commanding officer find himself greatly outnumbered and in severe straits, show decision and at once take a decisive line toward extrication . . .

Buller got up and put his arms around Clemmie, conscious even at this difficult moment of her thinness. "Darling, it wasn't the countess that he meant. I met Whitney Campbell in Germany, and he told me that he loved you but had been trying to persuade you to come back to me." She knew what was coming. He could feel that in the stiffening of her body, and her fingernails were sharp against his neck. But he continued, speaking quickly to get it over soon.

"They found out I knew more than I should and had pricelessly valuable photographs. They tried to shoot me, but they murdered Whitney by mistake."

No word passed between them for a time. Then Clemmie pushed Buller away. She was laughing and crying, both gently. "The poor, sweet chump," she said at last. "Why did that have to happen to him? But I'm glad it wasn't you, Archy. This is a time for the truth, my dear. I did love him. It began here, as I expect you know. That's why he left. It was a bad time. I was feeling restless, you were away for such ages, and there was the reaction when you were nearly killed in the battle, and Lucy was being awful, and along came this nice, gentle American who fell in love with me. Of course it was ridiculous. But then I was told about this German countess and how you were showing her off in society. I'm not making excuses, but I was sick and angry." She looked at him in silence for a moment, the tears still trickling down her cheeks. "But I never saw him again. I wanted to but he never let me. Poor Whitney. He was always very unselfish. It was like him to die for someone else's cause."

They went for a long ride together before it became dark, talking very little, allowing the wounds to heal. Searching for a crossing in a river swollen by recent rains, Buller drew in beside his wife and said, "Clemmie, I had better say this and get it over. It was not all naval duty with the countess—not by any means."

Clemmie laughed and flicked her riding crop at him. "Archy, you're so innocent I wonder you ever grew up to be a captain. Do you think I didn't know that?" She dug her heels into the flanks of her stallion so that he cantered toward the riverbank and into the water. He swam easily, his head held high, with Clemmie, soaked to her waist, laughing. Halfway across, she turned in her sidesaddle and called out, "Race you home, Archy."

Chapter XI

⚓

Buller's Dreadnought

SHE BEGAN LIFE in Elswick Slip 3 in January 1910, and was code-named by the yard 691B. Everyone knew that she was be even bigger and faster than the *Invincible*, which this yard had built in such secrecy and with such speed between April 1906 and May 1908—the first of Fisher's "ocean greyhounds" with the teeth of a tiger. The keel plate was laid by January 21, a bitter winter day on the Tyne with an east wind, typical of this thundering, smoke-infested industrial port. Then the wooden staging—scaffolding and planking—began to rear up, climbing higher and higher above the keel strake, so that people living across the river had an ever-changing picture of the big new ship. Soon her curved ribbing was dominating the riverside skyline. Steel plates were bent into shape by hydraulic rams under the heat of furnaces, and forged and stamped in the frame shops and platers' shops. In anglesmiths' and blacksmiths' shops, the great steel plates were punched, drilled and countersunk, scarfed and joggled. The pattern shop and the riggers' loft, the sawmill and joiners' shops, all contributed in small or large measure to the multitude of parts, from minute valves to hawsepipes, watertight doors and gantries, that make up the complex mechanism of a great fighting ship.

By March 1911 she was plated and framed out and decked. In the mast yard the steel tripod masts were laid out, along with the shrouds and stay wires from the rigging loft. Her funnels and casings were ready for hoisting on board, her Parsons' turbines and boilers already installed. Four circular holes in her deck, fore and aft and on either beam amidships, like toothless cavities in a long gray gum, marked the location of the trunks and turrets, the *raison d'être* of this 19,000-ton man-o'-war.

Not far distant, in the Armstrong ordinance shops, where Rod Maclewin's father had worked back in the 1860s, the eight twelve-inch, fifty-caliber guns were cast and forged, hardened, bored, and wired. Then they were taken out to the Armstrong proof range at Ridsdale high up on the Northumberland moors, where old Tom Maclewin had been blown to pieces while his son, Rod, was still an infant.

In December 1911 Lady Clementine Buller traveled north from London in a railway coach specially reserved by the Armstrong Company for the launching ceremony. With her were her husband, Jackie Fisher, the Fourth Sea Lord, and senior directors of the company. The 575-foot-long battle cruiser was ready for launching. Shipwrights had performed the setting-up with molten tallow, soft soap, and train oil on the surfaces of the slipway. On the morning of the launch, by means of wedges the weight of the ship had been transferred from the building blocks to the launching ways.

On December 10, on a draped platform above the bows of the ship, the assembled company, full of good food and (according to Buller) only indifferent champagne, with the patriarchal figure of Sir Andrew Nobel in command, made small talk until the signal was given that all was ready.

Clemmie Buller looked nearer twenty-seven than forty-seven, the taut gauntness of her unhappy years now quite gone. She was dressed, as always, just right for the occasion in a long Astrakhan cape over a green, fur-trimmed tweed suit, and a matching Astrakhan hat fitting close around her ears.

Clemmie stepped forward, made a little speech about Britannia continuing to rule the waves and the small part mere women could be expected to take in preserving our sea heritage, and concluded: "I name this ship *Incontestable*, may God bless her and all who sail in her." She almost added, "Especially my husband," but instead turned to Sir Andrew Nobel and said, "Isn't this exciting—I've never launched a ship before." But he was too old and deaf to hear her and merely smiled beneath his vast white beard.

There was never any risk that Clemmie would have to hurl the champagne bottle twice. It exploded with a mighty crack first time. The dogshores were knocked out under the supervision of the shipyard manager, and Buller's future ship gathered speed down the slip amidst cheering and the sound of rattles and brass band music. Her stern entered the water, not too fast, not too slow, sending up a wave that quickly sped across the Tyne, slopping onto the quays and slipways and causing many small boys to run away shouting and pushing.

Clemmie turned to Buller. "Well, I did enjoy that," she said. "I do hope you will let me do it again." The *Incontestable*, looking twice the size now that she was in the water, was being nursed by four paddle tugs, smoke streaming from their funnels, to the Walker yard for fitting out. The members of Mr. H.G. Amer's brass band put away their instruments, and the workers of Elswick and their wives made their way back to their homes. Among them were Rosie Maclewin, whose husband was serving on the China Station, her two daughters, and her son, Tom, and his wife.

"That was a beautiful sight," commented Rosie. "I've seen so many launchings, but they are always exciting, like the birth of a child."

"All right, mama," said Tom Maclewin dourly. "If it's a child, it was conceived by sweated labor—a capitalist ship for the capitalist war to come."

"Oh, Tom, why can't you ever enjoy *anything*?" asked one of his sisters.

At which Tom Maclewin steered his unhappy-looking wife away at the next street corner toward Groom Road, and the rest of the family made for the nearest tram stop. "Wasn't Lady Buller looking lovely!" exclaimed Rosie. She had thought of sending her a message of good wishes, even of inviting her and her husband to "Balmoral." In the end she had been too shy to do either.

But when the family arrived home, a telegram awaited them, from Lady Buller, inviting them all to the Royal Station Hotel for dinner that night.

In accordance with custom in the Royal Navy, Archy Buller lived with his ship during the final stages of her construction. The most important operations, like the hoisting in of her guns, her twelve-inch "teeth," were outside his responsibility. But every day, as the complex and honeycombed interior was built up, Buller was consulted about arrangements, from the position of the hatchways, the siting of latrine doors, and the position of the chart table in the chart cabin to the layout of his own quarters at the stern.

Like an architect as a house nears completion, he had to approve or correct a thousand details, so that everywhere below decks in the big battle cruiser the Buller stamp was to be seen.

By early April 1912 Buller was able to live on board and moved his belongings from the Royal Turk's Head Hotel, which had been his home for so many months. On April 5 he received a signal from the Admiralty: "First Lord, First Sea Lord, Admiral of the Fleet Lord Fisher, and First Lord's Naval Secretary arrive in *Enchantress* April 22 to inspect progress of men-o'-war building on Tyneside and detailed tour of *Incontestable*. Confirm."

It was an uncoded message, and the news of the visit was soon known throughout Newcastle. Since the *Incontestable* had first been laid down, Britain had suffered a series of crippling strikes. The railwaymen, the Welsh coal miners, the dockers, and the countless more skilled workers had withheld their labor. Somehow at the Armstrong works and shipyards the work on the many men-o'-war under construction continued according to schedule, although there were temporary shortages of some materials.

The Geordies of Tyneside were fully employed for the first time in many years as the pace of rearmament increased, and there were even shortages of some tradesmen, especially riveters. With the city continuing to prosper, the work of political extremists in Newcastle became more difficult. The men worked in two shifts, the night shift's acetylene lamps and fires lighting up the quayside and cranes and workshops reflecting in the waters of the Tyne.

As soon as Buller received the signal from the Admiralty, he called in the carpenters' foreman and gave instructions for accelerating still further the work so that the guests could be welcome on board in proper style. This was going to be a big occasion for Buller, who was looking forward to being promoted to flag rank as soon as he had worked up the *Incontestable* and had shown his qualities as a commander in the Battle Cruiser Squadron.

Events occurred rapidly and dangerously after this. The carpenters were already working a ten-hour shift six days a week, and their wives were worrying that they were tiring themselves out unnecessarily. Debts had long since been paid off, and there was money in the traditional teapot on the shelf above the kitchen range.

At this point, Tom Maclewin and his friends, who made up the exteme element in the various trade unions within Armstrong's, decided to take advantage of the situation and cause trouble. Working first through the wives of Elswick, Tom Maclewin began a campaign for double pay for all the overtime the carpenters had to put in to do this additional Admiralty work. "This is your chance to get some real money out of the bosses," he told them at street corners, in pubs, and when the men in their clogs clattered home from the works' gates in the evening and early morning.

Certain that he could succeed, Tom and his caucus worked hard to spread disaffection, with such success that a week before the *Enchantress* was due in the Tyne, there still remained a lot of finishing work, day and night, if the *Incontestable* was to be ready for her guests.

The company refused to bow to what they regarded as blackmail, a carpenters' strike was started, and Buller cursed and called the senior foreman to his own half-paneled day cabin.

"We've got to get the men back to work," he told him. "It isn't just this ship or my pride that's at stake. If the First Lord sees signs of trouble and delay at Elswick, Armstrong's are not going to see any new contracts for a long time."

The head foreman was in despair. The carpenters were now convinced that they could not fail to get their double money for this work—the word had been spread that they could not lose—and the management of Armstrong's would not yield.

"In that case, we'll bring in the 'chippies,' " said Buller.

"Sir?"

"Naval carpenters. I'll find a party of two hundred without any difficulty—I'll bring them in from Rosyth, Yarmouth, Gravesend, Portsmouth if need be. This ship is going to be ready on time."

The first naval party arrived the following evening in a train from Scotland, all in uniform. Word had spread through the railwaymen's union. The sailors were booed and hissed, and were given the first taste of some rotten eggs as they marched from the station down the cobbled streets to the yards.

The following day, more arrived. Acting on the principle of solidarity, other unions joined the protest and failed to clock on for work. A riot threatened on the dock alongside the battle cruiser, the police were called out, failed to disperse the strikers. Except for the sounds of hammering and sawing by the naval carpenters, the *Incontestable* was silent and deserted of all workers. When the sailors were seen from time to time, and when more arrived, they were pelted with stones and rivets. The crowd increased and now included women and, here and there, a red flag was raised above the shouting mob.

Buller was hard put to conceal the dismay he felt at what he had started. As he watched from the ship's bridge, the old, powerful, uncontrollable anger that had caused him so much trouble as a boy and young man began to flow like molten steel in the Armstrong plate shops. Rapidly he descended to his cabin, changed into his uniform, and strode ashore unescorted and unarmed, carrying only a standard naval megaphone. This time, the megaphone was not for raising his voice above the sounds of high winds and high seas, but above the baying and shouting of the mob.

The police superintendent at the bottom of the gangway tried to send Buller back to his ship. "They're in an ugly mood, sir." Buller brushed him aside, seized a wooden box in his other hand, and walked toward the crowd, now numbering several thousand. He looked the personification of pride and authority as he broke through the police cordon, and for a few steps the crowd opened up before him.

Buller climbed onto the box, his six-foot-two figure dominating them, and held the megaphone to his lips. "You're all mad," he began unwisely, his voice traveling far above the temporarily subdued massed men and women. "You've never been so rich in your lives. And we've all got to work together to make our fleet stronger, or . . ."

It was at this point that the voices rose about him and the brickbats began to fly. Buller shouted one last appeal before his cap was knocked off, his megaphone was snatched from his hand, and a stone struck him hard on his right cheek. He began fighting a lonely battle against those close about him, punching men in cloth hats with handkerchiefs around their necks, all smaller than he was but countering every one of his hard blows with a dozen aimed at him.

They were afraid of him, there was no doubt about that—or so Buller told himself. He seized one young man, lifted him up as if he were a child, holding him like the red banner he was carrying, above the crowd. "You don't care twopence for work and your country," Buller shouted into his face. "Lazy cowards, the lot of you."

The man, in spite of his humiliating position, shouted back gamely, "And you're a capitalist swine, grinding down the workers—and then you'll be sending us off as cannon fodder to your capitalist war!" His face was twisted with hate and passion. In spite of that, Buller knew he had seen this face

before, many years ago. He bore a close likeness to his
father.

Buller shouted at him, like a challenge, like a clarion cry of
hate for all that this young man stood for—anarchy, revolution, anti-royalism, antipatriotism, and, worst of all, family
disloyalty. For Buller had in the grip of his powerful hands
Rod's boy, Tom Maclewin. He knew it as he tossed him aside
contemptuously.

At once, Buller was thrown to the ground by a dozen men
and was kicked where he lay on the cobbles, the weight of his
assailants holding him down. The jabs of pain struck him like
shell splinters, one of them on the old Mauser bullet wound
from Colenso. This inspired him with a final thrust of fury,
and he struggled to his knees, pulling down three men,
feeling a woman's spit in his face.

The police were closing about him, the thud of truncheons
on the men's heads like drumbeats into battle. They were
sparing no one, working in silence, and Buller was aware of
the relief of pressure on all sides. Then there were arms under
his arms, and a voice said, "All right, sir. We have you
now."

The Admiralty yacht *Enchantress* swept up the Tyne as
contemptuous and graceful as the riverbanks were humble
and ugly, a swan gliding disdainfully to its destination—
white upperworks and glinting brass, jet black hull, single
raked funnel. At the east end of the Walker yard, she came
alongside the quay; lines were thrown and seized by the
dockyard mateys, hawsers secured to the capstans.

Buller, in frock coat, and morning waistcoat, with plain
blue trousers, undress belt, and sword, only a black eye
detracting from his dignity, strode up the *Enchantress's*
gangway and was piped on board. The captain greeted him
and took him below, where the party was drinking midmorn-
ing coffee in the smaller of the two lounges. It was an
oak-paneled cabin with an electric mock-coal fire, seascape
and landscape photographs and paintings on the walls,
cretonne-covered armchairs and settees arranged in groups.

Buller shook hands in turn with Winston Churchill, his

Naval Secretary, Captain David Beatty, Admiral Sir Francis Bridgeman, the new First Sea Lord, and Jackie Fisher, retired now after his tumultuous and eventful six years as First Sea Lord. Buller distrusted Churchill, a politician who had crossed the floor of the House of Commons when his own party appeared to be weakening, then preached naval economy until he achieved his ambition of becoming First Lord of the Admiralty. Buller glanced at the full, round face, the wide-set, clever eyes, brown hair receding, full lips formed into a knowing smile. He wore a white shirt with wing collar and bow tie, yachting jacket, and white yachting shoes. His yachting cap lay on a table beside him.

Churchill had glanced at Buller's D.S.O. and now remarked, "You were at Colenso, captain, is that not right? That was a lively affair, eh? Shortly after I was captured."

"Yes, sir, and I think Captain Beatty and I have both had our fill of land battles. We'd prefer to fight at sea next time." Buller turned to the handsome man on Churchill's right who was also wearing the D.S.O. ribbon, an award he had gained in the Sudan sixteen years earlier. He was six years younger than Buller, but had caught Churchill's eye who saw in him a future Nelson.

Beatty smiled at Buller's observation. "I think we shall have that experience," he said. "And before long." He glanced more closely at Buller's face. "It looks as if you've been in the wars again. A proper shiner, eh?"

Buller laughed. "That's what comes of taking on a revolution single-handed."

"It's not revolution we're to expect," boomed Fisher, "it's Armageddon. Armageddon will break out in 1914. By that year the kaiser will have completed widening the Kiel Canal to take his dreadnoughts. Yes, war will begin when the harvest is in and the kaiser can switch his Battle Fleet from the Baltic to the North Sea in hours. My old friend, John Jellicoe, will command our fleet in the North Sea. There will be another Trafalgar and my dreadnoughts will sweep the German High Seas Fleet off the high seas."

Fisher chuckled, and Churchill laughed with him, lighting a large cigar and declaring between puffs, "Jackie has never been known to be wrong. We'll have to have him back in the Admiralty instead of growing cabbages at Kilverstone. 'The First Lord's oracle'—that shall be his title.''

Fisher's rule at the Admiralty had ended humiliatingly in an official inquiry, engineered by Beresford, into the conduct of the administration under Fisher. He had been cleared of most charges, but enough of the mud had stuck for his position to become increasingly difficult. King Edward had privately supported him throughout this ordeal, but the Prince of Wales less privately supported Beresford. The naval civil war came to an end with Fisher's resignation. The king died six months later in May 1910, loyal to his old friend to the end.

But Buller recognized that Fisher's presence on board the Admiralty yacht proved that his influence on naval affairs, through his great admirer Winston Churchill, was still powerful. Fisher had come to see his latest ''greyhound'' and preach the gospel of the battle cruiser to the First Lord and the up-and-coming younger generation represented by David Beatty.

Now Churchill, speaking with an attractive slight lisp, asked, ''And when may we examine your great ship, Captain Buller?''

''At your pleasure, sir. Thanks to the stout work of naval carpenters, the wardroom and my quarters are comfortable enough for me to entertain you for luncheon.''

Clemmie had come up from Gloucestershire with the Wyston Court cook and two parlormaids for the occasion. She had bought food and wine locally, and the cook had conquered the technique of cooking on a ship's new and untried galley. Clemmie was at her best, quite undeterred by the unusual and unfamiliar circumstances. Churchill, after some gallant remarks to Clemmie (''What an admirable name! The same as my wife's. And what admirable hock!''), talked navy without a break to the end of the meal. He shot questions at Fisher, the veteran and the inspirer of the battle cruiser, and at Beatty and Buller, the men who would fight them in Fisher's ''coming Armageddon.''

''And the Germans?'' Churchill demanded over the tender

stuffed spring lamb. "The Germans—what of their battle cruisers? What do you think of the *von der Tann*, Captain Buller?"

"A fine, strong ship, sir. Not the match of this, and I shall see to it that our gunnery is superior to theirs."

"And the *Blücher*?"

"A hybrid, sir. Neither one thing nor the other—neither armored cruiser nor battle cruiser. We can outrange her, outgun her, and outpace her."

Fisher broke into the conversation from the other end of the table. "Thanks to Captain Buller, sir, the *Blücher* has only eight point two-inch guns—from Captain Buller and his wonderful camera we learned *that* before the Germans wished us to."

Churchill raised his eyebrows questioningly, and Fisher continued characteristically, "The Germans said to Captain Buller, 'Hitherto shalt thou come, but no further'—Book of Job, thirty-eight, eleven. And Captain Buller went no further. He had no need to. For he had a camera of unprecedented power—and made in Germany. Do you not like that, sir?"

Churchill laughed. "You're a wicked old man, Jackie. Encouraging our officers in the arts of deception and spying."

After luncheon Buller took his party on a tour of the *Incontestable*, from the engine rooms to the armored conning tower. On the bridge wing he pointed down to the midships turrets. "You will see, sir, that they are spaced apart much more widely than in the earlier *Invincible* class."

"And that will give your guns a wider arc of bearing," Churchill said quickly, keen to demonstrate his recently acquired knowledge of gunnery and ship design.

Churchill replaced the cigar between his lips and spoke through it, "Ah, Captain Buller, I would dearly love to hear those great brutes firing in anger."

Later that day Clemmie visited Rosie Maclewin and returned in a disturbed state. "Archy, Tom is in the police cells! He is being charged with riot and battery. Rosie has been told that he will almost certainly be sent to prison.'' She looked pleadingly at Buller. "Do intercede for him, Archy. For Rod's sake. She has telegraphed him in Hong Kong, but he won't be able to do anything.''

"I'll go and see him,'' Buller promised. "The first thing is to learn what state of mind he's in.''

Tom Maclewin's state of mind, Buller learned at once when he was shown into his cell that evening, was unrepentant and hostile.

Buller arrived in a suit instead of his uniform and sat down on the other side of a deal table after he had sent away the police officer.

He had begun in a light tone. "Well, we exchanged some pretty pleasantries the other day! But now that neither of us has an audience, I hope we can talk plainly.''

Tom said he did not wish to talk at all, and that the meeting was against his wishes. He quoted Marxist jargon until Buller snapped in with the question, "Do you *want* to go to prison?''

"It is part of the price of revolution.''

Keeping his temper but speaking sharply, Buller said, "If I do not press any charges against you, they may drop the case. And then you'll be able to go about rabble-rousing instead of wasting your time in a cell like this.''

Until this moment Tom Maclewin had not met Buller's eyes. Now he glanced at him and asked, "Are you doing this for my father?''

"Yes. And your mother. If you go to prison, you'll lose your job and you won't be able to spread all this rubbish about revolution to your workmates. A police cell for a day or two is nothing. My daughter has done that twice.''

This raised even higher Tom Maclewin's curiosity. "Your daughter? Have you got a daughter in my party?''

Buller laughed. "Yes, in a way. The cause is revolutionary. She wants votes for women and chains herself to railings in London. You ought to meet her one day.''

Tom Maclewin, suddenly transformed, sitting up straight

on the wooden chair and with his face expressing eagerness, said, "Yes, I'd like that. She must have some courage."

"She's a Buller. In the same way that you're a Maclewin. Your ideas may be half-baked, but neither of you is a coward."

The sound of new dreadnoughts thundering down their slipways echoed in shipyards all over Europe—at Vickers in Barrow; at Krupps, Vulkan, Blohm and Voss and Schichau in Germany; at Elswick on the Tyne; in the yards at Clydebank, Wallsend, Devonport, and Portsmouth, and at Brest and St. Nazaire; at Lorient and La Seyne in France; Galerny in Russia; Fiume and Tecnico in Austria-Hungary; Ansaldo, Odero, and Orlando in Italy.

Their names matched their guns, provocative and belligerent: *Thunderer* and *Audacious*, *Conqueror* and *Implacable*, *Moltke*, *Seydlitz*, and *Derfflinger*. The size of the battleships and battle cruisers grew with their guns, which were fifteen-inch by 1914, hurling a projectile two and a half times the weight of the *Dreadnought's* twelve-inch shells, and with unprecedented range and penetrating power.

Dreadnoughts were superseded by super-dreadnoughts, battle cruisers by super-dreadnought battle cruisers. Hundreds of thousands of skilled men were employed in designing, building, fitting out, and manning these monsters. Millions of tons of coal were torn from the earth, transported to naval bases, and consumed in the ships' boiler rooms; and their appetite for shells was insatiable.

Unlike Clemmie's mild patriotic speech at Elswick for the launch of the *Incontestable*, the tone of other launch speeches became more and more fervent, especially in Germany. Here the kaiser and his brother, Grand Admiral Prince Henrich, Admiral von Tirpitz, and a number of grand dukes and grand duchesses, counts and countesses, sent the ships down into their element amidst cheers, and predicted for them a victorious future. On a bright spring morning in 1913, the Countess Reitzberg-Sönderlong broke a bottle of champagne over the bows of a German super-dreadnought at the naval yard at Wilhelmshaven after pledging that the ship would destroy any enemy of the German Empire with her *grosse Geschütz*. Among those at her side who applauded loudest was Konteradmiral Klaus von Klusshaven, age forty-four, six feet four inches tall, and Miranda's powerful paramour for almost two years.

In England a special event was the ceremonial launch of a super-dreadnought by the king in October 1911. The hierarchy of the Royal Navy was there for the occasion, and Clemmie and Archy Buller were among those at the royal reception after the event. When Buller was presented to the king, he discerned no sign of a return to their old friendly and informal relationship. Even now, nearly two years after Fisher's retirement, the bitterness of the division in the senior service still hung heavily at naval occasions. Perhaps if he had heard of Buller's risky espionage in Germany, the king might have relented, but knowledge of those events had been confined to the inmost recesses of the Admiralty's intelligence department.

So it was "Your Majesty" and, in a chill voice, "Ah, Captain Buller"; a rapid turnaway after a nod toward Clemmie, who was outraged on Buller's behalf. "Considering that you once saved his life and defended him against those terrible bullies in the *Britannia*, I think it's disgraceful!" Clemmie said loyally, and privately, after the event.

By an ironic twist of naval strategy and international politics, as relations between Britain and Germany grew worse and the naval race became more intense year by year, the small world of naval families benefitted and separations became fewer and less far away. Distant squadrons and fleets were reduced to a scattering of vessels "to show the flag" and no more, in order to concentrate men-o'-war protectively in home waters. As Beresford had warned, the Mediterranean Fleet became scarcely more than a token force. The South American, North American, South African, and Indian Ocean forces shrank to a few old cruisers or gunboats. The reduction of the China Fleet brought Rod Maclewin back from Hong Kong long before the end of his commission.

Rod was thankful to be within easy reach of Newcastle. At "Balmoral," Grosvenor Gardens, Jesmond, both the girls were engaged to suitable young middle-class men. But while Tom had kept his job and, thanks to Buller, had been spared a prison sentence, he remained a daily anxiety to Rosie, who had also increasingly to nurse Rod's mother.

No influence, no appeals to high authority, could save Lucy Buller from prison after she was caught smashing windows in Whitehall on November 21, 1911, in the cause of women's suffrage. Along with several others, all from the educated and privileged classes, she declared a hunger strike and went through the appalling experience of being force-fed.

"Thre is nothing—absolutely nothing—we can do," Buller said, trying to console Clemmie as they read in the newspapers of their daughter's activities. "She'll get over it in time."

But the restlessness and violent passions of Lucy Buller in London and of Tom Maclewin in Newcastle-upon-Tyne were, in their individual ways, expressions of a restlessness and a latent hysteria that were building up all over Europe, as if rising temperatures must one day lead to the explosion Fisher had predicted for the late summer of 1914. In Germany the Reichstag was closed after socialist attacks on the kaiser. In Britain the coal strike intensified, the transport workers joining it; the troubles in Ireland became more violent along with suffragette marches in London and other cities; there were riots in the docks; Turkey went to war with Montenegro, Bulgaria, and Serbia; the king of Greece was murdered; and the king of Portugal fled his country. In Russia there were food riots and more rumblings of a massive revolution.

On June 28, 1914, a fuse was lit in the obscure town of Sarajevo with the assassination by a Bosnian revolutionary of the Archduke Francis Ferdinand of Austria and his wife. As people asked, "What interest is this unhappy event to us?" the little flame spread along the wire like a vengeful snake hissing venomously, ominously.

On July 17 and 18, 1914, the British Fleet assembled at Portsmouth for a grand royal review. Many officers besides Lieutenant Maclewin and Captain Buller remembered earlier fleet reviews, for the Golden and Diamond Jubilees of Queen Victoria. Impressive they certainly were and at the time the greatest assemblies of naval power in history. But as these two officers, chief gunnery officer and captain of the *Incontestable*, stood side by side on the bridge of their battle cruiser, the lines of dreadnoughts, armored cruisers and light cruisers, destroyers and torpedo boats and auxiliary craft, appeared to have no end—as if the British Fleet stretched clear around the world and back again.

Rod glanced up at the White Ensign fluttering from the *Incontestable's* mainmast, above the spotting top and searchlight platform and the three stout steel legs of the tripod mast. His eyes followed the line of the battle cruiser's twelve-inch guns—*his* guns—to the ship's bows, the 13.5-inch guns of the new battle cruiser ahead, and beyond her to Rear Admiral Sir David Beatty's flagship *Lion*, to the heavy guns of the dreadnought ahead of her, one turret superimposed above another, and more turrets, more guns falling away into the distance.

Three hundred feet above, a pair of Wight seaplanes banked away and then flew in formation side by side down the line of dreadnoughts, omens of new weapons of sea warfare, like the insignificant little submarines tied up inshore.

The royal yacht hove into sight, streaming a thin trail of black smoke, the seaplanes dipped in salute, the first twenty-one-gun salute cracked out.

"Do you think this is the last time we'll see the fleet at peace?" Rod asked.

Buller nodded. "I don't see how war can be avoided now. Are we ready, Midge?"

"The men are ready, and my guns are ready," said Rod slowly. "But I'm not sure that my mind's ready. I don't think it will be until we really are at war."

Buller did not understand. He reckoned that his mind was ready, as ready as the whole of this giant fleet, mobilized at the command of Winston Churchill and his First Sea Lord. War at sea was the inherited birthright of every generation of Bullers for centuries. Of course he was ready.

Chapter XII

⚓

The Clash

ROD COULD SEE the smoke rising from the anchored Battle Cruiser Squadron far away up the Forth, beyond the great railway bridge which spanned the wide waters west of Edinburgh. It rose from every funnel of every big ship in the Rosyth anchorage, and from the light cruisers and the flotillas of little destroyers, and was carried away on the northeast wind as a single gray-black cloud.

He said to his Welsh friend and fellow gunnery officer, "There goes up another few thousand tons of your land and heritage, Jonas."

"The Grand Fleet wouldn't put to sea without the black gold of our valleys," Jonas Jones added. "And there's more of it going up in smoke than an hour ago."

Rod looked more closely at the line of battle cruisers. Their ship, the *Incontestable*, was the most distant, and the volume of smoke rising from her three wide-spaced funnels told him what he had feared: The squadron had been ordered to sea, and the ramparts of Edinburgh Castle upon which they were standing was about the most distant place within sight of their ship.

The two officers ran down the stone steps three at a time, Rod cursing himself for being so sure that there would be no need to return to their ship until dusk. After all these months of false alarms and fruitless pursuits of the elusive German High Seas Fleet, it would be a fine thing for their ship to go to sea without her chief gunnery officer and one of his lieutenants.

There was still a reassuring number of sailors in Princes Street, wrapped up against the cold wind and hurrying towards the railway station. There were many more at Queensferry, and chief petty officers were calling out and gathering their men together like sheepdogs, and officers and ratings were leaping aboard their respective steamboats, three of which were already on their way upriver toward the ships. On the slipway and in the boats the talk was all speculative—was it a flap or just another buzz? Would they come to grips with Hipper at last? Was the "baby killer" on the rampage again?

Twice in recent weeks the German dreadnought battle cruisers had swept across the North Sea, appearing without warning off the English coast to bombard towns. Scarborough, Whitby, Hartlepool, Yarmouth, had all be indiscriminately shelled, and hundreds of civilians had been killed or wounded. The outrage in the British Fleet was as strong as in the British public, who reacted by demanding, "Where was the fleet?" and named Admiral Franz von Hipper, commander of the German battle cruisers, "the baby killer." Until these raids the average British sailor had thought that the war at sea would be fought with old-time chivalry. Now, like the soldiers in Flanders who had heard of the outrages against Belgian civilians, there developed a real venom and hatred for the enemy.

Rod, while fearing for the safety of his family in Newcastle, felt awkward and remained silent when talk in the wardroom became fiercely "anti-Hun," as it so often did now. He felt no love for the enemy, believed as strongly as his fellow officers that their cause was strong and just, but also believed that it was futile to have "rules" in war which sooner or later were certain to be broken. If the German High Command calculated that they were more likely to win the war at sea by killing Englishmen in their homes, then that was that. But Rod also felt that every man in the *Incontestable* would fight that much harder now as the only way to stop these raids; certainly he would.

All the battle cruisers were hoisting in aboard their steamboats. The massive, complex organism of the dreadnought was coming rapidly to life, from the raising and lowering of signal flags to the rumble of the torpedo nets coming in, the drone of the dynamos and fans, and then the rattle of the anchor chains followed at once by the deepest sound of all—from far below the Parsons turbines spinning into life, all 45,000 horsepower.

Rod climbed to the signal bridge. It was already dark when they steamed slowly under the Forth Bridge, the 6:12 P.M. train to Inverness pounding overhead, the glow of the engine's firebox and the brightly lit carriages streaking above the *Incontestable* like a comet. The passengers would see the masthead lights and the dark silhouettes of the battle cruisers beneath them moving slowly towards the sea. That would be something to tell their grandchildren: "I saw the British Fleet sailing out to its victory over the Germans!"

The signal lieutenant put a piece of paper under the shaded light above the chart table. "Take a gander at that. It really looks as if you'll be using your guns this time."

Rod read "Four German battle cruisers, six light cruisers, and twenty-two destroyers will sail this evening to scout on Dogger Bank. All available battle cruisers, light cruisers, and destroyers from Rosyth should proceed to rendezvous . . ."

"Sounds promising," Rod said. "But how the deuce do they know at the Admiralty—even before they sail?"

"Spies," said the signal lieutenant darkly.*

Before turning in, Rod summoned the four gunnery

---

*He was wrong. Copies of the German Navy's cipher books had been found on a drowned German signalman following the sinking of S.M.S. *Magdeburg* in the Gulf of Finland. They were described by Churchill as "sea-stained priceless documents," and their capture was known to only a handful of senior officers. Intercepted German wireless signals were rapidly decoded and acted upon.

lieutenants commanding the twelve-inch turrets and told them the news. "It looks like action at dawn," he said. "And it won't be only light cruisers and destroyers."

Rod was referring to the first time the battle cruisers had fired their guns in anger, back in August 1914, when they had surprised German light forces deep in the Heligoland Bight, and in a few minutes had sunk three cruisers and a destroyer. The odds were more likely to be even this time. Fisher's "ocean greyhounds" had proved themselves again in December on a far distant ocean, although the *Incontestable* had played no part in the destruction off the Falkland Islands of Admiral von Spee's powerful squadron. The *Invincible* and the *Inflexible* had sent to the bottom two big armored cruisers and two light cruisers: "It was not a victory," declared Fisher triumphantly, "it was annihilation!"

Buller left the bridge at 8:00 P.M. with May Island safely past, and went down to the wardroom. He wanted no formal assembly of his officers, but most of those not on watch would be having a pink gin or two before dining late. They put down their magazines and glasses when he entered, and stood up.

"I don't want to disturb the best time of the day," he said, indicating that they should sit. A steward brought him a glass of champagne, and he raised it to those who had gathered around him, including Rod.

"You've all seen the Admiralty signal by now," he told them. "I think they know what the Hun's doing this time, so stow your gear away tonight—and, like Nelson, write your last letter to your mistress." They laughed quietly, and Buller added more seriously. "Tyrwhitt'll be reinforcing us at seven A.M. with thirty-five destroyers, which'll be handy, and his three light cruisers. And the c-in-c will leave Scapa in an hour's time with the Battle Fleet, though I fear Admiral Jellicoe will miss the fun again."

Buller glanced around at his men, his team which he had brought to a fine pitch of fighting efficiency and ability, fifty officers and under their authority, 820 midshipmen, petty

officers, and men. "You thank your lucky stars we can do
twenty-eight knots—is that right, 'Turbs'?" he asked his
lieutenant commander (E), who smiled and said, "At a
pinch, sir."

"Good luck to you all." And Buller drained his glass,
handed it to the steward, and left them—a man with heavy
responsibilities who felt in his bones that he was within hours
of the crowning moment of his life.

Before turning in, Rod had ordered his servant to call him at
5:30 A.M. so that he would be up on the bridge by the middle of
the morning watch. According to custom, Marine Thomas
was shaking Rod's shoulder at 5:25 with a pot of extremely
strong tea.

"It's bitter up top, sir."

"You haven't been up on deck since we left Rosyth," Rod
replied. "I know you, Thomas. Skulking in the galley with a
mug of cocoa since you turned out."

Rod had slept in his underclothes and now dressed rapidly
between sips of tea. He drew aside the red curtain dividing his
cabin from the gangway. The *Incontestable* was rolling
steadily and not too acutely, making (Rod calculated) about
16 knots. He still experienced surprise at the lack of the
steady beat and pulse of reciprocating engines, replaced now
by the drone of turbines, whose revolutions were more difficult to estimate.

He hurried along the dimly lit alleyway, past more cabins
and Buller's dining room and sleeping cabin, up a spiral
staircase, and though a steel doorway. Even if he had not
tested it himself, his servant's statement was correct about
the rawness of the morning. In spite of his thick overcoat,
Rod felt the wind strike him like a blow. He paused for a
moment beneath the dim blue light above the doorway to
catch his breath and adjust to the blackness beyond. Spray
flicked his face, and he caught hold of a rail as the *Incontestable* gave a heavy lurch. With the strong wind from the
northeast and the ship on a southeasterly course, the sensa-
tion of speed was stunning.

Grasping the rail of the steel ladder which would take him to the upper four-inch gun deck, Rod gave a thought to his son, who was serving in destroyers at Harwich. On the very day war had been declared, and to his parents' and wife's astonishment, Tom Maclewin had cast aside all his revolutionary beliefs and pamphlets and had marched wordlessly to the recruiting station in Pilgrim Street to sign on as a naval rating. The only comment anyone had heard him mutter, almost inaudibly, was "The revolution'll have to wait!" And now he was somewhere in this same North Sea, not far to the south, with the rest of Commodore Tyrwhitt's flotillas, closing in on the rendezvous with Admiral Beatty's battle cruisers, and making heavy weather of it in a ship one-twentieth the size of the *Incontestable*—Ordinary Seaman Maclewin, T., with less than five months of training behind him.

There was a certain definition in the darkness now, the foremost funnel and its streaming smoke, the vague outline of the tripod mast, and the piled-up superstructure just forward of it. Rod walked past Buller's sea cabin and up another ladder to the searchlight platform, and at last to the signal bridge and to the first men he had seen since leaving his cabin. At each signal lamp stood a muffled figure, staring into the night, and between them and moving about beating his hands, the signal lieutenant.

"Morning, Barney. Any news?"

"Not a wink, ol' boy. Silence is golden. We're not like the Huns, who can't stop chattering away—thank goodness."

Rod looked ahead over the screen, shading his eyes against the icy blast. Surely there could be only empty ocean for miles and miles out there in the blackness! But though there was not a blink of light, even from the stars above, Rod knew that a mere four cables distant, a battle cruiser even bigger than theirs was pounding through these same seas, and beyond her another, and another—all hell-bent on a duel to the death with other machines as massive as these, also manned by thousands of men.

The signal lieutenant came up behind him. "Did you see a

flash over there, bearing about ten degrees east?''

Rod said, ''No—no such luck. And no one else seems to have done.''

Rod made his way up again to the exposed compass platform, where the wind swept more fiercely than ever and the personnel—the officer-of-the-watch and his sublieutenant, the signalmen, and the lookouts—crouched behind the canvas screens and the compass binnacle.

Here, at 6:30, Buller joined them, his tall, bulky figure immediately recognizable in the improving light, camera and binoculars slung around his neck. Everyone present straightened themselves from their half-crouching stance. ''Signals are beginning to come in from the Harwich boys,'' Buller announced. ''They're dead on course and about eighteen miles south of us.''

''Any news of the enemy, sir?'' someone asked.

''Not yet—but I've ordered the bugles to sound off 'Action' at seven A.M. They won't be far away by then.'' Buller glanced at the illuminated compass dial and disappeared as quickly as he had arrived.

It was almost as if the Admiralty, far away in London, had laid on the show for peacetime maneuvers. Within a few miles of the predicted position and a few minutes of the predicted time, a message in code was received in the *Incontestable's* wireless room from the light cruiser *Aurora*: ''Am in action with High Seas Fleet.''

Simultaneously, flashes of gunfire appeared on the eastern horizon—there was no doubt about it this time. It was like far-distant searchlight beams switched on and off again in one movement.

Rod made his way rapidly to the big Barr and Stroud rangefinder, whose fine lenses set fourteen feet apart would provide the first and most accurate figures on the distance of the enemy when sighted. Well-wrapped against the cold were the chief petty officer and his assistants, with headpieces already fitted for passing on the range as soon as a reading was possible. Here was the single cyclops eye of the *Incontestable*.

But aloft below the foretop in a small armored drum were the director crew, including trainer and gunlayer, and Rod's lieutenant. It was this officer who, when informed that all the heavy guns were ready, electrically fired the salvo or full broadside when the uproll of the *Incontestable* brought the crosswires of his telescope on the target.

Raising his voice above the wind, the chief gunner, a heavily bearded Devonian and surely a direct descendant from Francis Drake, asked Rod, "Any more news, sir?"

"The destroyers are taking station ahead of us," Rod told him. "But their smoke shouldn't bother you with this wind. And I don't see how the Hun can get away from us. Not in this weather."

Over the next half hour as the light in the east increased, it became evident that this was to be a morning of exceptional visibility, a gunner's dream morning when only the curvature of the earth seems to limit the range of one's eyesight. And as another ripple of gun flash splashed the horizon to the northeast, it also became clear that the enemy was in a highly disadvantageous position, ripe for being cut off from his base by Beatty's battle cruisers.

Ahead, a hoist fluttered from the *Lion* and was as quickly hauled down: "Increase speed to 24 knots."

Rod turned back to his petty officer. "It looks as if the chase is on, Mr. Broadhurst."

7:45 A.M. January 24, 1915. Position 54.58 N. 3.16 E. Course S.S.E. Speed 23 knots. Visibility unlimited. Five miles distant on the port bow, British light cruisers and destroyers streaking through the water at over 25 knots.

The British battle cruiser line was headed by the *Lion* flying Beatty's flag, the *Tiger,* and the *Princess Royal*—"the big cats," as Beatty proudly called them, and all with the latest 13.5-inch heavy guns; then in the second division, the *New Zealand,* flying the flag of Admiral Sir Archibald Moore, and astern of her, the *Incontestable*.

Buller, hands clutching the bridge rails of his ship, had been silent for several minutes. Behind him the routine func-

tions of supervising the speed, course, communications, and
readiness for battle of his ship were being conducted by his
officers and petty officers, who knew exactly what to do. The
wind beat at his cap and when he raised his binoculars,
threatened to tear them from his grasp.

Buller turned his head and saw Rod at his side. There was
no need to ask if everything was ready in his department.
Buller knew as well as Rod that in the four twelve-inch gun
turrets, the trainers, gunlayers, and sightsetters were in their
places behind the heavy armor plate, the men at the breeches,
the men at the loading-cage levers; below in the working
chamber, the second captain of turrets; many more men
under petty officers in the shell room, handling room, and
magazine, ready to send up in the swift-moving cages the
projectiles and charges which would be fired at the rate of two
a minute when shooting began.

Instead, Buller nodded toward the distant specks of destroyers beneath the smudge of smoke. "Your boy'll be over
there, Midge. I hope he's found his sea legs."

"He'll be all right." Rod spoke gruffly, finding it hard
after all these anxious years to speak with pride of his son.
And yet he felt it, deeply.

A signalman saluted and handed Buller a message. Rod
read it with him: "Enemy sighted are four battle cruisers,
speed 24 knots." It was from Admiral "Barge"
Goodenough in the light cruiser *Southampton*.

Odds of five to four in their favor. But those odds were
outweighed by the advantage to the Germans of holding the
initiative, of threatening to lure Beatty's force onto
minefields, into submarine traps, or of dropping mines in the
path of the pursuers and sending in destroyer attacks. And
first Beatty had to catch them, for it was a foregone conclusion that the enemy would flee as he had fled on every
occasion when a clash was threatened.

The captain of the *Incontestable's* A turret forward of the
bridge was turning his 400-ton turret from side to side and
elevating and lowering the twin guns like a boxer flexing his
muscles in his corner. Over the next half hour one hoist after

another indicating a speed increase was hauled down on the flagship, until at ten minutes before nine o'clock, 29 knots was ordered. Probably not even the *Lion* or the even more powerful *Tiger* could log that speed, but it gave the engineroom staff a figure to aim at. The *Incontestable* had made 27.1 knots for a brief moment on her trials, and already, Buller was proud to see, his ship was making well over 26 knots. At this rate and in this weather, surely they must soon sight the enemy. One of the fastest destroyers had already got within four miles of the last of the German big ships and had reported that she was being fired on.

Then, soon after 8:30 A.M., the wireless room picked up Admiral Beatty's signal to his commander-in-chief, Admiral Jellicoe, still far to the north.

"Enemy sighted consists of four battle cruisers, four light cruisers and destroyers, bearing S 61E eleven miles. My position 54.44 N 3.44 E, course S. 40 E."

Buller had his glasses on the sharp and brightly illuminated eastern horizon. Yes, there they were. The war was six months old, but for the first time the enemy's heavy ships were in sight of one another, dreadnought to dreadnought. The picture was neater than Buller had imagined it would be: four triangles of black smoke, four close-spaced dark bases, and smaller smudges of smoke from the accompanying light forces in the van.

A white stab of flame from one of the German ships, like a man far away striking a match. The first shot, a sighting shot. Buller glanced at his wristwatch. Five, ten, fifteen seconds, twenty seconds. It would be close now. At twenty-five seconds, a tall column of water appeared at least a mile on the port bow of the *Lion*.

"Check the range, Midge."

The figure came back from the petty officer at the rangefinder, and Rod repeated it to his captain: "Twenty-two thousand five hundred yards."

"Do you want to try a ranging shot?"

"I'd like to leave it for five minutes, sir."

The gap was widening between the *Incontestable* and the

New Zealand and the faster, newer "big cats." But the *Incontestable* was showing a better pace than anyone could have thought possible, resulting in a signal from Beatty, "Well done, *Incontestable*."

"Get that message to the engine room right away," Buller ordered. He could imagine the scene deep down in the bowels of his ship, the stokers in the choking atmosphere of dust and heat throwing shovelful after shovelful of coal into the furnaces in a steady, back-breaking rhythm. Like any Phoenician galley of two thousand years earlier, the speed of this battle cruiser depended in the end on simple muscle power.

And they were gaining on the enemy. The Germans had assiduously spread word before the war that their battle cruisers were faster—oh yes, 30 knots with ease. But even under the pressure of imminent battle and the urgent need to seek the security of their base, the German ships were steadily losing their advantage. "Twenty-one thousand," Rod reported. "Twenty thousand five hundred, twenty thousand."

Buller saw the puff of cordite spreading from the fore turret of the *Lion*, now two miles ahead. The flagship's first salvo. Then, almost half a minute later, the hundred-foot-high fountains of spray and water, higher than the bridge of the rearmost German ship. The sound of the detonation was like a light slap across the face. Then B turret opened fire, then X and Y.

There were shells falling all around the *Lion* now, some very close. All the first division ships were firing, gray cordite fumes streaming with funnel smoke to starboard on the northeast wind. Until now, it could have been battle practice. But at gunnery practice, your ship did not steam through the falling spray of near-misses from twelve-inch guns a dozen miles away. Nor would your flagship suddenly throw up yellow flame, tentlike, tall as the mainmast, then with flame extinguished, but emitting instead a pall of dark gray smoke, a different shade to cordite or funnel smoke, and more of it—much more.

"The *Lion's* taken a nasty knock," the navigator said.

"Things are going to hot up for us, too. Do you want to go below, sir?"

"To the conning tower?" said Buller. "Not on your life. Can't see anything from the conning tower, and they haven't hit us yet."

"Range seventeen thousand seven fifty," said Rod. A shell exploded 200 yards on the port beam, and the spray whipped across the bridge, soaking every man.

"Are you going to open fire?" Buller need not have spoken and knew that he need not have spoken. And when Rod said, "Yes, sir," those were wasted words, too. Both knew that orders were not necessary, and both went through the polite formality. It was like Buller's great-great uncle finding his ship close alongside a Spanish frigate.

"Shall we board the enemy, sir?" he had called out to his first lieutenant. "Yes, sir, I think we should board the enemy now," both remarks spoken as they were in midair, leaping from ship to ship, swords drawn . . .

The A turret guns below them were at maximum elevation, bearing on the four still-distant dark spots. Buller raised his glasses and focused on the last of the German ships, which appeared to be losing ground, the gap between her and the next one ahead wider than that between the *New Zealand* and *Princess Royal*. Had she been damaged, or was she unable to keep up with her consorts? A yellow flash on the forward part of the German ship registered a hit by one of Rod's guns— and not the first hit. Beyond, a great sheet of yellow flame arose from another of the German dreadnoughts, 100, 200 feet into the sky, remained like a memorial beacon to those who had perished in the flames, died to a deep red, and was replaced by a giant cloud of black smoke.

But as Buller lowered his binoculars, he saw another sheet of flame rising only a mile or two ahead, from the *Lion*, which was tearing at close to 30 knots through a forest of waterspouts. The flagship was taking a drubbing, too. And the action was becoming general with every ship within range, and only the fastest M-class British destroyers capable of keeping up with the battle cruisers.

Buller spared a thought for Jackie Fisher, recalled to the Admiralty by Churchill: "My beloved 'New Testament' ships," as he also called them, tearing after the enemy, and exchanging this furious fire.

Buller's commander repeated the navigator's question. "Do you think we should retire to the conning tower, sir?"

Buller "did a Nelson" and pretended not to hear amidst the ever-increasing racket. They were both soaked through by near-misses, but the ship had not been hit, and Rod was firing steady two-gun salvoes, the recoil shaking the *Incontestable* from stem to stern, the blast like express trains tearing out of a tunnel in rapid succession.

The guns of B turret nosed the air, settling on bearing and elevation, thundered out with a double flash that was reflected in the water washing about the forecastle from German near-misses. The cordite stench, acrid and heavy, swept across the bridge. When it cleared, Buller put his glasses on their target again. She was noticeably nearer, much nearer. Fourteen thousand yards, Rod confirmed. Fire again. The noise was becoming murderous to the eardrums. Buller steadied himself, tried again to bring the German ship into the lenses of his binoculars, and for a second got a crystal-clear picture: tripod foremast, big swan-neck cranes amidships, twin tall funnels, well spaced. Could it be . . . ? The irony if it was!

Then, before smoke from another hit on the German ship obscured the length of her starboard side, he saw the yellow pinprick flashes of four guns firing from amidships. Yes, it could only be the *Blücher*, the silhouette he had once photographed with his 400-mm. Zeiss when she was fitting out at Kiel, and had lingered over at leisure in the Admiralty. There was no mistaking her, and she was the *Incontestable's* target. Not only was she the nearest enemy, but Admiral Beatty had just signaled, "Engage the corresponding ships in the enemy's line . . ." The destruction of the *Blücher* was Buller's reponsibility, Rod's responsibility. "You'll blow her out of the water!" Jackie Fisher had predicted all those years ago.

Now the running battle assumed a new shape, with the four ships ahead of Buller concentrating on the leading German battle cruisers, the *Lion* zigzagging from time to time to avoid the intense and concentrated fire of all the German ships, and the *Incontestable* pouring in her twelve-inch shells at the badly damaged *Blücher*.

The *Blücher* continued to fire fast and accurately, her shells clearly visible as they descended at the end of their parabola, but their inadequate size was measured by the relatively small splashes they made as she straddled the *Incontestable* time and again, but proved unable to hit her at their extreme range.

Rod had climbed up the inside of the foremast to join the director crew. All the big guns were making hits now—deep yellow lyddite-shell hits that were penetrating deeply into the *Blücher*, twisting and tearing her steel plates, burning and shredding her crew. Already her upper decks were a shambles of torn metal and destroyed platforms, ventilators, and boats, funnels riddled, and masts, signal yards, wireless aerial antennae all shattered. A sudden spread of flame from another hit on the after part of the ship left a terrible smoking gap like a volano's mouth where the 8.2-inch turret had been.

But two other turrets were firing with a wonderful steadiness under the awful circumstances. Buller focused his camera on the stricken vessel. "Two points to port, navigator. Let's get this over with."

"Two points to port, sir . . . Two points to port."

"Aye aye, sir. Two points to port."

By 10:30 the *Blücher* was a blazing, smoking hulk, abandoned by her friends, a victim of the *Incontestable's* twelve-inch guns, yet still with way on, still firing her surviving 8.2s as well as her six-inch secondary armament from time to time. She could still do damage and she showed no signs of surrendering, so Buller had no alternative to continuing a steady rate of fire: rending, pulverizing, igniting, killing again and again, the armor-piercing shells exploding against the hulk with a deep orange glow.

"My God, she's a tough nut!" Buller said to his comman-

der, taking a photograph of the tragic sight with his small
Zeiss. As if the fire of the *Incontestable* were not sufficient to
send her to the bottom, three of the other battle cruisers had
turned to help finish her off. Far away to the south, Buller
could see the *Lion*, listing, smoking, and apparently out of
control. So the battle had not gone all their way!

It was midday. The skies had clouded over in funereal defer-
ence to the dying *Blücher*. The German ship lay wallowing in
the swell, surrounded by British destroyers like pallbearers.
Buller kept the *Incontestable* at a mile distant, bows on to the
German ship, still alert for a possible last-minute torpedo
attack. From time to time, a twenty-four-pounder spoke with
pathetic defiance.

Then she began to go, flags still flying, very slowly turning
over on her port side, the volume of smoke and steam increasing and rising in a massive cloud as the water poured in
through shell holes and vents and open hatchways. At the
same time, while one minute she had been no more than a
dead log, the next she was alive with moving figures like
alarmed termites suddenly aware of the water creeping up
and threatening to engulf them.

From below decks the hundreds of survivors, from mess
decks and flats, from gun turrets and engine rooms, from
deep-down magazines and upper-deck 24-pounders, the
Blücher's men swarmed out and, as she turned over, began to
run down her starboard side, over the stowed net booms, over
the side armor plating, onto the red and rusting underside of
the great vessel, from which the water trapped inside now
burst forth like a dozen waterfalls, some of it carrying the
men into the sea, while other men ran and jumped or slid.

Buller saw several of them, seized by apprehension, turn
and attempt to climb up the steeply listing side of their ship,
finding the gradient easier as she listed more steeply, then—
suddenly facing being taken down on the other side—
reversing their direction and joining the hundreds of other
seamen, heads bobbing, in the icy North Sea.

"Lower boats!" Buller ordered.

"D'you mean that, sir?" It was the commander, who suddenly lapsed into the familiar "For God's sake, Buller, remember the *Cressys*." In the early days of the war, a single German U-boat had sunk a British armored cruiser not far from here, and two more had been torpedoed while helping to pick up survivors. The tragedy of the *Aboukir, Hogue, and Cressys* had made everyone wary of picking up survivors, especially enemy survivors.

Buller would have none of it. "I'm not watching those men drown after what they've been through," he said. "Just post double lookouts for signs of a periscope, and I'll give the boat crews fifteen minutes."

Destroyers with nets lowered were moving slowly through the bobbing heads, and already two of the *Incontestable's* boats were heading for the capsized hull of the *Blücher*. She went down steadily, slipping gently below like a reverently lowered coffin, bows held high, with a twelve-inch shell hole clean through below the hawsehole. There was an angry hissing noise of escaping steam and quenched fires, a moment of quietness, and then a strange blend of sounds—of cheering and singing from men clinging to wreckage, and the beating, crashing sound of top hamper and loose wreckage shooting up from the seabed under pressure, riding high into the air, and falling back onto the surface of the sea, killing and maiming both from above and below.

They got the first boatload on board, a dozen men, shocked, blue with cold, shivering, and vomiting. Buller's surgeon lieutenant and his team dealt with them speedily, sorting out the wounded, wrapping them, wiping the oil and coal dust and cordite powder from their faces. A second party of ratings were giving them rum from mess mugs. "Never you mind, matey, soon have you warm and all right!"

Buller stood by and watched, taking a series of photographs as the second boatload was helped onto the deck—the squalid side of war, the wounded, the filthy, the demoralized, the defeated.

"There's an officer 'ere, sir. Says 'e's the captain. A bit touched, if you ask me, sir."

Two ratings were lowering a man onto a stretcher. His uniform under the life jacket was torn, stained and unrecognizable, his face smeared in blood and coal dust.

"I thought captains went down with their ships—seems not these 'uns."

"Oh, stop yer gob, Charlie. Let's just get 'im below."

The German was shouting—sitting up on the stretcher and shouting in English—"Why don't you go for more? There are more of my men in the water."

He was still calling out and gesticulating when the sound of his voice was drowned by engine noise immediately above. Buller looked up and saw a seaplane no more than 300 feet high, banking steeply above the *Incontestable's* foremast, the black cross clearly visible on its fuselage. It skimmed low over the sea above the *Blücher's* floating wreckage, and Buller heard the sound of a machine gun and saw the line of spurts cutting through the bobbing black heads in the water.

Then the plane turned steeply and flew back over the same area. Two stubby objects fell from its wings, and the bombs exploded, sending up tall columns of water.

The shock of an attack from the air, a German attack on German survivors, paralyzed all who witnessed it for several seconds. Then individual initiative and ordered discipline took over. Several machine guns began firing at the seaplane as it sped away, almost skimming the sea. But, surely, more seaplanes would soon arrive.

The destroyers needed no orders to get under way, drawing in their nets and leaving hundreds of men still in the water. The *Incontestable* was also moving, heading away from this area of wreckage and suffering, everyone on deck scanning the skies for seaplanes and the surface of the sea for periscopes.

Back on the compass bridge, the officer-of-the-watch told Buller that Admiral Beatty had shifted his flag to the *Princess Royal*. The *Lion* had been so badly damaged, her wireless antennae destroyed, her halyards shot away, that neither his captains nor Admiral Moore had read his last signal ordering the chase to be continued. Instead, all the battle cruisers had surrounded the *Blücher*, which could have been dealt with by light cruisers and destroyers and the *Incontestable*, the only ship to follow orders correctly. A great opportunity had been missed.

"Signal just in, sir. We're to take the *Lion* in tow."

Beatty's ex-flagship was a sorry sight. The most famous of "the big cats," the most admired dreadnought in the whole Grand Fleet, lay wallowing helplessly in the North Sea swell, all her engines, all her electrics out of action, a ripe target for any passing U-boat. It took two anxious hours, during which two hawsers snapped, to get a line passed between the ships, and it was not until five in the afternoon that the *Incontestable* was able to get under way with the *Lion* in tow, the two battle cruisers surrounded by protective destroyers.

All through that night, the next day, and the following night the laborious tow continued, back over the reverse course they had steered with hopes and expectations of victory so high two days earlier and at four times this speed. Although the *Incontestable* had shot brilliantly and Rod had every reason to be proud of his gunners' performance, and they had been most responsible for the sinking of the *Blücher*, Buller was aware of a deep sense of anticlimax. Something had gone seriously wrong for three out of four of Admiral Hipper's ships to have escaped. But it had, after all, been a British victory—a Buller victory—to notch up on the records at Weir Park. It just should have been a bigger victory.

Late on the next afternoon, just before the second dog-watch, Rod came up to the bridge. "Are you getting any sleep?" he asked Buller.

"Not yet. It's been a busy time, Midge."

"You get some. If there's a crisis, you'll be no good all knocked up."

"I'll get some tonight. Your men shot well. You'll be up for a decoration. You said your guns were ready—remember, back in July? And you said your mind wasn't ready."

"That was a long time ago. A hundred years and a hundred rounds of twelve-inch shellfire ago."

A messenger appeared, saluted, and awaited an opportunity to present Buller with an envelope. Buller tore it open. It was from his surgeon lieutenant. "Can you spare a moment in the sick bay? I'd like your advice."

A corner of the sick bay was occupied by a dozen German wounded. They had been cleaned up, given nightshirts, and lay in bunks. "The one at the end is the only fellow giving us trouble," said the surgeon. "It's not his broken leg. He says he's the captain and must have a cabin and attendant. Says he's got a right to see you."

"You know I've all the time in the world, Quack," Buller said wearily. "I ought to have held an enemy's complaints' parade."

Buller paused by the bunk and looked down at the German. He was heavily bearded, his hair cut short in the Prussian style. His broken leg in splints and plaster protruded from the blankets and rested on a pillow.

"What can I do for you?" Buller asked.

The German did not reply for a moment, and Buller was about to repeat his question impatiently, when he heard the voice—a recognizable voice, redolent with memories of formal meetings, of informal meetings, of the most exciting mistress he had ever had, of the imperial presence of the kaiser, of boar hunts in the Harz Mountains. "How do you do, Captain Buller." A slight guttural accent, a note of provocative sarcasm.

"Well, so it's you, Sonny. It's quite time you were my guest—I owe you hospitality." Buller laughed and bent closer. "I didn't recognize you with all that fuzz on your chin. So you're a real sailor, now."

There was no lighthearted note in the reply. "As commanding officer of His Imperial Majesty's Ship *Blücher*, I demand three things," said the count harshly. "I demand a cabin of my own, as befits my rank. I demand to know the names of my surviving officers and men. And I demand an explanation of why the rescue operations were halted when my men were in the water, and why your air force bombed and machine-gunned them.''

Buller drew up a stool beside the bunk and waited for the wave of fury to pass before he spoke. Yes, he told the count, he could have a cabin if he did not wish to be tainted by the presence of his men. In due course a list of survivors would be presented—there were some two hundred. ''As to the rescue operations, after Admiral Hipper left you and your men to sink or swim, these were carried out under the most dangerous circumstances in a sea thick with your U-boats, and finally they were bombed and machine-gunned by one of your seaplanes—yes, yours. I have a photograph of it, and it flew back toward Borkum. The pilot thought he was going to earn an Iron Cross by machine-gunning helpless English sailors. But they were his own countrymen.''

The count turned his head away from Buller, too weary and demoralized to say more. Buller rose to his feet. ''I have the responsibility of two dreadnoughts, Sonny. But I hope to see you again later. Meanwhile, your men are being cared for, as you can see.'' He turned to an attendant. ''Will you please have this officer moved into my day cabin when the suregon says he is fit to be carried there.''

Buller allowed himself an hour's sleep that night and for the rest of the time, between mugs of burning hot cocoa and a beef sandwich, remained on the compass bridge or checked with the towing party at the stern. Signals from Rosyth and Hull suggested that the weather would hold, but every lurch in these North Sea rollers put a severe strain on the great hawser linking the 19,000-ton *Incontestable* with her 26,000-ton disabled consort.

Dawn spread a dark gray light over the sea, and one by one the destroyers became visible, rising and dipping, tossing the water from their forecastles, their smoke tracing out the complex protective pattern of their U-boat screen.

''I'm going below for an hour,'' Buller told the officer-of-the-watch. ''Call me if there's any trouble—the smallest trouble.''

Count Sonny had been moved into his cabin, with a Royal

Marines guard at the door. The German was asleep but woke up when Buller came in, following his movements with his eyes.

"How do you feel?" Buller asked.

"How would you feel, a prisoner with a broken leg, after losing your ship?"

"I would be sorry for my wife. This is going to be a long war."

"Miranda will be all right. She is always all right, as you know, Captain Buller." He took the cigar offered to him and lit it from the match. "But for you she had a special fondness. Did you know that?"

"I had a great fondness for her, although our relationship led to many complications." Buller was about to laugh until he noticed unmistakable signs of tears in the eyes of the count. The reaction to the battle has been too much for him, and the Germans are sentimental people, Buller told himself in explanation.

Sonny said in a low voice, "It led to most of my men being dead, and to me lying here your prisoner. In the *Kriegsmarine* we were proud of our first dreadnought battle cruiser until we saw we had been tricked. After that most unfortunate accident at my schloss, always the blame came on Miranda and on me for the design of the *Blücher*. I was not reappointed A.D.C. to His Imperial Majesty, not promoted konter-admiral as was my due, and instead given this command—to the how do you say? to 'the lame duck,' the sacrificed sheep, which would one day be left behind without the speed and the gunpower. Ah, my poor *Blücher!*"

To Buller's acute embarrassment, Count Sonny began to cry quietly. "My poor *Blücher,* my poor men . . . You cannot imagine what it was like at the end. I tried to throw myself into a great fire forward of the bridge, but my secretary and first lieutenant held me back, and then some sailors seized me and dragged me into the sea."

Buller was at a loss to know how to comment, how to sound sympathetic, and then recalled sharply that the guns which had proved inadequate against the *Incontestable* had proved quite adequate to blow up houses and women and children in several English East Coast towns early on the morning of December 16.

The count raised himself on one elbow and pointed his cigar at Buller, grief and self-pity quite gone, and his expression now one of surly defiance. *"Ach,* but Captain Buller, if my ship had twelve-inch guns, like our flagship and like your ship, I should have blown you out of the *Nordsee."* There was not a trace of warmth or humor in his harsh laugh before he replaced Buller's fat cigar in his mouth. "And you would be lying here with a broken leg, a defeated prisoner—yes?"

Because he needed it, and thought it fit to complete in full measure the Royal Navy's hospitality, Buller poured out two extremely stiff single-malt whiskies and handed one to his ex-antagonist.

"No," Buller said emphatically. "No—that is not so. Not with Lieutenant Commander Roderick Maclewin C.G.M., R.N., as my chief gunnery officer. With Midge, no guns could have sent this ship to the bottom."

"Who is this lieutenant commander—this Midge?" the count asked scathingly.

"Oh, he's just the best damn gunnery officer in the fleet. And an old friend of mine."

Buller observed the signs of strain and weariness in the king's face. He was only forty-nine, a few months older than Buller himself, but the stress of war had left its mark more damagingly on the monarch than on the dreadnought captain. Buller thought, "There's not much of the old skylarking and mischief of the *Britannia* days left in poor Georgie."

Eight months of the bloodiest and most critical war his country had ever endured, the need to keep the spirits of his people high, the optimism alive, the will for victory strong, the compassion for the wounded and bereaved warm in people's hearts—all this with the taxing visits to the Western Front, the fleet, casualty clearing stations, and hospitals, an endless round of inspections and parades and investitures (like this one), had borne down heavily on the king's stamina.

There were deep lines about his eyes and across his

forehead. Buller repeated to himself, "And he's the same age as me—this terrible war is aging us all." But he also knew that the king's greatest concern was about the wave of anti-German hysteria still sweeping across the country—shops with German names being smashed and looted, and even German Dachshund dogs pelted with stones. A few months earlier the king's cousin and Buller's friend, Admiral Prince Louis of Battenberg, a stout patriot and servant of the people if there ever was one, had been hounded out of the office of First Sea Lord because of his German roots.

And now even the king's own family had come in for increasing suspicion and attack because of historic German associations and because the king's aunt—long since dead—had married the kaiser's father. In certain sections of the public, a new prorepublican and anti-royal campaign was being pursued, which was deeply wounding to the king and his family.

"Well, Archy, I think it's high time we buried the hatchet."

Still cautious, Buller replied, "Thank you, Your Majesty."

They faced one another on the velvet-draped dais, two middle-aged sailors who had once, as the king had described it, been "great chums," Buller a full five inches the taller. Now, with the threat of divorce and the Fisher dispute long since past, Beresford senile and long since discredited as a politician and naval officer, the sinking of the *Blücher* to Buller's credit, and with the white star on purple cloth of the Grand Cross of the Order of the Bath pinned to his chest, it was hardly possible for the king to keep up the old coolness.

In fact, his smile could not have been warmer. "I can't give you the Bath *and* continue calling you Captain Buller. How are you, Archy?"

"Very much the better for seeing you, Georgie. Even if this meeting is rather public."

Behind Buller in the great hall there sat in rows several hundred service men with their families—men of ranks from generals and admirals down to ordinary seamen and private soldiers, all present to receive decorations for valor from the Victoria Cross to the D.C.M., many of them from the Battle of Neuve Chapelle and the Battle of the Dogger Bank.

"Yes, I must get on with my day's work—a word or two with each man. But you and Clemmie must dine with us soon. I shall make arrangements."

With his tricorn under his arm, Buller formally bowed low, turned, and made his way down the steps. The next man to be decorated—an officer from Beatty's flagship—was already walking toward the dais.

The Bullers had all come to watch what Clemmie called "Daddy having his Bath": Clemmie herself in a broad-brimmed hat with a posy of spring flowers tucked into the brim, pretty Lucy, twenty-six, now in nurse's uniform and completing her training as a V.A.D., Harry, twenty-four, a lieutenant in the Grenadiers just back from the front, and Richard—the apple of Buller's eye—just home from distant seas.

Buller's brothers were at Scapa Flow and had been unable to get away for the investiture, but they had contributed to the deluge of telegrams piled on the drawingroom mantelpiece in Clarges Street, where Randolph, soon to join the colors, would have plenty of Mumm's Extra Dry on ice ready for opening.

As Buller sat down, Clemmie fingered the velvet of the Order. Harry, looking absurdly young in Buller's eyes, and very proud in the lieutenant's uniform he was wearing in public for the first time, smiled at his father and said nothing; and Lucy sitting on his left touched his hand for a moment.

As for Buller himself, for the first time in his life he was not looking forward to the celebration laid on by Clemmie when they returned home. In an uncharacteristic moment of introspection, he had thought that the Dogger Bank battle was an event to mourn rather than to celebrate. He had been thinking of the last photograph he had taken from the compass platform of the *Incontestable* just before they had been forced to steam away.

He had glanced at this gray print in his dressing room

before leaving for the palace. It showed the *Blücher* capsizing, in such pathetic contrast with that early secret picture he had taken with the big Zeiss of her fitting-out at Kiel, the pride and wonder dreadnought of the *Kriegsmarine*. Now men attempting to save themselves were clambering or running down her hull. In the water there were bobbing heads and waving arms, men already drowning—and all, within minutes and with their great ship, to become victims of the icy North Sea.

And how many more dead would there be, in Germany and Russia, Austria and Italy, France and Britain, before this most terrible of all wars was won?

Outside the palace, in warm early spring sunshine, the Maclewin family joined them, Rod now wearing the white and gold cross with the red center of the Distinguished Service Order. A small crowd gathered around them, these two heroes of the Dogger Bank battle, while the cameramen called out to them to smile.

Buller took from Richard the small Zeiss he had been carrying for him and joined the cameramen in order to take a photograph of the Maclewin family, including Tom in his jersey and bell-bottoms. He glanced at the big box camera held by the man from *The Daily Mail* standing beside him. "You'd be better on f/8 in this light," Buller said.

The man laughed good-humoredly. "Get away with you, sir. I'm a professional—I knows my stuff. You go on back to sea, that's where you belong."

Buller rejoined the two families. "Did you hear that?" he asked Rod. "He told me it was time I got back to sea."

"And he's right—that's what we always say after a spell ashore."

Author's Note

The fate of S.M.S. *Blücher* at the Battle of the Dogger Bank in January 1915 was not only a great personal tragedy for the relatives of those who succumbed to the shellfire or icy seas. The moral and tactical effect on the whole German Navy was profound.

The *Blücher* had been built in great secrecy and at great speed in order to confound the British, who were at work in equal secrecy on their first all-big-gun battle cruiser. The deceit, espionage, and counterespionage which led to the inadequate gunpower of the German ship have never been explored, and it is probably now too late to discover, in that murky world, the truth behind the affair.

My explanation is purely fictional, as are the chief characters directly involved—Buller, of course, and Rod Maclewin, and Captains Campbell and Holly, and the Count and Countess Reitzberg-Sönderlong.

The main sweep of events spanned in *Buller's Dreadnought* is in accord with history, as are the leading royal and naval characters, such as Edward VII and the Prince of Wales, the kaiser and Prince Heinrich of Prussia, Admirals Beresford and Fisher, and members of the Board of Admiralty.

The ships in which Buller serves are also fictional, although based very closely on real men-o'-war of the time. The *Incontestable*'s resemblance in design and career to the battle cruiser *Indomitable* will be clear to naval historians. My apologies are therefore due to the descendants of the *Indomitable*'s company who performed so gallantly in their action with the *Blücher*.